S0-BTR-420

The Cardiac Cartel

Donna
I Hope you enjoy
THe Book
Best wishes
David Mucci

1 | CHAPTER ONE

Dr. Anthony Collas sat hunched over at his desk. His blood shot eyes, blurry at times, fixed on his computer screen. Until recently, his shoulders were normally squared and solid, but tonight they drooped under tremendous stress and tension. A winter storm charged outside in unrelenting gusts. Despite the frigid air that flowed through the partially opened third floor window, the room felt like a steam bath and he sat drenched in sweat. Beads rolled down from under his loose prematurely gray hair and continued under the bridge of his thick glasses. Occasionally the drips veered into one, or both, of his eyes causing him to blink hard from the sting of the salt. Otherwise the coalesced beads formed on the tip of his short, stubby nose. He ignored them now, and let them fall where they splattered onto the keyboard, his sleeve long since saturated from blotting them away.

The studio apartment that he had lived in for the last year was compact, not much larger than an efficiency unit. The bedroom, separated by a partial panel, allowed the landlord to charge full apartment rates. That didn't bother him. He was not one to place much emphasis on a place where he only ate and slept. Until a few days ago, all his free time had been spent at the hospital.

A pizza box hung off the edge of his small dinette table. Its contents were cold and untouched. A coffee pot, drained and refilled four times in the last three hours sat filled with its warm brew. Coffee

9

was the only thing Dr. Collas had consumed from 11:00 PM to the present 3:10 AM, but it wasn't the caffeine that made his heart pound faster with every swallow. It raced more from what his light brown eyes danced over on his computer. His palms, damp and clammy, tightly gripped the mouse and guided the cursor across the screen with expert precision as he checked and rechecked his data.

Startled, he snapped his head around to the left. The sound was sharp and quick like a twig snapping. He panted with fast, short breaths as he scanned the room. The double-bolted door remained locked. Computer spreadsheets covered the stacks of Cardiac Journals that littered the floor. The window shade swayed with the suction from the winter storm that raged outside. The room lit only by the computer screen and a side desk lamp was empty. The apartment was too small for anyone to hide in. He rubbed his throbbing temples. The rhythmic pounding in his head made him think of his heart pumping the blood through the dilated vessels just below the surface of his scalp. That made his headache unbearable. Assured he was alone he attempted to calm down by taking three purposeful, long, deep breaths, then he turned his attention back to the computer screen.

He mumbled to himself as he clicked the mouse and advanced the screen, "These numbers aren't even close. How did they get away with this for so long?"

Suddenly, like a shot, out of his peripheral vision a shadow moved. He spun around ready to defend himself, hands clenched, again only to find an empty room. The shade fluttered slightly and the street lamp across the street cast a moving shadow on the opposite wall. He rubbed his temples again. "I've been doing this too long." He looked at the clock and realized he wasn't going to get any sleep this night.

The steaming hot shower relaxed his tense muscles, though only momentarily. By the time he was dressed and ready to leave for the hospital the spasms in the nape of his neck had returned. He backed out of his apartment glancing before he left at his computer to ensure that it was off and the disks were hidden away. He pulled the door tight behind him and spun around, but his heart stopped and he gasped as he ran head on into a tall muscular man draped in a heavy winter coat. Their arms intertwined in a brief moment of struggle. Dr. Collas gave out a yell, pushed the man away and held his hands up ready to strike out to defend himself.

"Hey, hey, hey! Collas, what the hell are you doing?" Dr Yasito, a fellow resident, called out as he quickly retreated.

It took Collas a few seconds to recognize Dr Yasito's face and voice. He lowered his hands. "Oh God, sorry. You scared me. Shit, you almost gave me a heart attack. I thought you were attacking me."

"No, not today Collas. I'm just heading in for a shower then back to the hospital." He gave Collas a funny look. "Are you alright?"

"Yah, just a long night writing a report. Listen, I gotta go. See you in the hospital."

Five in the morning was an eerie hour in the Cardiac Care Unit, the limbo between day and night when the body's normal circadian rhythm shuts down the adrenal glands. This is the time when one's body should be asleep, and the ones that weren't experience chills and shakes that at times resemble early narcotic withdrawals. Dr. Collas felt nauseous and involuntarily shuddered. He felt relatively safe inside the confines of a patient's intensive care cubicle as he glanced over the patient's chart, illuminated only by a dim side light. Out of the corner of his peripheral vision he again saw a shadow, but he was nonplused. No one would be around at this hour, he thought, other than himself and the nursing staff. The firmness of the hand gripping his shoulder told him otherwise. He turned his head and was horrorstruck to see a hand clutching a syringe swiping at him in a downward arc. Terror filled his face and his eyes grew wide. In that moment a protective instinct took over, he raised the medical chart to shield himself and deflect the syringe. The needle struck it and bent, rendering it useless. Collas stared at his attacker in disbelief.

"You've been given a momentary reprieve Dr. Collas. But make no mistake about it, today you will die." The attacker reached into his coat and pulled out a gun fitted with a silencer.

Collas swung the chart and struck his attacker on the nose, stunning him momentarily. In that instant he jumped out of the room and into the dark hallway. He looked in both directions but saw no one; no nurses, no technicians, and no secretary. Where were they? he asked himself. With no time to think he broke into a run down the hall, each second expecting to feel the searing pain of a bullet in his back.

He rounded the corner and heard, between gasps for breath, the soft pounding of footsteps behind him. When he reached the elevator bank he pushed every button there was, willing, pleading for one to open. The footsteps were closing in and no elevator had arrived. On the opposite wall he saw a door to a stairwell and he reached it in two strides. He threw the door open and charged onto the landing dismayed to find that the stairs only went up. Furious with his lack of choices he entered the isolated stairway and ran up two steps at a time. At the top of the steps he stopped, but he heard the pounding of footsteps not far below. With no choice he ran though the door onto the roof. The storm had reached a feverish pitch and the swirl of wind and snow instantly blinded him.

Fear engulfed him as his vision was reduced to being barely able to see three feet in front of him. Despite that he moved forward, away from the door. He had to find a way off this roof. He knew the howl of the wind would disguise the sound of the door when his attacker arrived. His only solace was the fact that if he couldn't see his attacker his attacker couldn't see him. He bent forward at the waist and struggled in a random direction hoping to come to another door or a fire escape that would lead off the roof. The stinging wind-driven snow blinded him but when his hand touched something hard and rough he knew he had reached the three-foot high cement border of the roof. He stopped to think, and quickly realized how intensely cold he was. He had on only thin hospital scrubs and his lab coat offered no protection from the wind, and snow. His fingertips stiffened and he knew that he was in as much danger from the cold and hypothermia as he was from his attacker.

He edged along the roof squinting in a vain attempt to see. Suddenly two strong arms spun him around. Chilled to the bone his muscles shivered in spasms and he stiffened further. Unable to protect himself he stared at his attacker. "Why?" was all he managed to yell over the howl of the wind.

"Why am I going to kill you? An interesting question Dr. Collas," the voice yelled back. "I'm going to kill you because you got too close, way too close. And I can't have you jeopardizing my future."

"But I trusted you." His voice weakened fast.

"That, Dr. Collas, was your biggest, and last, mistake."

The two hands suddenly gave him a hard push. He fell backwards over the cement retaining wall and off the roof. In a surrealistic swirl he fell through a snow filled void. His vision instantly lost the figure above him in a snowy haze as the distance between them quickly increased. An instant later it was over.

2 | CHAPTER TWO

A sudden blast of Arctic air slammed into Peter's face causing the moisture in his nose to freeze instantly. Unaffected by this blustery cold he eyed the building up and down. Peter Pavano stood outside Connecticut General Hospital in Hartford, Connecticut. He had worked far too hard and been through much worse discomfort on his road to this point. He threw back his shoulders and hurried through the front door. The lobby, though cavernous and filled with echoes, felt overheated and claustrophobic. Peter unbuttoned his Chesterfield coat, took it off and draped it over his arm. He took a moment to get the feel of the place. Hospitals had personalities, which were all different, and all unique. The lobby nearly always gave them away. This one's personality was tough to identify though. It was too big, and while chaotic might be too strong a word, there was an undercurrent of frenzy.

Peter paused. He checked his reflection in the huge mirror that served to make the lobby look even bigger. His hazel eyes gave away a hint of fatigue. It had been a long trip. His sandy hair lay flat for once, and his chalk-striped suit appeared understated but professional. Satisfied with his initial impression he headed for the information counter and asked directions.

Connecticut General Hospital, otherwise known as C.G.H., was a thousand bed hospital. It was large, impressive and impersonal. Too big for the warmth of a small rural community hospital, it was more like a city in and of itself, cold and overbearing. Each section, or floor, appeared independent of the next, oblivious to the fact that others existed. Somehow, they were inherently connected, and very much dependent on what happened around the next corner.

To get the true pulse of a new hospital Peter always visited the Emergency Room. This gave him a sense of how well their systems ran. The Emergency Room today was in full chaos. The staff sprinted between patients with crushing chest pain, to patients vomiting over the side rails and onto the floor. It didn't surprise Peter that they left him alone to observe their rolling turmoil. If his interview went well, he would be spending a lot of time doing cardiac consultations in this place.

Suddenly a voice boomed above the constant din of voices, "Who in God's name is in charge of this ZOO?" A stocky six foot three inch man with oarsman shoulders emerged from behind a curtain. A white coat hung to his knees.

The buzz in the ER stopped.

"What's the problem, Doctor?" The charge nurse approached him. "I hope you are not going to start this early in the day?"

The Doctor stepped forward until he stood only six inches from her. His fists convulsed with suppressed rage as he towered a good foot over her. All the nurse could see was the middle of his tie on his broad chest. With each word his face grew redder, contrasting the black hair, trimmed in silver, and stone cold chocolate eyes.

"What's the problem?" he mimicked her. "The problem is where is the Retavase? I ordered it over fifteen minutes ago. The problem is I can't dissolve the blood clot in this man's heart without the Retavase. That's what the god damned drug was invented for. The problem is I can't reverse this man's heart attack without the Retavase. The problem is he needs emergency angioplasty but refuses. The problem is the patient's stupid and the entire staff in this goddamned zoo is equally incompetent. That's the problem!"

15

He stared down at her. His nostrils flared with each breath and waited. Their eyes locked in mortal combat.

A nurse ran breathlessly around the corner. "Here's the Retavase."

He took it and shoved it at her. "Here. You're the charge nurse. I'm charging you with giving it to that idiot patient. Or is it too much to assume that you know the protocol for giving it?"

"I know the protocol, Doctor. And we will take up the issue of your unprofessional rudeness later." She turned to enter the patient's room.

"Don't waste your time," he replied. "And try not to drop it on the floor."

Peter shook his head to himself. From his vantage point he could see the entire staff cower in fear. The only one who stood up to him was the charge nurse.

"May I help you?" Peter turned with a start and faced a staff nurse.

"Oh . . . I'm sorry," he replied. "I'm Doctor Pavano. Peter Pavano. I was just looking around the hospital before my interview."

"What are you interviewing for?"

"For the Invasive Cardiology Fellowship," he said, "With Doctor Barbosa and his associates."

"Have you ever met the good Doctor Barbosa?"

"No."

"Well, you just got to see him in action. I'd leave this place and never look back if I were you. The last fellow wasn't so lucky."

"What do you mean?" Peter asked.

"Two days ago he jumped off the roof. Have a nice day." She turned and walked away.

Ten minutes before his appointment Peter entered Barbosa's office. One would never know the hospital was downsizing from the looks of it; large and spacious, beautifully appointed. And this was only the waiting room.

"Good morning," Peter smiled. "I'm Dr. Peter Pavano. I have an interview with Dr. Barbosa at ten o'clock."

"Welcome, Dr. Pavano. I'm Beth, Dr. Barbosa's secretary." Her tightly cropped brown hair highlighted her well-defined cheekbones. She had a manner that was soft and exuded professionalism. "Please, have a seat. Unfortunately, Dr. Barbosa will be delayed. Dr. Clayton, one of his associates, will start your interview." Peter noticed a slight hesitation, "I'm sure Dr. Barbosa will join you shortly."

Peter found a corner chair, and placed himself in it with deliberate ease. He sat and glanced around the outer office. Unintentionally his eyes returned to Beth. She wore a well-tailored navy blue dress. He figured her to be in her early thirties. She looked up and their eyes met. She smiled then went back to her work.

"Doctor Pavano, can I get you anything? A cup of coffee maybe?"

"No thank-you." He sat back and relaxed. He had four other highly regarded programs bidding for him and he was not about to work for someone like Barbosa. He'd use this interview as a practice. It was thirty-five minutes before any one entered the office.

"Dr. Charles Clayton here. You must be Dr. Pavano." A lean English gentleman with thinning brown hair and round wire-framed glasses extended his hand to Peter with the grace of a British gentlemen receiving guests properly for afternoon tea. "Come. Let's go into Dr. Barbosa's office where we can talk."

Clayton wore an expensive tailor made suit. It accentuated his five foot nine inch frame. His physique was that of a marathon runner. He didn't have an ounce of fat on him.

Clayton walked around the desk and sat down. It was then Peter had his first opportunity to look past Clayton's eyeglasses and into his eyes. They exuded self-righteousness.

"My apologies for keeping you waiting," Dr. Clayton said with a brisk British accent. "But you know . . . patient care comes first."

"Yes, I understand. Please, there's no need to apologize."

"Right then, down to the interview. I reviewed your resume last night. You are a graduate of Georgetown School of Medicine."

"Yes," Peter replied. He fidgeted ever so slightly in his chair in an attempt to get comfortable. "I also did my three years of Medical Residency there."

"Yes, I am aware of that. And currently you're in your third year of Cardiac Fellowship at Cook County Hospital. Tell me, why do you want to come to Connecticut General?"

"Connecticut General has a wonderful reputation for training. It speaks for itself." He laughed to himself at his canned answer.

"Are you active with a church?" Clayton's eyes bore down on him.

The question took Peter by surprise. "No."

After a moment's thought Peter continued, "I'm Catholic, but with the long hours and responsibility with the present fellowship, I just can't seem to find the time to go to church every Sunday."

"Responsibility? How can you ignore your responsibility to your almighty creator? I am a good Christian, and that means I take my responsibility seriously."

A silence hung in the air.

"I agree," Peter finally replied. "But, I think that being a good Christian goes far beyond just going to church every Sunday."

Clayton's finger shot through the air. "Not only do I actively worship under His watchful eyes every Sunday, I teach Sunday morning Bible class. And, if we hire you, you will be required to be in the hospital covering me during that time." He thumped his chest. "I also run a mission in Ecuador. I travel there for one month every year. I not only tend to their medical needs, free of charge, but I also help them heal their spiritual pain. Yes, medicine and religion are intertwined. We truly do God's work."

Clayton jumped up. "Well I've got another procedure to do. It's been a pleasure talking to you. Remember what I've said."

He shook Peter's hand and rushed out. Peter stood for a moment, stared at the open door and ran a hand through his hair. *What the hell kind of an interview was that?* he thought. Finally he walked to the open door and peered out at the secretary.

"Excuse me," he said. "My interview with Dr. Clayton . . . I guess . . . is over. He had to leave to do a procedure." He raised his shoulders in a question.

Beth looked up, half smiled, and half laughed. "I guess you had an interesting interview with him." She put her pen down. "Anyway, Dr. Kyle's on his way up. He just called and said he finished his angioplasty. Please have a seat back in the office. He'll be in soon."

Peter returned to Barbosa's office.

Ten minutes later Dr. Kyle strode in. "You must be Dr. Pavano?"

"Yes, I am." Peter stood and they exchanged firm handshakes. Dr. Kyle was in his early fifties and wore a warm smile on his bird-like face.

"I'm sorry if I've kept you waiting. Our practice is so busy we don't know if we're going or coming. Sometimes I think it's too busy. I understand you've had the pleasure of talking with Dr. Clayton first," he laughed.

"Yes, I did." Peter couldn't help but smile.

"Well, did you get the fire and brimstone lecture?"

"I think I did."

"I'm surprised you stayed. Regardless of his holier than thou attitude he's a very competent physician. Anyway, you must have a few questions. Go ahead, shoot."

Peter took a moment to get himself back on track. Despite no interest in the program, he pressed on. He wanted to ask about the fellow's suicide but thought otherwise. "Mostly I'm interested in the dynamics of the Fellowship. Its responsibilities and your expectations." He left it there and hoped Kyle would fill in the blanks.

Kyle perched on the edge of the other chair. "Fair enough. To start off, we are a three-man group. Despite the large number of cardiologists in the hospital, which I think are fourteen or fifteen, only the three of us do angioplasty. Between us we do close to two thousand per year. And the responsibility of the Fellow is solely to our group. There are three other Cardiac Fellows in the hospital, but they are non-invasive. That program is much like the three-year program you're presently in. They deal with all the other cardiologists."

"Do they work with you at all?"

"No. And our Fellow doesn't work with any of the other cardiologists." Kyle stretched his arms, and then continued. "If we choose you, and you decide to come here, you'll work your tail off. You'll be expected to be in house making rounds on all patients seven days a week."

"I can handle that."

"You'd also be first call on weekends. You'd get one weekend off a month without call and two weeks vacation a year. You'd be completely responsible for any research project we're involved in. And, be required to compile and keep track of all data for articles being written."

Peter nodded.

"All data and journal articles are the property of our group. We approve everything before submission to any journal for publication. The Fellow is required to write two articles to graduate, though neither have to be accepted for publication, just submitted."

Peter had heard all this before. Every interview said basically the same thing, all work, no sleep and definitely no time for fun. "How many procedures does your Fellow do?" Another standard question.

"Our Fellow graduates with five hundred angioplasties. By the time he graduates, he'll be completely proficient in it."

The next ten minutes of conversation was pleasant. Peter relaxed. He found Kyle warm, witty and generally an all around nice guy. Too bad his associates were both dysfunctional.

"You have to understand," Kyle brought them full circle. "Your year of invasive Cardiovascular Fellowship will be like no other, no matter where you end up. It will be more intense and demanding than anything you've been through. The egos you'll be working with are tremendous. We have to be available to supply angioplasty to anyone within minutes of their diagnosis of an Acute Myocardial Infarction. (A.M.I.) No ifs, ands, or buts. No excuses. You have to remember it's only one year and we're your drill sergeants."

Kyle looked up. There was a loud commotion in the outer office.

"I think Dr. Barbosa's arrived," Kyle said. "I heard he's having a bad day. Listen, don't take anything from him too personally. He can be a little harsh at times."

The door to the office flew open. Peter looked up but remained nonplused.

"I'm God damn tired of having to deal with idiots." Barbosa stormed in and sat behind his desk, his face crimson with rage. He swiveled in his chair to face Kyle.

"Problems with the ER again?" Kyle asked.

"I think I've reached my limit with that hell hole. From now on, I don't give a damn what the problem is. I will not do a primary consult in that place. It's damn chaos down there." He opened a desk drawer as if looking for something, then slammed it shut. "Every time you ask a nurse to help you she's running off to do something else. No one helps you in that God damned place. I told that little shit charge nurse that when I come into that ER I expect to be assigned a nurse to work solely with me and only with my patients. Do you know what she said?"

"I can imagine," Kyle said.

Peter listened with interest. He knew what he would have told him if he was that nurse. He noticed Barbosa's eyes. They were cold and insensitive.

"That little shit," Barbosa continued, "told me she didn't care who I was or who I thought I was, that there was no way in hell she'd ever assign a nurse to work with me. She said most of her nurses would quit before they would work with me one on one."

"They are responsible for multiple rooms and patients—"

"That's what that bitch said. She told me if I wanted my own private nurse I should hire one myself."

Kyle laughed. "She's got big ones."

"Not when I get through with her. She needs to be taught that I am the Doctor and she is nothing but a God damn nurse." He slammed his fist onto his desk. His eyebrows, continuous from one side of his face to the other, buckled with his frown.

"Before we plan this war let me introduce Peter Pavano. He's here for the fellowship interview."

Peter made eye contact, smiled and extended his hand. Barbosa left his on the desk forcing Peter to retracted his awkwardly. "Pleased to meet you, Dr. Barbosa."

"So, you want to be our fellow?" Barbosa's tone conveyed no interest in the upcoming answer.

"I'm looking at a few places. I want the best place where I can get the best education."

Barbosa glanced up. "You think you have what it takes to be a fellow under me?"

Peter stared into Barbosa's lifeless shark eyes. "I could only try."

"You could only TRY?" Barbosa bellowed. "Let me tell you, mister, trying in this program is unacceptable. Succeeding is the only thing that is accepted, and tolerated. Trying and a dime won't get you a cup of coffee anymore. The competition is too stiff. Are you married?"

"No."

"Engaged?"

"No."

"Have a girlfriend?"

"No."

"What are you, fuckin' gay?"

"No."

"Fine. If we accept you, you'll have to keep it that way. Sue me if you want. I don't give a shit. We don't accept married men

22

into this fellowship. We interview them, but if they're married, or engaged, tough. We won't take you." Barbosa leaned forward. "Do you know why?"

"No, I don't."

"Because my fellow is expected to eat, sleep and breathe angioplasty. And if you have a wife she'll resent the amount of time you'll be in this hospital. And if she resents that she'll resent you. And eventually you'll resent this program and me. And I won't have that. For one year if you want to be married, it's to me. Do you understand what I'm saying?"

"Yes I do." They stared at each other, neither blinked.

"Do you disagree with me?"

"At the moment, I'm in no position to disagree, sir."

"Then, knowing that, you'd still come here?"

"If those are your rules, and I decided to come here I'd—"

"You mean if we decided to offer you the position."

"Yes, of course. If I ended up here knowing the rules I'd be foolish not to abide by them." Peter rearranged himself in his chair. "I'm curious . . . has anyone tried to get married?"

"Only one," Kyle said. "He tried to hide it from us. That lasted about five months until we found out."

Barbosa continued. "He tried to threaten us with legal action when we confronted him. That was a bad mistake on his part. We worked that bastard so hard he didn't last. He left less then one month later, on his own. He learned his mistake the hard way. Do you know what that mistake was, Dr. Pavano?"

Peter sat stone-faced.

"He challenged me. He actually thought he could beat me." His fingers shot through the air at Peter. "If we offer you the job, just remember, don't ever fuck with me. I'll cut your balls off. I'm a god damned good cardiologist. I didn't become Chief of C.G.H. without being the best. I know that and God damn anyone who forgets it."

Peter sat unmoved by Barbosa's bravado. He'd seen worse and survived.

"Well, Dr. Pavano, that's it. I'm sorry I can't talk to you more but I'm very busy." Barbosa waved his hand in dismissal, then opened a file on his desk.

Kyle stood and walked Peter to the door. "Thank you for coming." Peter shook his hand and remained stoic. Inside, he tried not to laugh. The door behind him closed as abruptly as his interview had ended.

Moments later Peter was back in the lobby. He dialed a number using his calling card. "Hi. It's me."

"Hi." The reply was soft, female, and very sexy. "What's wrong? Did you miss your interview?"

"No. It's over."

"What do you mean? They usually last all day. It's only ten thirty."

"Believe me, it's a long story. I'm just glad I have four other interviews. This place is nuts. There is no way I'd ever consider coming here. Listen, I'll leave for Boston now. I'll be there in two hours. Can you meet me at the Marriot Long Wharf for lunch?"

"See you then."

The line went dead and Peter walked out of the Hospital and never looked back.

At the same time Peter was on the phone, Kyle and Barbosa continued their meeting. "Have you spoken to Joshua today?" Kyle asked.

"No!" Barbosa said.

"I'm telling you, Joe, the two of you have to get beyond this thing you have for each other. It's becoming detrimental."

Barbosa rose out of his seat. His dark eyes widened. "Let me tell you about 'this thing'. It is deep rooted and won't go away until he does. If that son of a bitch had done his job in the first place we wouldn't be in this mess. I told him over two years ago to take care of the problem. Now we have both barrels loaded and shoved up our asses. And you want me to get over 'this thing' we have for each other. He forgets that he's where he is today because of our hard work. We hired him, not the other way around."

Barbosa's private line rang. He picked it up and sat down.

"Barbosa," the voice on the other end said.

"What do you want Joshua?" The fine hairs on the nape of his neck stood up.

"Your boy Collas, the senator, and the feds had been dancing a slow song together. Our source confirmed he struck a deal. Collas met with the senator three times." Joshua lapsed into silence.

"That's wonderful. I'm glad he's dead." Barbosa sat forward. "Did he give them anything?"

"We don't think so. He's also met with Agent Sloan."

"And what information did he give him?" Barbosa barked.

"We don't know."

"Why not?" Barbosa demanded.

"For the same reason you didn't know what your own fellow was doing. And let us not forget he was under your nose almost twenty-four hours a day. Here's the bottom line. He accessed some files."

"How lax was your security to allow him near anything that could be dangerous to us?"

"We know what information he got hold of." Joshua continued, "We don't think he turned any of it over to Senator Demind or Agent Sloan. We think he was trying to sweeten the deal they were making with them. So for the moment it appears we're fine. The matter is completely under control. Neither Demind or Sloan got anything from Collas," Joshua said with confidence.

"Then what about Demind?" Barbosa. "We have to stop it with him."

"I'm working on something at present," Joshua said. "Tell me about Pavano."

Barbosa held his hand over the mouthpiece and turned to Kyle. "You talk to him. I've had enough of this for one day." He reached down and punched the speakerphone button. "Ask Kyle." His voice degenerated into a guttural rasp.

"Dr. Kyle, what did you think of the candidate?" Joshua's voice sounded as if it was in a tunnel. Barbosa sat and listened with seething eyes.

"There isn't that much to say. He was straightforward and honest. His resume was excellent. He's published a number of papers. He went to a prestigious school and has had good training."

"Cut the bullshit," Barbosa said. "All the candidates are qualified otherwise they wouldn't have made it this far. The bottom line is what do we know about him? Will he do what we want him to do, when we want him to do it? Will he keep his mouth shut or cause trouble? That's what we need to know. And that, Joshua, is what we pay you to find out. So why don't you tell us what *you* think of our candidate."

A long silence permeated the room. Barbosa's pupils dilated as they raked the speakerphone.

"Pavano is clean," Joshua said. "There is nothing to speak of. He graduated from Brookline High, went to the University of Michigan for pre-med, Georgetown Medical School. Both on full scholarships. He did his Internal Medicine residency at Georgetown and at present is at Cook's County for his Cardiac Fellowship. His nose is clean. He's never been in any trouble. As far as we can tell he's never even gotten a speeding ticket. As far as I am concerned he's the one."

"Fine, we'll take him. Make sure no one else offers him a contract. Let's see if you can at least do that without screwing up." Barbosa reached over and punched the disconnect button on the phone.

3 | CHAPTER THREE

July 1st came too soon for Peter. It was 8 a.m., his designated starting time, and he found himself sitting in Dr. Barbosa's office. The package had arrived in mid March. The introduction letter informed him Connecticut General Hospital chose him to be their fellow. The package contained a contract and a note instructing him to sign it and return it as soon as possible. By the first of April, and only after four disheartening calls to the other programs, the reality set in that his only offer was Connecticut General Hospital.

Peter sat in Barbosa's office resolved that it was only one year and he would survive it. Beth was still Barbosa's Secretary. He couldn't help quietly eyeing and admiring her features.

"Dr. Pavano, welcome." Clayton charged through the door and pumped his hand with vigor. "You are indeed a lucky young man to be starting your first day under my tutorage."

"Thank you Dr. Clayton. I'm glad to be here."

"Call me Charles. Well, if you're ready, let's start your first day as an Invasive Cardiologist."

"That's fine by me."

"Then let's go. Try to keep up. We are off to do God's work."

Peter followed him at a fast clip out the office and down the hall.

"Let me take you through your schedule," Clayton said as they rounded the corner and headed for the elevator. "I arrive at the hospital at eight a.m. sharp, unless some catastrophe calls

27

me in earlier. In which case I expect you to be present waiting for me. Anything other than that would be bad form. As I said, on a normal day I arrive at eight. You will be expected to have rounded on all my patients, which are now our patients. I require every patient to have been examined, evaluated, treatment plans decided on. And, all notes, and orders written."

"Yes sir," Peter said.

"By 'all patients' I mean patients that are the pre-angioplasty, post angioplasty, and any patient in the hospital that we've already done consultations on."

"I understand."

Clayton stopped and pointed a finger at Peter. "I mean all patients. Without exceptions."

"Dr. Clayton," Peter said calmly, "I do understand what you mean."

Clayton looked down his nose at Peter for an instant. "Good." He restarted their forced march towards the elevator bank. "I also expect a complete list of those patients that require our consultation. That will be your primary morning responsibility. By that, I mean you will see, evaluate, then present your evaluations and recommendation plans to me. After, of course, you have finished your aforementioned task. Any questions?"

"No. I would say your explanation has been extremely clear so far."

They boarded the third elevator in the bank of six.

"Splendid. We are alone," Clayton said. He stared straight ahead as he talked. "You will be assigned two angiograms a day for the present. I will pick them and assign you. You will observe two angioplasties in the afternoon. I will also assign you to those. Understand?"

"Without question." Peter said. He turned to make eye contact with Clayton but found himself looking at the side of his face. So, he continued. "During my cardiac fellowship I had my own service. You know, the typical staff service patient, the indigenous patient that didn't have insurance. I assume I will have. . ."

"You will have no such thing." Clayton shot him a dagger stare. "There is no staff service with us. Do you understand?"

"Actually, I don't," Peter replied. "How can you not accept patients that don't have insurance?"

"Let me explain, so you understand. We are not in the habit of giving free service to uneducated, lazy, heathens who refuse to work or pay their bills. This," he waved his arms around the empty elevator, "is a business. This is our livelihood. Those lazy un-Christian leaches on society refuse to stop abusing themselves with their smoking, drinking, and drugs. Why, then, should I come to their rescue when their coronary arteries are clogged shut? Let them first pray to God almighty for forgiveness and attempt to better themselves, or they can see the cardiac surgeon," he laughed. "If they want to cut them open and do bypass surgery for free, let them."

"Remember," Clayton shot a finger into the air. "God helps those who help themselves."

Peter shook his head. "How do you get away with not helping them? There are laws."

"That is correct. And within those laws there are quotas and ratios. We know what they are and that sets our limits. Don't misunderstand me, we do give free care."

"But you dole it out through the year until the quota is reached."

"Again correct. And once you become proficient in angioplasty those patients will be yours. Though we," he fingered his chest, "will hand pick those cases for you."

Clayton shoved his index finger into Peter's chest. "And you are never, I repeat never, to book or do a case without prior approval."

"What if they need it and all of you are tied up?" Peter said.

Clayton shrugged his shoulders. "Sometimes it is in God's hands. What can I say?"

The elevator door opened they stepped onto the floor and into one of seven telemetry units at C.G.H. Fluorescent lights bathed the surroundings with shadowless light and the hue of multiple monitored banks sat behind the nurses' station. Every patient's chest was wired and data was relayed about cardiac rate, rhythm, along with blood pressure and oxygen saturation to these stations. One glance at each screen gave a reasonable indication of the stability of each patient.

Peter and Clayton rounded, talking with and about each patient. Lastly, they jotted a quick note on each patient's chart appraising their situation.

One hour and twenty minutes later they finish their rounds. Peter had a list of the patients and memorized all the idiosyncrasies that Clayton liked to have done on his patients. At least, all those displayed today. He was sure there would be more. Peter's beeper sounded. He glanced down and read the number displayed.

"At 10:15," Clayton said, "Mrs. Cininski is scheduled for angioplasty. I will see you angiosuite No. 3. Until then you have a few moments to collect your thoughts." He started to walk away then abruptly stopped. "I would check with Beth if I were you. See if there are any consults." He walked away at a fast clip.

Peter pick up the nearest phone and dialed the number on his beeper.

"Peter. Welcome to C.G.H."

Peter recognized Dr. Kyle's voice. "Thank you."

"I'm in Coronary Care Unit No. 2. Join me, I'll wait for you."

Peter hung up the phone and walked off the unit.

"Are you one of the new doctors?" Peter was face to face with an employee. He was short, had a flattened nose, curved fingers and slightly protruding tongue. But the most prominent feature Peter saw was an outgoing smile.

"Yes, I am." He returned the smile. "I just started today. My name's Doctor Pavano, but you can call me Peter."

The young man held up his little hand and gave a slight wave. "Hi, Peter. My name's Dusty. I work in housekeeping. You need anything, you ask me. OK?"

"Yes, I will. Thank you."

"Bye." Dusty turned and quickly waddled down the hall.

It took Peter a few minutes longer than expected, but he finally found the C. C. U. #2. Kyle was waiting patiently.

"Sorry, I got lost."

"That's OK. I don't expect you to know your way around on day one. I finished my two morning angioplasties, why don't we make rounds. I usually make them between procedures. I like to make life easy on myself, and that means not getting up at six in the morning to start at seven. But," he put a hand on Peter shoulder, "life isn't that kind to the fellow. Even though you are assigned to Dr. Clayton for your first month you will round on my patients. I usually see them between nine thirty and ten thirty. As I said, between procedures, on days when you are free I'll expect you to round with me. But every day you will see them before me."

They both walked into the first patient's room only to have Kyle interrupted by a beeper page. Moments later, he returned. "Peter, I'm on call for the ER. They need me to see a patient. Why don't you finish up with your notes on this patient and join me there."

A short while later, Peter walked at a fast clip towards the emergency room. It had been many months since his interview and his visit there, but he immediately recognized a few faces. Upon entering the ER he stood for a moment and looked around. It was relatively quiet but he knew that could change instantly.

"I see you didn't take my advice."

Peter turned to face the ER nurse.

"Excuse me?"

"You didn't take my advice. You were in the ER a few months ago. Dr. Barbosa threw one of his special temper tantrums. You were on an interview. I told you to skip it and leave."

Peter smiled, "No, I didn't take your advice. I really didn't have much choice."

"Good luck." She held out her hand. "I'm Joan. If I can help you anytime, call me."

6-MUCC

"Thank you, I will." He walked over to where Kyle stood.

"Well, Dr. Pavano," Kyle handed him two EKG's, "they are five minutes apart. The first one is thirty-five minutes after the onset of constant chest pain."

Peter perused them. "The first EKG is suggestive of an early inferior wall MI. The second EKG confirms it. There are more ischemic changes consistent with a rapidly progressing inferior wall infarction. Was the pain relieved by IV Nitroglycerin?"

"No."

"If there's no confrontations to angioplasty, that's the way I'd go."

Kyle stared at him. "You're awfully confident for a person who's never done one."

Peter knew the look. His dad had stared him down so many times he'd become immune to it.

"I'm sorry, I didn't mean to be presumptuous. This is a very clear-cut case. Angioplasty is the appropriate therapeutic modality."

Kyle smiled. "Agreed, Doctor. Let's talk with the patient."

* * * * *

The angioplasty suite was a room loaded with every imaginable piece of high-tech equipment, computer, EKG machines, cardiac monitor, echo-cardiac machines, and an X-ray machine. The equipment was stacked and squeezed into every available space. In the center of these cold dead machines, on a cold hard table, lay a warm-blooded, air-breathing, terrified human being.

Kyle, dressed in surgical scrubs and a protective gown, addressed Peter, who dressed the same. "OK, Dr. Pavano let's test your knowledge. I assume you have at least read about how the procedure is done."

"Yes sir. I have, many times over," Peter said.

"Good. Then I want you to teach me. . . to talk me through this procedure as if it were my first. I hope you are as confident and capable as you were in the emergency room, because this patient's life may depend on it. What do you want me to do first?"

Peter fixed his eyes on the patient, who stared back, a look of terror in his eyes. Terror of the upcoming procedure, terror of the rapidity with which his life had changed. Two hours ago he was safe. Now he was on the brink of death. Terror of the partially relieved pressure that squeezed his chest and worst of all, terror at the game his trusted cardiologist, whom he just met, proposed to play with his life.

Peter approached the patient and squatted down so they were eye to eye. "Dr. Kyle will be doing this procedure from start to finish. This is only my first day. He just wants to test my knowledge. He will not do anything wrong, no matter what I tell him to do. To be able to describe the procedure is part of the training. OK?"

The patient bit his lips and nodded his thanks. But his blue eyes watered over and told Peter how we really felt.

Peter stood up. "Dr. Kyle, the first thing I'd do is give this patient five milligrams of Verced intravenously."

"Verced? Why Verced?"

"Why? Because he's terrified. I'd be, too, if one minute I were driving to work then an hour later I was told that if I didn't have this procedure I might not survive the day let alone lead a normal life. Yes, Doctor, I want to give Verced."

"Good. I agree. I'm a sympathetic doctor. I'm glad you are too."

The muscles in the back of Peter's neck tensed though he did not respond.

* * * * *

"How accurate is your source?" Barbosa stoically stared out of his office window at his domain below.

33

Joshua's voice rolled out of the speakerphone. "Very accurate. Pavano has already been targeted."

Barbosa spun. His voice attacked the phone. "If your source is so accurate why didn't he know about Collas until it was too late?"

"Collas did all his work independently. The key being, Collas approached them after he found something. Until then no one knew of any breach. This time though they've decided to go after Pavano."

"That doesn't make any sense. This is Pavano's first day. He knows nothing. They wouldn't go after him unless they have something on him. You said he was clean."

"Squeaky clean," Joshua said.

"Obviously not." Barbosa sat down at his desk. "Find out what they have on him." He punched the disconnect button.

At 5:03 Peter walked into Barbosa's office. He was three minutes late.

"Lets get one thing straight, Pavano," Barbosa clenched his jaw. "When you have a meeting with me you show up ten minutes early."

Peter took a seat in front of Barbosa's desk without saying a word. "I hope that in the future you are more proficient in seeing my patients in the morning . . . before I arrive." His eyes bore down in Peter. "I do not enjoy doing your work for you." His voice started to rise. "That is why I hired you. That is what I pay you for."

"Yes sir," Peter replied without any annoyance in his tone. "I had intended to get a list of your patients when Dr. Kyle called me stat to the ER. He had to do an emergency angioplasty and he wanted me there. He told me to finish my rounds later."

"How nice of him." Barbosa changed his tone. "Dr. Kyle did mention the procedure. He was impressed with your compassion and knowledge. Don't get cocky. It takes a whole lot more to impress me."

"When will I be working with you?"

The Cardiac Cartel

David Mucci

Copyright © 2001 by David Mucci.

Library of Congress Number:		2001117097
ISBN #:	Hardcover	1-4010-0489-X
	Softcover	1-4010-0490-3

All rights reserved. No part of this book may be reproduced or
transmitted in any form or by any means, electronic or mechanical,
including photocopying, recording, or by any information storage
and retrieval system, without permission in writing from the
copyright owner.

This is a work of fiction. Names, characters, places and incidents
either are the product of the author's imagination or are used
fictitiously, and any resemblance to any actual persons, living or
dead, events, or locales is entirely coincidental.

This book was printed in the United States of America.

To order additional copies of this book, contact:
Xlibris Corporation
1-888-795-4274
www.Xlibris.com
Orders@Xlibris.com

ACKNOWLEDGMENTS

I am very grateful to Louis Graff M.D., F.A.C.E.P. for sparking the idea behind the book's plot. My thanks to Robert Borkowski M.D., F.A.C.C., F.A.C.P., for his tutorage in angioplasty. Any misrepresentation of what is involved in real angioplasty is poetic license or oversight on my part.

My special thanks to Virginia Wolf. Her encouragement, editing, and character development ideas helped me persevere through the years I've worked on this story. Thanks to Barbara Van Bramer for the editing and reassurance in the final stages.

And finally to my wife and soul mate, Jeanne–your love, support, and efforts are the foundation for all the wonderful things that happen in my life.

Cover design by Brian Schmitt. My appreciation for all your research and creative talent.

"When I say you will."

Peter marveled at Barbosa's resemblance to his father. He'd come full circle.

Barbosa continued, "I apologize for not meeting you earlier today. I'm sure that after the busy morning you've had you can understand how busy I have been also."

Peter nodded. Barbosa's sudden collegiality set off alarms.

"I wanted to talk to you and explain the expectations I have for you for the upcoming year. First, I want you to consider my door open to you at anytime. I don't want you to fall into the same trap my last Fellow did."

"I've heard just a little about him. What happened?"

"He killed himself. Instead of walking through that door and telling me he was having problems, he jumped off the roof. I hope you won't snap under the pressure."

"No, Dr. Barbosa. I can assure you I won't be killing myself anytime soon."

"There will be a lot of pressures placed upon you in the near future," Barbosa said in an unusually fatherly tone. "If anything does bother you I want you to come to me."

"I promise I will."

"Good. Now let's get down to business. I arrive at the hospital every morning at eight, sharp. I expect you to have made rounds on all of my patients."

"That is not a problem," Peter said with confidence.

"The only restriction is under no circumstances are you to see them or wake them before seven in the morning. I think one hour should give you enough time. Don't you?" His eyes locked onto Peter.

Peter was running through his mind the schedule he had to concoct to meet everyone's demands for morning rounds. He looked at Barbosa and smiled. "Yes. I can handle that."

"I'm glad you agree. Your duties were light today. Tomorrow you will start one week of Angioplasty training at the Cardiac

Institute in Boston. When you return, your duties, and our expectations will increase."

Barbosa's body language relaxed.

"I look forward to it." Peter stared unflinchingly at him.

Barbosa's phone buzzed. "Yes."

"Dr. Barbosa, Bill Wilder is on line one." Beth's voice came over the speakerphone.

"Dr. Pavano," Barbosa continued, "always remember, you, and you alone, are in charge of your destiny. A case in point, Bill Wilder is a highly influential, wealthy, stockbroker. Yet he sits on hold waiting for me to answer his call. He most likely has some stock tip he wants to sell me on, hoping I'll buy or sell something so he can earn his commission. He occasionally gives me a good tip."

"What if he's wrong?" Peter asked.

"Then I have no one to blame but myself. That's because I," Barbosa thumped his chest, "make all the decisions. I tell him how much to buy and at what price. I tell him what to sell."

"I'm surprised you use a broker. In this day and age of on-line brokers why not do it yourself?" Peter said.

"Oh I do. But you miss the point of power and wealth, Dr. Pavano. When I buy and sell anything on my own, he gets nothing." Barbosa glanced at the blinking light.

"I have ninety million dollars in my account with his firm. That keeps Wilder on his toes to be on top of my account. Have a nice day. Enjoy your week at the Cardiac institute," Barbosa said. "Shut the door on your way out."

4 | CHAPTER FOUR

The Cardiac Institute was built on the Cambridge side of the Charles River. The side that faced the river was fitted with an expanse of mirrored windows that gave those inside, and out, a spectacular panoramic view of Boston on the opposite shore.

Annually during the first full week in July, the incoming invasive cardiology fellows arrived at the Institute for a mandatory week of angioplasty training.

The Institute was founded for the advancement of cardiac knowledge, and is sustained by an annual gift from an anonymous benefactor. Hapless medical students, as well as skilled cardiologists, migrate through the marble arched entrance throughout the year to participate in many of the lectures and training labs. Using the newest computers, and virtual reality imagery, along with robotics, they are given hands on experience without the risk of harm to real patients.

Peter stood off to one side of the glass foyer. Trees and shrubs filled the large atrium, and the soft splash from cascading water soothed all those nearby. It was a beautiful setting for a training institution.

Peter scanned his program for the day's events. To his surprise he saw Barbosa listed as one of the keynote speakers. He leaned against a marble column in the lobby and watched groups of participants stroll by. Occasionally, he looked past their heads to the Boston skyline not far away.

37

How he missed Boston. It was good to be back. How long had it been? Sixteen? Seventeen years? Either way, it had been too long.

On the drive up from Connecticut, he had decided to find time to visit Ethel. He owed her that bit of respect. After all, if it weren't for her he would most likely have stayed a homeless runaway, in jail, if not dead from drugs. He wanted to show her what he'd become.

It was just about eight in the morning when he entered the auditorium and took a seat off to one side. Precisely at eight, and to Peter's amusement, Barbosa walked up to the podium and stood there. He didn't utter a word. He simply stood there straight in his thousand dollar tailored suit filled with poised arrogance. The only movement was his eyes. They slowly scanned from one side of the room to the other then back again, momentarily grabbing on to those that dared make eye contact with him. A dense silence quickly fell over those seated. All eyes locked on him. Despite everyone's undivided attention, Barbosa continued to stand there in silence.

Then with slow, melodramatic movements, Barbosa placed both hands on the podium and leaned into the microphone. "So, you are all cardiologists." He slowly looked around the room at the nodding heads. "So what. Who cares? . . . Let me tell you. You are a dime a dozen. You push your pills, maybe on a good day you get to give thrombolytics and dissolve a blood clot in an artery. You feel great because you've reversed a heart attack. And on one of your better days you do an angiogram. You inject dye directly into a coronary artery and take a picture of a blockage."

His words hung in the air as he smiled sardonically. This time Barbosa nodded his head. "Again I say, who cares? . . . You find the blockage . . . But you can't do a God damned thing about it . . . until now, that is."

Peter looked around the room. Barbosa had them in the palm of his hand.

"Up until now," Barbosa continued, "you were nothing more than gophers, and technicians, for the cardiac surgeons. You found the lesions and they fixed them. They got the big bucks, the glory, and the thanks. But . . . no more. Today, you are beginning your journey to becoming invasive cardiologists. In a great majority of cases, you'll be able to compete directly . . . for those of you who missed it the first time, I'll repeat myself . . . you'll be able to compete directly with the cardiac surgeons.

"You!" Barbosa pointed to a physician in the front row. "What do you think your patients will say when you tell them they can either have their chest split open like a chicken breast for by-pass surgery, or that you can pass a thin wire up a vessel from their groin and have their blocked artery opened up again?"

Now in a low tone Barbosa continued. "And what do you think they'll say when you tell them angioplasty costs only a few thousand dollars compared to the twenty-five thousand or more dollars a cardiac surgeon will charge?

"I'll tell you what they'll say." He leaned forward on the podium and placed his lips against the microphone. "They'll say, 'Do it, Doctor'. And they'll say 'Thank you, Doctor'. And the cardiac surgeons will get angry with you for taking away their business. But I say . . . who cares? WHO CARES! Learn hard, learn well, Doctors. God knows my Fellow will. Isn't that right, Dr. Pavano?"

Peter's only reaction was a slight nod of his head in agreement. He marveled at Barbosa's driving eyes.

* * * * *

Barbosa strutted down the hallway, the arrogance of power evident in every step.

"I was moved by your speech. It made me feel like I was at a pep rally."

Barbosa spun around to face Joshua Kleinman. They were alone in the corridor. Joshua stood eight inches shorter than

)6-MUCC

Barbosa. He also wore a finely tailored suit. He meticulously parted his hair just right of center, and had perfectly manicured fingernails. The tan, lean, toned body indicated he was partial to outdoor activities.

"Joshua," Barbosa nodded and waited for him to approach.

"So, Barbosa, we start one more year."

"It's Doctor Barbosa."

"Ah . . . sorry . . . Dr. Barbosa. I forgot you need your title to remind yourself of how important you are."

"Don't push me. What do you want?"

Joshua clenched his teeth. "We meet in forty-five minutes."

"I'll be there."

"I can't tell you how happy that makes me." Joshua spun one hundred and eighty degrees and started to walk away.

"One moment," Barbosa said.

Joshua stopped but didn't turn around. "What do you want, Dr. Barbosa?"

"I am curious. When and how are you going to take care of that little gnat that continues to bite at our feet?"

Joshua kept his back to him. "Barbosa, canceling a crusade against us is not as easy as you think. You don't waltz into his office with a suitcase filled with a few million dollars, hand it to him, and tell him to leave you alone."

"So the war continues then."

"At this point. Yes. There is very little we can do about it. Unless you have a brilliant idea."

"I thought that was what we paid you for. Is it time we re-evaluated your contract?'

"Barbosa, don't ever threaten me." Joshua took a few steps away from him.

"Don't walk away from me until I'm through speaking to you."

Joshua stopped, his back still to Barbosa. "You're right. My mother did teach me better manners."

Barbosa walked up to him, leaned down and spoke into his ear from behind. "You were lucky with Collas. But your internal investigation caused me quite a bit of embarrassment amongst my colleagues. You should have come to me privately. And the matter should have been handled that way also. Just a word of warning, I'd let this be the last time you turn your back to me."

"Ah, so now the good doctor resorts to threats."

All Joshua heard was the sound of footsteps receding behind him.

* * * * *

They received only one day of lectures. But it was a day of intensive instruction. The history of angioplasty, the successes, the multiple failures, it was fascinating if you were a history buff, but Peter rarely found a patient who asked about the history and development of a procedure. They were more interested in the doctor's history. How many had he done? How many were successful. And, more importantly, how many were failures. So the next day when his group moved into the actual practice lab Peter felt a tingle of excitement.

There were twenty-three labs, all identical. Peter found his assigned room, and entered.

"You must be Dr. Pavano." A man in a clean white lab coat approached.

"Yes. You are Dr. Citrullo?"

"That's right."

They shook hands.

"Come. Let me show you around."

They walked over to equipment that looked similar to that which Peter had used during cardiac angiographies.

Dr. Citrullo started in, cheerful and enthusiastic. "We have your standard equipment, fluoroscopic imaging, regular x-ray, heart monitor, and blood pressure monitors. And, of course, the angioplasty catheter."

41

Peter scanned the room. His eyes focused on the dummy mannequin that lay on the procedure table. "You've gone through a lot of trouble to make him look so real."

"Oh, but he is real," Dr. Citrullo smiled. "Let's start with Bill here." He pointed to the dummy. "The general public is very familiar with 'Resuscitator Annie' from CPR courses given at the YMCA. Well, let me introduce you to 'Dilate-me Bill'. Bill is the closest thing to a real patient you could work on. His vascular tree from his groin to his heart functions realistically. His heart pumps a liquid that is red, and has the same viscosity as blood. Bill's heart, controlled by a computer, regulates the pressure inside its fake vasculature."

"I'm impressed," Peter said.

"There's more. The computer controls Bill's pump, giving it a rate and rhythm. It will increase, decrease and if you really make a mistake, stop. And then Bill dies."

Peter glanced at the monitors.

Dr. Citrullo continued, even more enthusiastic and animated than before. "That monitor is fed by the computer. It will give you an EKG that correlates to Bill's pumping heart. But, what's most impressive is you'll actually do angioplasty on Bill's coronary arteries."

Peter looked at Bill then Dr. Citrullo. "I assume there are small tubes attached to the pump and we catheterize them."

"Yes . . . and no. We have multiple tubes attached to the base of Bill's heart. Similar to where the coronary arteries are attached in real patients. You will catheterize these tubes and the computer will give you an image that looks like a real heart on the fluoroscopic screen. With the computer we can make that image look like a thousand different variations with multiple different lesions."

"But, how real will it feel for me? Watching a screen is fine for video games. But I'll need to get the feel in my fingers for the actual procedure."

"And you will," Dr. Citrullo said. "You will actually be doing the procedure. Bill is completely lifelike. His heart moves and jumps like a real one. You'll have to thread the guide wire into the tubes at just the right angle, similar to real life. All the while, the heart is bouncing all over the screen, and in his chest. And off those tubes are multiple smaller tubes. The computer will open and close them depending on the configuration we set up. And the computer will constrict any area of any vessel, realistically giving you a blocked coronary artery to dilate."

"Virtual reality takes over medicine," Peter smiled.

"That's for sure. The recorded image of Bill's monitor is indistinguishable from a video of a real angioplasty. In fact, if you were to give me a video of a patient's angiography I could feed it into the computer and it in turn would set up Bill's arteries to look the same."

"In essence," Peter said, "you could practice a difficult procedure before performing it on your real patient."

"Exactly. Let's get started."

Over the remainder of the day, and week, Peter found himself immersed in saving 'Dilate-me Bill'. From stable to crashing vital signs and dying patients, the computer and Dr. Citrullo put him through the paces. At week's end, he'd simulated twenty-six procedures with varying degrees of success.

Nonetheless, after his last procedure he felt ready to try it for real. He knew he'd get that chance within a few days.

On the afternoon of the last day of the conference, Peter stood in the atrium of the Institute and took in the view. The conference was over but he still had two obligations to fulfill. One was an appearance at the evening's farewell banquet and dance. Before that, he wanted to visit Ethel. Then he'd have Sunday to enjoy Boston.

He walked out to the curb and hailed a cab. Twenty minutes later the cab pulled over and stopped. Peter didn't get out immediately. Instead he sat in the back seat with his arms resting on the open window. Deep in thought, he stared at the wrought iron gate that surrounded the finely manicured lawn.

"How you gonna get back?" the cabby asked.

"Huh . . . ah, do you mind waiting?"

"How long?"

"Twenty minutes. Maybe thirty."

"It'll cost you thirty bucks. A buck a minute for waiting."

"Fine." Peter got out and walked through the gate. He thought for a moment. Was she to the right or left? He felt ashamed. He'd forgotten. He walked to the right and after a while instinct took over. Finally, he stood before Ethel Pavano's grave.

"Hi, Ethel." He sat down on the grass. "It's Peter. Doctor Peter. I did it." He felt a bittersweet happiness. "I want you to know I owe it all to you. I couldn't have done it without you. I only wish you were here to see it. To share it with me."

"She was a good woman, wasn't she?"

Peter turned and saw a man he guessed was about fifty-five years old standing close to the grave. He wore denim slacks and a soft cotton pullover. He had a hard face with chiseled features.

"Did you know her?" Peter asked.

"No. Never met her."

"You said she was a good woman like you knew her."

"She had to have been."

"Why?"

"Look what she did for you."

"Have we met?"

"No."

Peter stood slowly. He looked around at the rolling landscape of Auburn Hills Cemetery. It was majestic, so calm and serene. His eyes fell on the headstone.

"Who are you and what do you want?" Peter asked.

The man stood a good six inches shorter than Peter. He pulled out a cigarette and placed it between his lips.

Peter calmly took it out of the strangers' lips and handed it back to him. "No smoking," he said. "Ethel didn't allow smoking around her. It's the least I can do to respect her wishes."

The man put it in his pocket. "My name's Dack Sloan. I work with the FBI". He pulled a picture identification from his back pocket and held it up for Peter to read.

"What does the F.B.I want with me?"

"Your help."

"With what?"

"Come walk with me. I need a cigarette."

When the two were fifty feet from Ethel's grave he lit up and inhaled. "My partner and I are on special assignment. Have been for over a year. We saw that you were the new boy with Barbosa and company and thought we should talk."

"I didn't know accepting a fellowship broke any federal laws that required the FBI to investigate," Peter said.

"It's not you we're investigating. It's Barbosa and his crew. They've formed a private little society."

"So, it's not unusual for groups to form societies. And I hate to break it to you, it's not illegal." Peter stopped and turned to Sloan. "Unless they're doing something illegal. Do you want to tell me why you are so interested in them that you followed me into a cemetery?"

"No." Sloan paused and took a deep drag off his cigarette. "At the moment, I'm just going to tell you to be careful. Don't trust any of the Doc's you're working with."

"Tell me," Peter said, "why should I trust you? All you've given me is a loose accusation with no explanation. I don't even know you. Why should I trust you?"

"Because your predecessor Dr. Collas didn't. And he is dead." Sloan took another hit off his cigarette and looked around. "And, it was no suicide."

"Agent Sloan. Let's get to the bottom line. You didn't come all this way just to warn me. What is it that you want from me?"

"Your help."

"First, I don't know how I can help you, and second, I don't know why I should help you."

"Oh, you can help us, Doctor. You can help us a lot. We need help on the inside. Someone to research a few things. There's a big scam going on. And as to why you should help us, it's simple. To protect yourself . . . and Ethel's good name."

"I don't think Ethel has anything to do with this conversation."

"Sorry, Woods. It is Steven Woods? Isn't it? And as far as Ethel is concerned, she is very much a part of this."

Peter stopped and sat on the nearest gravestone. He folded his arms.

Sloan continued, "Ethel was a good person. She loved to help students. She was a good teacher, well respected within the school system. So when her cousin's son came to live with her no one questioned when she enrolled him in high school. She presents his transfer transcripts to the school admissions board. They seem in order, so, no problem. He was allowed to finish his last year of high school and graduate. But, the problem is, when we looked into it we found Ethel didn't have a cousin with a son named Peter. In fact, those transcripts along with your birth certificate were fake. So the question is who are you, Dr. Pavano? Why the charade?"

"I've done nothing wrong."

"Falsifying high school records, which allowed you to enroll in college, then in medical school—"

"I earned my admission into medical school," Peter said.

"Yes you did. But I wonder how the Connecticut licensing board along with the American Board of Cardiology would react if they found out your past, and that your records were fake."

"You know damn well how they'd react."

"Yes I do. You'd lose your license and be an unknown again. What are you hiding? Who are you, Dr. Pavano? I wonder, do we need to dig deeper into your past?"

"No. You don't."

"No, I guess I don't. Go back to your conference, Doctor. I will contact you."

"Why me?"

"Simple. We need help. And you're in the right place. And you're vulnerable." Sloan walked away and left Peter amongst the headstones.

That evening, Peter stood outside the elevator and glanced at the invitation. Then he eyed his reflection in the mirror, Docker jeans and a button down shirt. The invitation had said casual. He'd never been a slave to fashion, and he wasn't about to start now. The ballroom was on the third floor. After showing the invitation at the door, he entered.

"Would you like a glass of champagne or wine?" A waiter dressed in cowboy attire asked.

"Thank you." He took a glass of Chardonnay. "This is quite an impressive layout."

"Sure is. The theme's the Wild West. All you can eat. Feel free to help yourself."

Peter looked around. "Why the Wild West?"

The waiter pointed to the back wall where a banner hung from the ceiling.

ANGIOPLASTY: THE BIGGEST FRONTIER
SINCE THE WILD WEST

Peter shook his head.

"Hey, I just work here," the waiter said. "I wear what they tell me."

Peter strolled around the ballroom, stopping at the food stations. He sampled chili at one, barbecued ribs at another. All in all, he kept to himself. His meeting with Sloan troubled him.

There were well over five hundred people in the room. Despite the size of the hall, with the people, the food stations, the band and dance floor, it was fairly crowded.

By complete accident he found himself next to Barbosa. Since the introductory speech, Peter hadn't seen him at all throughout the week.

47

"Dr. Barbosa," he extended his hand only to have it hang empty in mid air. His conversation with Agent Sloan was fresh on his mind.

"What do you want Pavano?" Barbosa said.

Peter returned Barbosa's deadpan stare. "I didn't see you at any of the lectures or labs. I thought you would have been one of the instructors."

"You'll be getting enough one on one with me throughout the year. Let's just say that was your reprieve from me, a reprieve you should savor. I'll ask you at the end of the year if you consider working with me a pleasure."

"Yes, time will tell," Peter replied without a blink.

Barbosa looked around the room.

"Did your wife come tonight?" Peter asked.

"No. She had some tennis match that she runs every year at the country club. If she's not spending my money, she's giving it away to one of her many charities."

Peter thought about Ethel and how she had made him her charity. "Do you have any charities that you endow?"

"I really don't think that's any of your business, Pavano."

"Sorry, I meant no disrespect."

"Enjoy the evening. Have my rounds done by eight Monday morning." Barbosa walked away.

Peter looked at his watch. Ten o'clock. It wasn't too late and the evening was pleasant. Why not go for a nice walk along the waterfront, he thought. He headed for the door, but stopped short at the display near the exit.

It was the only display in the entire ballroom. Set out on tables was a multitude of angioplasty and angiography catheters.

"Can I answer any questions?" The most attractive of the three women tending the booth approached. She wore a high riding cowgirl dress that displayed her perfectly toned long legs. Her ample breasts made the fringe on her shirt sway gently with each step. With her auburn hair and large chestnut brown eyes, she was the prettiest woman Peter had seen in a long time.

Peter looked at the display. Out of the corner of his eye, he noticed that Barbosa had only stopped ten feet away and stood alone. The catheters were all from the same company. For that matter, this was the only company represented tonight.

The young lady stood patiently in front of him. Finally, he looked back at her. "I'm surprised there aren't any competitors here."

She smiled. "American Standard Catheter Inc. sponsored this gala event. So we kept the competition out."

"Did American Standard Catheter Inc. also sponsor our week at the Cardiac Institute?"

"As a matter of fact, yes." Her smile broadened. "Doctor, you'll be seeing a lot of my company. We're pretty prominent in the field."

Peter looked at the display, at Barbosa, then back at her. "Yes, I see you are. If you'll excuse me," he said. "Have a nice night."

"You're leaving so soon? Aren't you having a good time?" She placed a hand on her hip seductively.

He cleared his throat. "Actually, no I'm not. This isn't my idea of how to spend an evening in Boston. I'd prefer to be walking along the waterfront."

"With a woman on your arm?"

Peter raised his eyebrows at her. "Yes."

"Well then, don't let me keep you."

Peter smiled at her and left without another word.

* * * * *

Kelsey watched Peter's back as he walked away, and then turned to Janice, her co-worker. "Could you excuse me for a moment? I need to visit the ladies' room."

When she turned the corner into the hallway, she found herself spun around and pinned against the wall. Peter leaned his weight against her tightly. With an explosive heave she pushed him away.

49

The two stared at each other defiantly. Kelsey looked both ways down the hall, but saw no one. Wide eyed she leaned forward, grabbed Peter around the back of his head with both hands and pulled him into her. They embraced in a long passionate, deep, kiss.

"Peter, how I've missed you."

"Not as much as I've missed you." His eyes bathed her with desire. Kelsey had transferred to Boston from the Washington, DC area. She wanted to be close to Peter during the upcoming year. And she hoped to settle in the area with Peter.

"We have to be careful, Barbosa is here. God forbid the Gestapo sees me fraternizing with a female."

Kelsey grabbed him between his legs. "From what you've said, he just might cut these off."

"There is no doubt he'd try."

"He'd have to fight me off first. These are mine," she grinned. "The display ends at 11:00."

Peter smiled, "I'll wait for you in the lobby.'

The evening air was hot and humid. A typical New England steamer. The walk along Boston Harbor was quiet and gentle, filled with hugs and kisses. They exchanged soft words of love. But not even Kelsey's presence could ease Peter's thoughts. Ethel's kindness, her lessons and righteousness, and what she had done for him haunted him. Now a stranger had come into his life and threatened to take away everything he'd earned, and he didn't have a clue why. He knew he couldn't let that happen.

5 | CHAPTER FIVE

Monday morning Peter entered the first full week of his fellowship. To his great surprise rounds went without a mishap or interruption. He was on his way to meet Clayton when he turned a corner and found himself face to face with him traveling in the opposite direction.

"Good morning Dr. Clayton. I was just—"

Clayton held his hand up in front of Peter's face and kept walking. "Sorry. Can't talk now, I'm busy." Clayton scurried around him and turned the corner.

"—coming to find you," Peter finished. "I think this is going to be a long day," Peter said as he turned to follow him.

Moments later, Peter walked into Angioplasty Suite #2.

"Well, good morning, Dr. Pavano." Clayton stared at him. "So good to see you. Our walking rounds will be postponed today. Are you up to snuff today?"

"I'll let you be the judge of that," Peter replied straight-faced.

"Good. Then let's begin."

The morning's procedures went smoothly and without incident. Clayton's skill and dexterity impressed Peter, but his lectures grew tiresome.

"'The value of wisdom', Dr. Pavano. 'Happy the man who finds wisdom, the man who gains understanding! For her profit is better than profit in silver, and better than gold is her revenue; She is more precious than corals, and none of your possessions can compare with her'. Proverbs, chapter three, Dr. Pavano."

6-MUCC

Peter just nodded.

"Back to the task at hand, Dr. Pavano."

Peter watched him introduce a burr bit and advance it to the partially occluded lesion in the patient's coronary artery. "The American Cardiac Invasive Journal, February last year. An article by Rostein and Blumfield entitled, 'Burring versus dilating'". While he pontificated about the article, Peter watched him advance the bit and shave the walls of the vessel open. "We are done. You should read that article. Someone besides me should. It describes a subgroup of lesions, which this one fell into. It says they do better over the long term with burr shaving over dilatation."

Clayton threw his hands into the air and stepped back. "For the lowly may be pardoned out of mercy, but the mighty shall be mightily put to the test." He threw a glance at Peter. "Pull the catheter out. I'm done."

Clayton spun and left the room.

Peter shook his head. "I can't believe this."

"What?" the technician asked. "You can't believe he left you to clean up after him? Hey, when you're an attending I'm sure you'll dump on your fellow also. Remember, it flows down hill."

"Wrong," Peter replied. "I can't believe how he twists the scriptures around. "Terribly and swiftly shall he come against you, because judgment is stern for the exalted-for the lowly may be pardoned out of mercy but the mighty shall be mightily put to the test. For the Lord of all shows no partiality nor does he fear greatness, because he himself made the greatness as well as the small."

"I don't get it," the technician said.

"It means the dumber you are the more you are forgiven. And if you are smart and powerful you will be judged on that level. A higher level, with a higher punishment. Dr. Clayton twisted it around to make himself look great and wonderful. It's about seeking wisdom and judgment, not about patting yourself on the back and saying how great you are."

"Are you going to tell him that?" The technician stared at him.

There was only silence.

"I didn't think so. Let's clean up and get out of here."

It was his third procedure of the day with Clayton. Between procedures he rounded with Kyle. And Barbosa called him with three more consults to do.

"Before noon," Barbosa demanded.

Peter knew it took a full hour per patient to do a new consult. The clock on the wall didn't allow that. Instead he cut corners, a skill all overworked fellows had learned. He would then go back in the evening and fill in the holes he had left. Anyway, he justified, few consults require immediate intervention. By ordering a few repeat tests, he could leave the work-up ongoing until that data had been compiled. Those that required immediate intervention were the easy ones. They were stat consults that involved the attending in a timelier manner, and they also provided him with one or more acceptable excuses for not finishing his multiple tasks. "Unstable patients requiring immediate life saving intervention always superseded all other work." He remembered many of his instructors saying.

Peter was hungry and thirsty when he entered Angiosuite #2 to assists Clayton in another procedure.

"Dr. Pavano," Clayton started, "know these words: Hear, O children, a father's instruction, be attentive, that you may gain understanding! Yes, excellent advice I give you; my teaching do not forsake. When I was my father's child, frail, yet the darling of my mother, He taught me, and said to me; "Let your heart hold fast my words:" keep my commands, that you may live! Dr. Pavano that is Proverbs Chapter five, Wisdom: the Supreme Guide of Men."

"Chapter Four. The Supreme Guide to Men is Chapter Four," Peter said.

"What did you say?" Clayton said.

"I'm sorry but Wisdom: The Supreme Guide to Men is Chapter Four, not Chapter Five."

There was a very long silence in the room. No one had ever dared contradict Clayton, especially with a challenge to his religious knowledge.

Clayton's mouth hung open for a moment. Then he broke the silence. "Dr. Pavano, you impress me. Somewhere in your past someone did you a world of good. You are right. It is Chapter Four. I stand corrected. You were schooled properly in the work of the Lord."

"That's one way of looking at it," Peter replied. His thoughts flashed back to his drunken father.

"You won't eat a damn thing until you recite that verse without a mistake." His tremulous hands slammed the bible down in front of Peter, who sat at the kitchen table. His father, with bourbon breath, had been liquored up all day and was in a foul, preaching mood.

"Do you practice what you recite?"

Peter jolted back to the present. "What did you say?"

"Maybe some day you'll consider joining me in Ecuador. It'll do your soul good to help those heathens. Remember, Dr. Pavano. Happy is he who has regard for the lowly and the poor. Psalm 41."

Barbosa sat back in his chair while he talked on the speakerphone. "Joshua, my displeasure with you is unchanged. I was not swayed at all by you sidetracking my questions concerning Senator Demind at our last meeting."

"At tomorrow's council meeting, I will present the plan I have been working on. You are just going to have to wait until then." The voice sounded hollow over the speaker. "On another note, how is Pavano working out?"

"Medically, the word is, he is impressing everyone. I'm told he can also out quote Clayton when it comes to scriptures. He corrected him earlier today. I'm watching him. I'm giving him so much work to do he has to schedule bathroom breaks. He won't be doing any snooping. He'll be lucky if he finishes the year."

"On that we agree. Work him as hard as you like. Last week Sloan was in Boston. I've had a tail on him since his last meeting with Collas. We followed him to a cemetery. And who do you think he met there?"

"Pavano?" Barbosa sat forward in his chair.

"That's right."

"I hope your source was able to tell us what they discussed."

"Not at the moment. We only know they met and walked and talked. We don't know about what. Hopefully, we will soon. I think, given the turn of events, bugging his apartment and car are the least we should do."

"Joshua, if you blow this one you know I'll make sure you're finished."

* * * * *

It was 11:17 A.M. the next day. Clayton and Pavano were mid-procedure. It had become one of those disasters, the kind that became worse with every attempt to fix the latest complication. The left main coronary artery had been blocked at two different sites. The first site had been dilated without difficulty but the second one had thrown Clayton into a verbal tirade. The beeps from the cardiac monitor mingled with the heavy breathing from Clayton and Pavano, tightening the grip of tension in the air.

"The Lord is making us repent, to suffer for our sins. Our moral fiber is being tested with this one, Dr. Pavano. If we are righteous, we will prevail. If this patient is to survive, we must prevail."

Clayton injected some intravenous dye through the catheter and watched it spread across the x-ray imaging monitor.

Peter was the first to notice and commented. "The artery has ruptured. The dye's leaking."

"Dr. Pavano, do you know what Nathan the Prophet said to David when he came to him after his sin with Bathsheba?"

"Yes. He said, 'Have mercy on me, O God, in your goodness; in the greatness of your compassion wipe out my offense. Thoroughly wash me from my guilt and of my sin cleanse me'."

"You are a wise man, Dr. Pavano. Today we need that goodness."

Clayton had attempted one too many times to dilate the second blockage. What he'd accomplished was to rip the artery instead of dilating it. Dye and blood leaked into the sac that surrounded the heart. If not stopped, the bleeding would continue until the sac filled with blood and squeezed the heart like a vise, unable to beat, unable to pump blood. The rhythmic beeps from the cardiac monitor increased in rate, announcing the insult the heart had just received.

"We are being tested," Clayton said to no one in particular. "For clearly this patient has done nothing wrong. It is we who must struggle. Doctor," he threw a glance towards Peter, "your suggestions."

"He needs a wire stent," Peter said.

"I agree. A stent." He turned to the angioplasty technician. "Get me a stent stat."

The process to repair a tear was a simple one. They would have to thread a small wire cage into the artery and expand it once it was in place. The tiny wire cage would press the artery outward like a frame that held a tunnel open. That pressure alone would press the torn edges of the rip together and seal off the leak. It was a tedious process they could do only once. There would be no second chance. If they placed the cage incorrectly the patient would need emergency open-heart surgery. That would not go over well with Barbosa, or the others.

The room became quiet while the technician laid out the equipment they needed. The monitor rhythmically interrupted the silence with synchronized repetitive beeps that announced each cardiac contraction. Peter's beeper broke that rhythmic cycle. "Excuse me," he asked the circulating nurse. "Could you call the Emergency Room? They're paging me stat. Please find out what they want."

It only took a moment for her to return. "They have a seventy-seven year old male in cardiogenic shock. He's had an inferior wall M.I."

That was a cardiac emergency. The patient's heart was in such bad shape from a blocked artery it couldn't pump enough blood fast enough, or hard enough, to maintain a blood pressure compatible with life. Peter knew that if they could do emergency angioplasty and open the blockage the patient would stand a much better chance of survival. The problem was they were already in the midst of a cardiac emergency.

Despite his religious rhetoric and apparent indifference to conversation other than his own, Clayton responded to Peter's thoughts and concerns. "Dr. Pavano. Go to the Emergency Ward and evaluate that patient. I will persevere without you."

Peter quickly pulled off his mask, gloves and protective gown and left the suite.

The Emergency Room was in utter chaos, the noise level well beyond a dull roar. A five-year-old child screamed at the top of his lungs, a psychiatric patient, hands and legs tied to the ambulance stretcher with plastic cord, spewed a tirade of vulgarities, a patient somewhere behind a curtain screamed for a bed pan, and a drunk, shackled to his bed, was singing the United States National Anthem in Polish.

"Where's the patient in cardiogenic shock?" Peter asked the closest nurse. Her reply before she ran off was a quick finger pointed towards room two.

He found the opening in the curtain and entered. One look told the story. They had the stretcher tilted and the patient's feet were two feet higher than his head. It was a last ditch effort at best. They hoped every ounce of blood that had pooled in his feet would flow downhill into the heart and help perfuse the brain and other vital organs. The patient had multiple intravenous lines in both arms. Powerful drugs flowed through

57

them in an attempt to squeeze blood from the arteries and veins and to raise and maintain a life-sustaining blood pressure. So far, they were failing. The patient's blood pressure was only fifty-five, not compatible with life for very long.

The patient was on a respirator. It pumped one hundred percent oxygen through the tube they'd placed down his throat and into his lungs. His breathing had long since failed. They hoped this would sustain adequate oxygenation. That wasn't working either.

Sweat drenched the patient. The washcloths placed on his forehead had long ago saturated. The staff was too busy to change them for dry ones. At the moment, that was the least of their concerns.

The Foley catheter in his bladder was dry. No urine. That told Peter the blood flow to the kidneys was beyond dangerously low. That was a bad prognostic sign. Peter looked at the ashen gray color that coated the patient's face and he knew time was of the essence.

"Who are you?" one of the nurses asked.

"Dr. Pavano. I'm the Invasive Cardiology Fellow."

"Thank you for coming." A doctor Peter's age quickly climbed over and under the tubes and wires that stretched from the patient. He spoke in rapid sentences that seemed to parallel the patient's quickening downward spiral. "He's seventy-seven years old. Eight hours of chest pain. Nitro intravenously didn't help. He was given thrombolytics, but it didn't help. I doubted it would. He has a known ninety-nine percent blockage of his circumflex. It was a matter of time before it became one hundred percent. There wasn't a clot to dissolve. Just sort of chicken fat clogging the artery."

"How do you know?" Peter asked. His eyes glanced towards the patient.

"He's Dr. Gold's patient. We did an Angiogram on him two months ago. We tried to get him into either elective angioplasty or by-pass surgery. He refused both."

"I don't think he has much of a choice now. He won't survive surgery. I just hope he'll live long enough to get to angioplasty."

"I agree. How soon can you take him?"

"Let me find out. Give me a minute."

"That might be all the time the both of you have."

Peter hurried out of the room and stood at the nurse's station and thought for a moment. His mind and heart raced.

Clayton was busy with his own crisis.

He dialed Barbosa's secretary. "Beth, this is Dr. Pavano." His breath was rapid as he tried to push the words out faster. "I have an emergency in the E.R. I need either Dr. Kyle or Dr. Barbosa. And fast."

"I'm sorry," she replied, "Dr. Barbosa's in Boston for the day at a meeting and Dr. Kyle took the day off. He's at the shore playing golf. I'm sure we can reach him, but it would take him over an hour to make it back to the hospital."

Peter shut his eyes and faced the reality of the situation. "We don't have an hour." He hung up the phone.

"What's happening to my father?"

Peter turned to face an anxious man in his mid forties. He anxiously shifted weight from one foot to the other. His drawn face displayed his concern. He wore his hair neatly to his shoulders. A single earring studded his right ear.

Peter backed himself into the counter and folded his hands at his waist in an attempt to appear calm and confident. "I'm Dr. Pavano. You're aware you father has had a very serious heart attack and is very critical condition?"

"Yes. What can you do to help him?"

"At this point angioplasty is the only thing that has a chance of saving his life."

"Then Godamnit, do it. What are you waiting for?"

"Dr. Clayton, my attending, is tied up with a complicated angioplasty. He won't be free for about an hour. The problem is, your father won't survive that long. The two other doctors trained in the procedure aren't available."

"What about you?"

Peter hesitated and took a deep breath. "I'm a Fellow in training. This is only my second full week."

"Have you done this procedure?"

"Yes."

The son grabbed him by the lapels of his lab coat and pulled him so their faces were only inches apart. "Then do it. I don't care if this is your first. If you don't, he'll die, and if that happens I'll have your license."

"Don't threaten me." Peter didn't blink. "I don't care if you go to a lawyer."

"I am a lawyer, and I'm not threatening, I'm promising. If you don't try, you can kiss your medical license goodbye."

He let Peter go, but stayed face to face with him.

"He still might die," Peter said.

"I'll accept that. I won't accept nothing being done."

The two stared at each other.

"Dr. Pavano." Peter faced Joan, the head nurse, who had juxtaposed herself between him and the attorney. "May I have a word with you?"

She walked him a few feet away. "I'm sorry, but I couldn't help hearing your conversation. You know you have to do the procedure."

"I haven't even finished my second week of training," he said. "I'm not qualified."

"So we write on that man's tombstone, 'Here lies so and so, who died because Dr. Pavano refused to try'."

"If I take him, it's not giving him much of a chance," Peter replied.

"If you don't he has no chance." She grabbed both of his shoulders. "Trust in yourself, Doctor."

Peter spun around and picked up the phone. The angioplasty technician answered the phone on the third ring. "Suite two. Roberto here."

"Roberto, this is Dr. Pavano. I need the Suite ready in two minutes for an angioplasty. I have a seventyish year old man in cardiogenic shock."

"Who's the attending staffing you?"

"No one. They're all busy. It's just you and me." Peter hung up the phone without waiting for a reply.

The patient rolled out of the Emergency Room sixty seconds later. An entourage of staff surrounded the bed like a protective cocoon. Portable monitors for heart and blood pressure hung from the bed rails. Intravenous pumps, pushed on poles with wheels by nurses on either side of the bed, continued to pump life-sustaining medicine into the patient. The bed, still tilted like a seesaw, moved quickly down the hall. A respiratory therapist assisted the patient's breathing, squeezing a bag to drive oxygen into his lungs. One nurse on each side of the bed monitored the intravenous pumps and monitors. Two aides pushed the bed at a steady pace. Finally at the end of the group, came Peter. A small bead of sweat formed on his forehead. His thoughts quickly raced through the upcoming procedure; all the while his subconscious questioned his ability.

6 | CHAPTER SIX

The thirteen members of the Senior Executive Council of the Cartel sat around an oblong mahogany table. Each of the twelve had arrived at the underground garage in inconspicuous sedans, the rear windows darkened to give the occupant anonymity. All came from different parts of the United States. Some had been picked up at the airport, others at hotels they stayed at, having flown in the night before. Barbosa had been picked up at his house in Connecticut, as had one other local cardiologist from the Boston area. Joshua arrived on his own. He ran the day-to-day operation for the group.

They met on the eleventh floor in one of the many buildings the Cartel owned. This building had a direct elevator from the private garage to the eleventh floor. There was a second, completely separate bank of elevators that serviced the rest of the building, headquarters for the American Standard Catheter, Inc. American Standard supplied over seventy-two percent of all the angioplasty catheters to hospitals in the United States, and forty percent of those used overseas. American Standard Catheter, Inc., along with its building, was completely owned by the Cartel.

Joshua called the meeting to order. They accepted the minutes from the last meeting and moved onto the new agenda.

"I think all of you have had time to review the quarterly financial statement," Joshua started. "As you can see, our profits decreased by two percent despite an increase of three point five percent in actual procedures over the last quarter."

He paused for a sip of water. The group leafed through the report while he talked. "That decrease in income reflects our annual endorsement of eleven million dollars to the Cardiac Institute, and our agreed upon decrease in procedure charges."

Dr. Weinsil from Seattle interrupted. "Why weren't we able to offset that loss by increased catheter sales? If we were up three point five percent in overall procedures from last quarter, I'd expect a three point five increase in sales."

"There are multiple reasons." Joshua had prepared for that question. To him doctors were a suspicious, greedy group. No matter how many millions of dollars they made, if their income dropped a single cent they demanded answers. "The first reason was, of course, the endowment. But, most importantly, we had an across the board decrease in the cost of our catheters to the hospitals. The bottom line is we cut our prices to them."

"Why? Who approved that?" demanded Blocknick from Boston.

"That would be two questions, Dr. Blocknick. Let me answer the why before the who. This country is in the midst of demanding health care reform. At times the inquisition in the Senate has the appearance of the Salem witch trials. Anything that gives the perception of gouging the consumer has to be avoided."

Joshua looked around the room. All eyes had stopped perusing the financial report and rested on him.

"And the who?" Barbosa demanded. "Who authorized this?"

"I did," Joshua replied.

Barbosa leaned forward on his palms. "What gives you the right to make a unilateral decision concerning my salary?"

"Dr. Barbosa, we're only talking about one hundred and fifty thousand dollars."

"One hundred and fifty thousand dollars is more than what ninety-five percent of the god damned general public makes in a year. We're not talking chump change here."

"No, we're not, but you'll get no sympathy from me." Joshua leaned forward and matched Barbosa's posture. "I know what

)6-MUCC

you make. You took home seven million three hundred and fifty thousand dollars this quarter. I really don't care if you want to cry over one hundred and fifty thousand, because in the scheme of things it is chump change."

"That's not your damned decision to make!"

"Yes it is!" Joshua shot back. "This council hired me to look after the overall interest of the Cartel. Medicine, and especially this group, is standing on the edge of a large precipice, just waiting to be pushed off, and it's attitudes like that that will cause us to fall. This is not the small secret society that was started fifteen years ago. We are a cartel of over five hundred physicians, and I've rarely seen three that can agree on anything for very long. You realized that," he slammed his palms on the table, "and that's why you hired me." He rose to his feet still leaning on his palms.

After a long pause he continued. "With a group this size, leaks are bound to happen."

"We've dealt with leaks before," Barbosa said.

"The days of burying our mistakes are over. We are about to be investigated again by a formal Senate inquiry. I'm more concerned about that than you losing one hundred and fifty thousand dollars of income." He and Barbosa locked eyes.

Dr. Blocknick broke in. "I think we all share your concern about the secrecy of our group. The leaks must be stopped. May I remind all of you that Al Capone wasn't put in jail for any of the murders he committed. It was for something as simple as tax evasion. A stupid piece of information got into the wrong hands. I don't want that to happen to us."

"So," Barbosa said, "what exactly do you suggest?" He looked at Joshua.

"We go public."

"What!" several doctors said.

Joshua kept his cool. "That's right. We go public. So far we've been able to shield ourselves from discovery. That, as I said, will eventually end. So we form a public group. We set stringent but obtainable guidelines for hospitals and groups to be able to do angioplasty. The governing board of accreditation, which is currently controlled by us, will stay the same. We still control the guidelines. Our referral system will be made public. We will face competition. That we will also control. Hell, our income will go down, but the God damned Feds won't be able to take it away from us."

"What sort of guidelines are you talking about?" Barbosa asked.

"If you'll open up the last packet in your file you can follow along."

After giving them a moment, he continued. "We are going to create a consortium of the finest hospitals in the United States. We will offer angioplasty to corporate America. We will guarantee them a minimal level of expertise, which we will standardize. We will offer open bidding from one center to the other for corporate contracts. Prices will drop. Unfortunately, Dr. Barbosa, income will also drop. But we give the appearance of open competition, thus avoiding anti-trust action. We open this up to other institutes. If they meet our minimal level of standardization, they're in."

"What's to stop these new institutions from starting their own consortium and competing directly against us?" Dr. Waverly from Miami asked.

"Cost," Joshua replied. "We will have to completely change the way we think about things if we are to survive the next decade. The success of this will hinge on all of us aggressively striving to lower health care costs. We will become the pinnacle of health care reform.

"We already control the Cardiovascular Norms Committee. We currently set the rules. We will encourage efficiency and lower cost, but still set extremely high levels of competency. We approve more hospitals to do angioplasty. They won't be able to compete in cost or competency. They'll be weeded out. We show the public that cost for angioplasty is varied around the country and the places that charge the most do not have the best results. They won't be able to compete with us from day one."

65

"What will stop us from getting trapped in an anti-trust suit?" Barbosa asked.

"Our fees, that is hospital and physician fees, will differ from institute to institute within our own group. We will set those prices and at times bid against each other. This will allay any fears of price fixing, even though that's exactly what we'd be doing. The employer will shop around and at times negotiate fees up front. It would then be the employer's obligation to guide that employee to the physician and hospital they contracted with."

"What about organization?" Dr. Blocknick asked.

"Despite what might appear as a decentralization of the Cartel, we will set up a core central corporation, separate from this group. It will contain a database, public relations and marketing group for this concept. However, it will appear to represent everyone to the public, not just us. That corporation will be the seller of services and this Cartel will continue to control it."

"What about the American Standard Catheter, Inc.?" a voice from the back of the room added.

"That will continue to be privately owned by us. Also, we should continue to fund the Cardiac Institute."

They made no finial decision. They agreed to think about it and put it on the agenda for the next meeting for a formal consideration.

They filled the remainder of the meeting with procedural questions that concerned the allotted number of repeat angioplasties. They decided to minimize their exposure to the Federal government by cutting back on their planned repeat procedures. Joshua felt this backing off and eventual end should coincide with the startup of the new Cardiac Group. He felt they could offset the loss of income by aggressive marketing that would pull patients away from cardiac bypass.

The meeting concluded with little fanfare. Each member entered the secluded parking garage where they were driven back to their starting points.

7 | CHAPTER SEVEN

The minute and a half it took Peter to move his patient, and the support team, to the angioplasty suite seemed like an eternity. Patients in cardiogenic shock aren't very resilient to further strain, and with every step Peter watched and waited for him to arrest. The thought of having to resuscitate a patient in the hallway did not appeal to him.

With a sigh of relief and the finality that he couldn't run away, Peter and company entered the procedure room. The long slow agonizing walk instantly became a hectic rapid sequence of events.

"OK! Let's move him," Peter called out the moment the stretcher came close to the procedure table.

"One, two . . ." one of the nurses called out. On three, they lifted the patient by the bed sheet and gently dropped onto the cold hard table.

"Nurse. Switch him over to the monitor," Peter called out. "Hey, hey, hey! Let's watch the lines. We don't want to pull any of them out."

Peter spun around. "Where's my technician?"

"Right here, Doc. I'm Roberto." A nicely tanned Puerto Rican approached. He had a diamond stud in his ear and his physique was thin with little muscle covering is bones.

"Roberto, I'm going to need your help on this. This is only my second week."

)6-MUCC

"Don't worry Doc, I'll take good care of you. Let's both take a Valium and chill a little."

"Let's just make sure he doesn't chill."

"Damned straight. Too much paperwork, Doc."

A nurse called out. "His heart rate's dropping!"

"Let's go!" Peter said to Roberto. "Forget the scrub and prep. Nurse, pour some Betadine on his groin."

Peter and Roberto donned their protective gowns while the nurse poured the antiseptic cleansing solution.

"Let's get him draped." He and Roberto had donned sterile gloves and threw the sterile waterproof drapes around the patient's left groin area, leaving only a small bit of skin in the groin exposed.

"Needle!" Roberto placed one into his outstretched hand. Peter felt for the pulsating artery, then plunged the needle directly into it.

"I'm in." Blood flowed into the syringe.

"Guide wire." Peter took it and threaded it into the artery.

"Introducer and dilator." Peter widened the skin and artery with a single pass of the dilator over the guide wire.

"Is the balloon tested?"

"Yes." Roberto handed the angioplasty catheter to him.

Peter took a deep breath, and then started.

"We're losing him, Doctor. His pulse is now twenty!" the nurse at the side called out.

"One amp of Epinephrine followed by an amp of Atropine." Peter replied, a quiver in his voice.

"Done," the nurse said. "Still no response. Heart rate still twenty."

"Put him on the external pacemaker!"

They slapped paddles onto the patient's bare chest and electric current pulsed, artificially stimulating the heart to beat.

"His heart rate is at sixty but his blood pressure is only forty-five systolic."

A bead of sweat rolled down Peter's nose under the mask. "It's the procedure or nothing for him." He slid the catheter through the introducer and advanced it up the artery towards the heart. Peter's focus was intense. He started at the fluoroscopic image of the catheter as it approached the heart that was so listless it barely moved with contraction.

With the catheter in place, Peter injected the dye then watched the image on the monitor. "We have a complete blockage of the left main coronary. I need the drill."

Roberto passed him the tiny drill that sat on the end of a tiny wire. Peter threaded it up the patient's leg via the catheter's sheath and then into the tiny blocked artery.

"Turn it on."

"By your foot, Doctor," Roberto replied. "The control pedal is to the right of you on the floor."

"Yes . . . yes thank you."

Peter depressed the peddle with his right toe and the burr on the end of the drill started to spin. He held his breath. "Please do not rupture the artery wall," he said in a low voice to himself. He bored through the clot to the other side. That done, he pulled it back and blood instantly flowed to the ischemic dying heart muscle on the other side.

Slowly the patient's heart rate rose. In a short time, they were able to turn off the external pacemaker.

The doors to the suite burst open. Clayton charged in. "Apprise me, Doctor Pavano. Apprise me of the patient's condition."

Peter turned around, his smile hidden by his surgical mask. "I'm happy to say, Doctor Clayton, that despite my attempts the patient survived and is alive."

Clayton walked up to Peter, looked at the monitors, then the patient, then at Peter again. "You, sir, are a virtuous man. One who has God on his side, helping you to do his work. 'I sought the Lord, and . . .'"

"'and he answered me and delivered me from all my fears'." Peter finished. "And how did your patient make out?"

"I must have done something wrong. I am being punished. He unfortunately passed on. Only the almighty Lord was able to raise Lazarus. Good work old chap. Carry on." Without another word Clayton turned and walked out of the suite.

A hand rested on Peter's shoulder. It was Roberto. "Doc, you did good work. You can take care of me anytime."

One and a half hours had passed since Peter walked out of the Coronary Care Unit. Only after he'd helped place his patient into the bed and seen for himself he was safe would he leave. Exhausted, ecstatic, and emotionally drained, Peter beamed with the inner satisfaction that came from persevering in the face of disaster. He hadn't walked around and boasted. He didn't have to. The word had spread to the C.C.U. long before he'd arrived with his patient. When confronted with praise and compliments, all he responded with was a simple, "Thank you".

For the moment, Peter sat alone in the coffee shop. He didn't really need the coffee, his success charged him, but he took advantage of the solitude to allow himself a private moment of inner gloating. Nothing he would openly express to anyone, other than a smile and a nod. He lifted his cup and took a long slow sip.

"Thank you, Dr. Pavano."

Peter looked up and saw the patient's son, the lawyer.

"You're welcome. I'm happy things turned out as well as they did."

The son extended his hand. "My name's Samuel Small."

Peter shook his hand. "You know he's still not home free yet?"

"I know. But at least you're off the hook." Samuel reached into his pocket. "Here's my business card. I practice general law. I owe you one. What you did for my dad took a lot of courage and guts. Everyone needs a lawyer sometime. When your time comes, call me. I'll do you right."

Peter placed the card in his wallet. "Thank you. If need be, I will."

"You're a damn good doctor, Dr. Pavano. You take care."

"Thank you, I will."

After Samuel left, Peter went back to his coffee and daydream about the procedure.

)6-MUCC

8 | CHAPTER EIGHT

The next day was hectic, but routine, for Peter. He breezed through rounds without incident. Lastly, he walked into his first recovering Angioplasty patient. He beamed with pride. The patient was awake and off the ventilator.

"Good morning." Peter walked up to the patient and took his hand gently in his. "I am Doctor Pavano. I was the one who did your angioplasty yesterday."

The patient looked at him and, though drowsy from the heavy sedation, responded in a low, slow, thick, speech. "Thank you, Dr. Pavano. Thank you for saving my life."

Peter felt his face flush. "You're welcome. Your morning EKG looks much better, though you're not out of the woods yet. Anyway, I think it is fair to say you are looking much better than yesterday."

Walking down the hall Peter felt satisfied. Then his beeper went off. It was Barbosa's office.

"Dr. Barbosa," Beth informed him, "wants to see you in his office immediately."

Peter sat across from Barbosa in disbelief. His euphoric morning vanished.

Barbosa slammed both palms onto his desk. "I don't give a shit what indication you have. You are never, and I mean god damned never to book an angioplasty without prior approval by one of us, let alone exposing this hospital and my practice by doing it yourself." His nostrils flared.

Peter kept his eyes focused on Barbosa, refusing to look down in submission. "I understand your concern and it won't happen again."

"It better not, or you won't happen again."

"Yes sir. I understand."

"You damned well better before I throw you out. Tomorrow night the Children's Hospital is having its dedication ball for their new wing in the auditorium. You will be expected. It is formal and you will be expected to bring a date. A female date."

Barbosa waved his arm and dismissed him.

* * * * *

The next night, Barbosa strolled through the crowded ballroom alone. His wife had long since abandoned him for a chat with other doctors' wives about their own charity functions, and only a small handful of colleagues approached him to say hello. He knew he was disliked, and that suited him just fine. He didn't want to be liked; he wanted to be feared. He also hated social chitchat.

For him, the whole evening was a waste. He really didn't care too much about the new pediatric wing. It had been the promotional darling of the greater Hartford news group for some time, but it had nothing to do with him. It might draw patients from all around the Eastern seaboard, but none of them would be candidates for angioplasty. The background music played by the symphony orchestra grated on his nerves, and he wasn't interested in food or drink. He had just made up his mind to leave when a voice spoke up from behind him.

"Dr. Barbosa, it's a pleasure to see you here supporting such a fine cause."

Barbosa found himself face to face with Senator Demind and his wife. The Senator had distinguished salt and pepper hair and wore a fine summer tan from many hours on the golf course. Despite his dedication to the links, he was not an athletic man.

73

In fact, he was severely overweight, more like morbidly obese. The two packs of cigarettes a day he smoked didn't help either.

"Senator," Barbosa smiled and nodded to the Senator's wife. "And Mrs. Demind." That was all he said. He had no desire to talk to either of them.

The Senator's wife filled the void. "Well, Doctor, this is a wonderfully successful event. The community has been eagerly anticipating the completion of the pediatric wing. I can't wait to take a tour of the facilities. Have you seen it yet?"

"No, can't say that I have." He looked around the room. "But I'm sure it's all it's advertised to be. If you would excuse me, I see someone I should say hello to." He politely shook her hand, ignored the Senator, and started to walk away.

"Dr. Barbosa. One moment please." The Senator turned to his wife. "I'll catch up to you in a moment."

The Senator walked up to Barbosa.

"What do you want, Senator?"

"A little cooperation would be helpful."

"Yes, I've heard about your little investigation. I just don't understand what you intend to accomplish."

"I intend to prove the existence of a Mafioso-style medical cartel that has a vise grip on a very lucrative piece of the medical pie and I intend to destroy it."

"For argument's sake, let's say this medical Mafia does exist. Who cares? The quality of medicine in this country is unmatched anywhere in the world. Advances are made daily, sometimes hourly. And those advances are available to everyone, no waiting list. That's all the public cares about. Why don't you go after the pharmaceutical companies that rape the little old retired people of their life savings so they can pay for pills that'll keep them alive? Or are you a stockholder with too much to lose?"

"You're barking up the wrong tree, Barbosa. Those are public companies, run by the public, the stockholders that is. Though I agree their profit margin is at times outrageous, there are ways of controlling that. The bottom line, as you like to refer to it, is controlled by the public. They have accountability. Does your group?"

"That is a very interesting point of view, Senator."

"Just remember, I agree with something one of your esteemed colleagues said recently."

"And what might that be?"

"Al Capone was put away not for murder but for something as simple as tax evasion. The wrong information got into the wrong hands. Leaks, doctor. They're inevitable. Enjoy the evening."

The Senator walked away and left Barbosa standing alone, red faced.

At the far end of the ballroom, dressed in a rented tuxedo, Peter attempted to waltz Kelsey around the dance floor. His steps were stiff, staccato movements that always seemed to be a half-beat behind the music. The more he struggled, the worse it seemed to get. He finally looked up from his feet, where his eyes had been focused and looked at Kelsey, who was trying not to laugh.

"I'm sorry," he said. He stopped on the dance floor and just stood there. "If I had two left feet that'd be an improvement."

"Just relax and move with the music."

"I thought I was moving with it."

She smiled. "You're listening to it and then reacting. You need to anticipate the music and the beat, so that your next step arrives at the same time the next beat does."

"That's too analytical for me." He took her hand and walked her off the dance floor. "Let's get a drink."

The orchestra played in the background while Peter and Kelsey sat at a side cocktail table for two.

Four hours later Peter lay naked in bed, Kelsey cuddled in his arms. He lightly caressed her back and marveled at how safe he felt with her. Their passion spent, he realized he hadn't felt this safe with a woman since he'd lived with Ethel.

06-MUCC

9 | CHAPTER NINE

Barbosa waited until Monday to call Joshua. "I told you that was what the son of a bitch said. He quoted Blotnick word for word from the council meeting. Find that god damned leak."

"I don't understand why anyone on the council would talk," Joshua said.

"That's a question you'll have to answer. I won't do your job for you. I also hope you come up with a better plan to contain the Senator than what you presented. That may be fine for the long term, but we need to stop him now." Barbosa hung up on Joshua and answered his page.

Seven minutes later the doors to the Emergency Room burst open and Barbosa stormed in. He stopped in the center of the room, fists clenched and jaw tensed. "Who paged me 'stat'?"

"I did," a petite nurse in her mid twenties said.

"Who gave you permission to page me to the E.R., let alone page me stat?"

"I'm sorry. I thought you'd like to know Senator Demind was here with chest pain."

He walked to within half a foot of her, his big six foot five inch frame towered over her. "Well, you thought wrong. Did you call the Cardiac Fellow?"

"No." She took a step back.

"No!" Barbosa stepped forward into her space. "You didn't call the Cardiac Fellow but you took it upon yourself to call me.

Do you know why I have a Cardiac Fellow? Better yet, do you even know what a Cardiac Fellow is?"

She just stood there, unable to speak. Tears welled up in her eyes.

"Well let me educate you. I hire a doctor after he finishes residency to work under me. I call him my Fellow. I pay him to come to the E.R. and see patients so I don't have to. But you decide to take it upon yourself to call me to the E.R. 'stat'. Fine, I'm here, give me the EKG, wipe your face and stop sniveling like a baby." He held out his hand.

She ran to the nurse's station and retrieved the EKG.

He studied it, then looked down at her. "Well nurse, or should I say Doctor, what does it show?" He handed the EKG back to her.

"I think he's—he's having a heart attack."

"You 'think he's having a heart attack'? So you call the Chief of Invasive Cardiology, instead of his Fellow?"

"I—I'm sorry, I didn't think—."

"That's right you didn't think!" he screamed in her face. "This EKG does not show an acute infarction. But instead of having the patient evaluated properly to determine that, you felt compelled to call me instead of my Fellow. Young lady, you are as useless as tits on a bull."

He stormed past a stunned and angry Emergency Room staff and disappeared behind the curtain that surrounded the Senator. The nurse, humiliated, turned her back and wept.

Behind the curtain Barbosa looked at the Senator and smiled. "So it comes down to this. Ironic, isn't it?"

"I feel like Daniel in the lion's den. Are you the lion or the hand of God that protects me?"

"You know how much I like playing God, Senator."

Moments later, Peter entered the Emergency Room. The astute E.R. secretary had taken the cue to page him. He sensed the tension and anger in the air and approached Joan, the head nurse and new friend. "What's wrong?"

)6-MUCC

"Gina," she motioned with her head to her crying in the corner, two older nurses trying to console her. "She paged Barbosa 'stat' for a patient instead of you."

"Oh God, I can picture the tirade. Where is he now?"

"Behind curtain number two with Senator Demind. The Senator is having chest pain."

Barbosa stepped out from behind the curtain and saw Peter. "Well, it's about time you showed up. I pay you to work for me, not the other way around. Senator Demind's in there. He's having pre-infarction angina. Go examine him and write him up. I'll call the lab. He's a good candidate for emergency angioplasty."

"Excuse me, Dr. Barbosa." An unfamiliar voice caused Barbosa to stop abruptly. He spun to face a clean-shaven, neatly dressed, student wearing a pristine lab coat. "I'm a third year medical student. I was wondering if you could review his EKG with me?"

"No, I wouldn't care to."

Without so much as a look to the right or left Barbosa walked past the student and the angry stares of the staff. When he reached the door to the hallway he suddenly stopped, turned and faced the group. "Why isn't the Senator on his way to the Angioplasty Suite?" he demanded. "Is everyone in this place as incompetent as that little crybaby nurse? Get him there A.S.A.P." He turned and stormed out of the department.

* * * * *

Senator Demind lay on the metal table and stared up at the surgical lights above him. His vision blurred from the intravenous Verced and Morphine given in the Emergency Room. His mind wandered from consciousness to a semi-stuporous state and back again. He tried to talk, to ask a question, but his speech slurred and sounded garbled.

Roberto leaned over the Senator. "Senator, don't worry. You'll be all right. Dr. Barbosa is the best angioplasty specialist in the state. I know you're scared, but trust me, you'll be OK."

The Senator smiled and reached for Roberto's hand. He mouthed, 'thank you', unable to speak.

Light bathed every corner of the Angioplasty Suite, creating a surrealistic, shadowless environment. The Senator, in one of his moments of clarity, focused on the bouncing line of light that flowed across the heart monitor. A beep toned from it with every heartbeat. Its rhythmic constancy blended in with the other background white noise. For the Senator, each beep gave affirmation that he was still alive and a constant reminder of his mortality.

Peter entered the suite, dressed in surgical scrubs, cap and mask. He walked over to the Senator. "Senator, it's Dr. Pavano. How's the chest pain?"

"Tha—that heavy pressure is almost gone but I still feel terrible."

"That's normal." Peter squeezed the Senator's hand. "Don't worry, you'll do just fine. We do this a lot here, you're not our first."

The Senator drifted off into a stupor.

Barbosa entered the room and looked over at the Senator who moved slightly on the table.

"Give him five more milligrams of Morphine IV. I want him snowed," he barked to the nurse at the head of the stretcher. "Pavano, get set up. You're doing this one."

Peter pivoted to face Barbosa. His eyes registered his surprise.

"You've wanted to impress me. Here's your chance. Set up, I'll check the catheter," Barbosa said.

"I already did," Roberto replied. His voice slightly muffled through his mask.

"Excuse me, but I am placing the Senator's life in Dr. Pavano's hands, not yours." He turned his back to them and checked the catheter's integrity by blowing up the balloon.

While Barbosa inflated the angioplasty balloon, Peter wiped antiseptic solution onto the Senator's left groin. Next, he carefully wrapped the area with sterile drapes. He left the groin exposed. With gentle fingers he pressed on the Senator's groin until he felt the distinct pulse of the left femoral artery. He inserted a needle into the artery and he slid a thin wire through the needle into the artery.

"Dilator." He held out his hand. His eyes never left the field of operation.

Roberto placed a soft plastic tube into his hand. Peter passed it over the wire into the artery. The hole in the artery widened. It was now large enough for the angioplasty catheter to pass into it without ripping it.

Peter slid the catheter over the wire into the artery. He advanced it and watched on the monitor as it approached the heart. Peter injected a small amount of dye. It squirted out of the catheter's tip and immediately got sucked into the dancing coronary arteries.

"I see the blockage," Peter said to Barbosa. "The left main is ninety-five percent blocked. He's lucky, if the artery had stayed in spasm much longer he would've infarcted. I'll dilate him now."

Peter slid the tip of the catheter through the tight blocked artery and engaged the pump that blew up the balloon and stretched the artery open to its normal position. That completed, he deflated the balloon, then pulled the catheter out of the coronary artery and away from the heart.

"He's in sinus tach!" the Cardiac nurse called out moments later.

The Senator's heart rate on the monitor rose to over one hundred and fifty beats per minute.

"Is the catheter out?" Barbosa said.

"Yes," Peter replied.

Suddenly, the Senator's heart rhythm degenerated from a stable rapid rate to a useless quivering flutter known as ventricular fibrillation.

"He's in V. Fib!" the nurse shouted.

Peter instinctively made a fist and slammed it onto the Senator's chest in an attempt to convert his rhythm back into a useful contraction.

"He's still fibrillating!" the nurse said.

Peter reached for the cardiac paddles, squeezed a large amount of gel onto them and rubbed them together. He placed them onto the Senator's chest and looked around. "Clear."

The nurse quickly looked around and made sure no one was touching the patient or the stretcher. "All clear."

Peter pressed the discharge button. The Senator's upper body momentarily jerked as the electricity coursed from one paddle through his chest muscles and heart and exited into the other paddle.

"He's flat line now!" the nurse called out.

The electrical shock had suppressed the deadly arrhythmia but replaced it with none at all. Immediately, Peter charged up the paddles and shocked the Senator again. There was no response. The heart remained stopped.

"Start C.P.R!" Barbosa demanded. "Give one ampule of Epinephrine followed by on ampule of Atropine, and bag him!"

Peter cupped his hands and pressed on the Senator's chest rhythmically. The nurse at the head of the stretcher placed a ventilation bag over the Senator's mouth and assisted his breathing.

Within moments, extra help burst through the doors; the nurse had pushed the cardiac arrest button that notified the appropriate people to drop everything and come.

"Tube him," Barbosa ordered the anesthesiologist, who immediately placed a tube down the Senator's mouth and into his upper airway. The Senator's breathing had just stopped and he now needed artificial ventilation.

Peter stepped aside. He let a medical resident replace him at doing chest compression's. Freed up for the moment, he pulled the catheter out of the Senator's groin and placed it on the

706-MUCC

equipment cart. He immediately moved over to the bank of monitors and assessed the situation.

Barbosa barked orders in a frantic attempt to revive the Senator. Peter saw Roberto back himself into the corner to get out of everyone's way. There wasn't much he could do at the moment to help.

Suddenly Roberto called out, "Dr. Barbosa! I think I know what happened!"

Barbosa turned. "Since when did you become a physician? Come here and do something useful."

"But I think I know what's wrong."

"When you graduate from Medical School then you can tell me how to run a cardiac arrest. In the meantime, take those blood tubes to the lab. Tell them I want the results yesterday."

Barbosa shoved a handful of blood tubes into Roberto's hands and pushed him towards the door.

Less then ten minutes later Roberto ran back into the Angioplasty Suite with the lab results and handed them to Barbosa. Barbosa read them, then tossed the sheets aside.

"Stop pumping for a moment. Anything on the monitor?" Barbosa asked.

"Nothing. He's still flat line," Peter replied.

"OK, everyone," Barbosa called out. "Let's stop. Thank you."

The room became instantly silent. It always did. Then the cardiac arrest team quietly filtered out of the room.

"You! Come with me." Barbosa hauled Roberto into a side room, leaving Peter by himself in the Angioplasty suite. He didn't know what was going on, it really didn't matter, a moment rarely passed with Barbosa when he didn't find someone to yell at or bully around. Peter reviewed the printed monitor strips of the cardiac arrest. He shook his head. He didn't understand what happened, why the Senator deteriorated so fast.

The door to the side room opened and Barbosa walked out. "God Dammit. If it's not the nurses tormenting me, it's the God dammed technicians. Pavano," he called back when he reached the door, "dictate this mess. I have to speak to the Senator's wife."

"Sure," was Peter's only response.

06-MUCC

10 | CHAPTER TEN

Three hours after they pronounced the Senator dead Peter walked slowly down the hall towards the auditorium. He walked with his hands clasped behind his back, and pondered the events just prior to and during the failed angioplasty. Long ago, he'd accepted death. He wasn't God. He didn't give life and hoped every day he was a doctor he wouldn't intentionally take it away. He functioned on the premise that physicians only postpone death. If a patient died under his care and he'd given it his best try, he accepted the outcome that nature had won, which it did many times. Nature was a powerful nemesis to battle.

"Dr. Pavano."

Peter turned. It was Clayton.

"You walk with such mournful steps. Are you doing penance for some wrongful deed?" he asked.

"No," Peter replied. "I was just reviewing a procedure."

"Ah, the Senator's death. You are a good doctor, though still naive. Just be strong. Repel Satan's thoughts. For the moment you doubt yourself, he'll take hold. Be humble, but have trust in your heart. Your soul is good."

Before Peter could reply, Clayton had turned and walked away.

Peter shook his head, as always, amazed at Clayton's rhetoric. Then he continued toward the auditorium. On the way to the auditorium, he reviewed the procedure moments before the

Senator's cardiac arrest. Once satisfied he hadn't made a mistake, he quickened his pace. There was a news conference in the hospital auditorium to announce the Senator's death.

Though Peter did the procedure, he wouldn't participate in the news conference. Barbosa would conduct it. He was the Chief, the best in the state. To have Peter give the conference would admit that Barbosa didn't do the procedure. Barbosa wouldn't allow that to be known to the public.

Peter entered the back of the auditorium at the same time Barbosa walked through the side doors and approached the podium. Simultaneously the multitude of television camera lights clicked on and bathed Barbosa in a wash of white. Unmoved, he stood behind the podium and stared out into the auditorium that contained three of the local networks, a CNN affiliate, along with members of the local and regional newspapers, and many curious staff members. In that moment of silence, Barbosa set the stage. He projected the image that personified him. He was the Chief, the boss, the best. It was in his stance, his posture, the simple way he addressed the crowd with his eyes. Gone was the arrogance, the rudeness, and the vile temper that surrounded him in his daily interactions with those in the medical field. In its place, was a powerful image of professionalism.

"Good afternoon ladies and gentlemen, members of the press. It is my sad responsibility to inform you that Senator Demind passed away at 2:11 this afternoon. His death was due to uncontrollable events with regard to an acute myocardial infarction. In layman's terms he had a massive heart attack."

While Barbosa pontificated to the cameras Peter leaned against the wall in the back of the auditorium. Beside him was Joan, the head nurse from the E.R., a few nurses and residents.

Joan smiled at Peter. "It's not every day we get to see God forced to stand before the masses and take credit for failure."

Peter just smiled back. He didn't want to tell her he'd done the procedure.

As they watched, Peter realized that only Barbosa could admit failure and still have people walk away thinking he was wonderful. The staff had gathered in the hope he would slip up. They prayed for that moment, but were quickly disappointed.

Unexpectedly Peter noticed a pungent whiff of body odor. He turned in surprise and saw Dusty nervously rocking from one leg to the other next to him.

Dusty faced Pavano and spoke with short excited stabs. "He killed him. I know he killed him."

Peter held a finger up to his lips. "Shh."

Dusty continued his nervous rock from one foot to the other. "He killed him. He killed him."

"What? Who killed who?" Peter finally asked.

"He did." He pointed to Barbosa.

"What are you talking about?"

"He killed him, killed the Senator."

Dusty turned and stared across the auditorium at Barbosa who looked blindly out into the bright television lights while he talked.

"He sees me! He knows I'm talking to you! He'll know I know!"

In a panic Dusty threw his arms in front of him for protection, turned and ran out of the auditorium, his hands flapping up and down.

Joan tapped Peter on the shoulder and whispered. "What was that all about?"

"Damned if I know."

* * * * *

Roberto rode his bike slowly through Frog Hollow. It wasn't far from the hospital, but it was the most dangerous section of Hartford. Puerto Rican gangs ran this part of town with impunity. It was their turf. Roberto never concerned himself with gang politics. He passed through here twice a day, to and from work. Long ago he'd been labeled "A Helper", a person who'd help any gang member with medical matters. He'd become their liaison with the clinics and doctors. He helped them no matter what gang they came from. In return, he had unmolested passage through Frog Hollow.

He rode and mused over the treatment he'd received in the Angioplasty Suite. Barbosa had crossed the line. What bothered him most was that he had no recourse. What was he going to do, demand an apology? Demand Barbosa be reprimanded? No, the reality of the situation was if he complained or even raised a concern about the Senator's death, he'd be the one tied to the whipping post.

Maybe it was time to look for a new job?

He rounded a corner and peddled slowly. He wasn't in a rush. He looked to his left for no particular reason, and saw a man in the alley. There was something wrong. His eyes locked onto a semi-automatic pistol, raised and pointed at him.

Instinctively he took his hands off the handlebars and held them in front of him. He let out a guttural groan as the first round of lead slammed into his abdomen. He flew backwards off his bike, his hands still frantically waving at the air in front of him.

The second and third bullets blasted through his right and left thighs. The fourth shattered his wrist, sending bullet fragments at different angles into his soft abdomen.

Roberto, wide eyed and numb, crashed onto the street. His bicycle bounced end over end away from him.

* * * * *

It was now six P.M. and Peter walked down the corridor. He had one final consult to do in the Emergency Room before he was through for the day. Though tired, he looked forward to a nice dinner and a rental movie with Kelsey. He couldn't wait to go over the events of the day with her. She had a way of putting things in perspective for him, of taking his pessimistic view of

06-MUCC

life and injecting it with some of her sunny optimism. He really needed a dose of Kelsey today.

When Peter turned the corner next to the Emergency Room, he saw Dusty run frantically out of the ER's entrance, his eyes wide with panic. He stopped in the corridor and hesitated. First, he turned right then left, then right again. Terror stricken, he ran down the hall towards Peter, arms flailing. He stopped inches from Peter.

Dusty's warm bad breath blasted into Peter's nostrils, with each new word spit spewed from his mouth, "They killed him! They killed him cause he knew!"

"Who did they kill?" Peter stepped back into fresh air.

"Roberto! Roberto! They killed. They shot him cause he knew!"

"Dusty, calm down. What do you mean they killed Roberto?"

"He's in there!" He pointed to the E.R. "They killed him!" Dusty swung around Peter and continued his wild run down the hall. "They'll be after me next, cause he told me! He told me! They know he told me! Gotta run, gotta hide!" Dusty turned the corner and disappeared.

Peter walked into the Emergency Room and up to Joan. "Do you have a gun shot victim here?"

"Yeah, back in the Trauma Room. They just wheeled him in. He's shot up pretty bad." She turned and walked away, a stack of charts in her hand, business as usual.

Peter walked to the Trauma Room. The automatic doors were open, so he entered. The patient lay naked on the stretcher while the Surgical Resident Trauma Team made their assessment and the senior resident barked orders. Peter moved to the head of the stretcher and looked at the patient's face.

"Roberto! My God, what happened?" He bent his face down close.

"He shot me." He looked at Peter bewildered. "Why?"

"Who are you?" the chief surgical resident demanded.

"Dr. Pavano, Invasive Cardiology Fellow. He's a friend. He works in the Angio Lab."

"Well if you don't get out of the way, he's gonna be a dead friend." The Chief turned his attention back to the patient. "I want a second IV in that arm, his blood pressure's dropping. I want four units of O negative, uncrossed blood here immediately. And tell them to type and cross eight other units. He's got a lot of holes in his belly. Bob, call the O.R. and tell them I want a room stat for a multiple gunshot victim. Hey!" He looked back to Peter, "What part of get out of here didn't you understand?"

Peter's eyes met Roberto's. They pleaded with him to come closer. Peter leaned over but a trauma nurse pushed him out of the way before Roberto could say anything. "We're losing his pressure!"

"Tube him!" the Chief called out. Peter slid to the rear of the room and watched the team elevate to a higher notch. Roberto was intubated and assisted with his breathing. They placed two more intravenous lines in his arm. They forced intravenous fluids into his veins under high pressure. Four units of the unmatched blood arrived and the Level One high-pressure infuser injected them into his system in minutes.

"I'm having trouble ventilating him!" the respiratory therapist called out.

"Sam! I thought you said his chest had clear breath sounds?" the Chief asked an intern.

"They were clear."

"Recheck them!"

The Intern immediately listened to Roberto's chest with his stethoscope. "No good, I think he's dropped the left lung. He's shifted his trachea, he has to have a tension pneumothorax."

Peter had seen that problem before, though not many times. The lung collapsed on one side but still leaked air. The air built up in the empty lung cavity and that created increased pressure on that side. If they didn't do something immediately to relieve that pressure, the heart and major vessels would continue to push

89

to the other side of the chest cavity, which would render them useless. This was a surgical emergency. They had seconds to react if Robert was to survive.

"Give me a 14 gauge needle!" the chief resident demanded.

Peter watched him take the large needle and jam it between the ribs into the chest cavity. The hollow needle entered the pressurized cavity. Everyone heard the air escape with a loud hiss.

Now blood was squirting out of the open needle. Along with the air, blood had built up under pressure.

"Shit!" the chief resident said. "We have a tension hemothorax. What's his blood pressure?" the chief resident asked.

"It's dropping."

"Damn! A bullet fragment must have entered his chest from his abdomen and hit something big. We need to crack his chest!"

Peter watched and knew they needed to stop the bleeding immediately. It didn't look good for Roberto. He watched the chief surgical resident pick up a scalpel and with one single cut slice open Roberto's chest between two ribs. Blood instantly poured out of the wound, off the stretcher and onto the floor.

"Suction! I need suction! I can't see a damn thing," the Chief called out in a controlled panic. "He's got a hole in his heart! Get me a stitch."

Peter watched the team suction and pull on the retractors between the ribs to give the Chief better exposure. He had only moments to find the hole and sew it up before all of Roberto's blood ran out onto the floor. Seconds, not minutes counted here. Peter stood mesmerized by the speed with which the team functioned. In all his years, this was the first time he'd seen someone's chest opened in the Emergency Room. Their white protective gowns were now crimson red with dripping blood.

"I need more suction. I can't see!" In a desperate attempt, the Chief felt in the pool. "I can feel a rip in the ventricle. Stitch!" He thrust his free hand into the air, palm up. "I need a zero-o suture. Dammit, I need it now! Come on team! Work with me!" he yelled. Blindly, in a last ditch effort, he attempted a few stitches, hoping to close the hole. In ten minutes, they had infused ten units of blood, but it poured out of Roberto's chest faster than they could replace it. Soon the color of the blood thinned out, becoming blood tinged intravenous fluid.

"We need more blood! I've got almost clear IV fluid coming out now," the Chief called out.

"We've gone through ten units already," a nurse said. "We're waiting for the lab to bring us some more. It's on its way. It'll be here in a few seconds."

"Cancel the blood," the Chief said as he took a step back. "Thank you everyone, there's nothing more we can do here. He's dead."

"Sorry, Doctor. We tried," the chief resident said to Peter as he dropped his blood soaked gown and gloves into a bin and left.

)6-MUCC

11 | CHAPTER ELEVEN

Peter stopped a few yards outside the entrance to D'Angelos' Funeral Home. A multitude of gang members, both male and female, crowded the sidewalk. A distinct neutral zone of four to five feet separated the two Puerto Rican gangs. Even here, they respected turf. Peter knew the history behind both gangs' wanton violence and disregard for the innocent. The atmosphere was uneasy, and Peter hoped they would refrain from any violence out of respect for Roberto.

He walked slowly between them, with his eyes focused downward at the pavement in front of him. He didn't want a look, or a stare, to be misunderstood. There were reams of charts at the Connecticut General Emergency Room that documented the Puerto Rican gangs' unprovoked violent outbursts. A multitude of nurses warned him when they heard he intended to go to Roberto's funeral.

Inside the funeral home, the atmosphere was different. The way Hispanics grieved amazed Peter. It went far beyond weeping and crying. He soon found the display of emotion ebbed and flowed with a cyclical rhythm. It peaked each time a new group of mourners took a turn at the casket. The women shrieked and screamed in rage. The men, at times, would fall in front of the casket and pound their heads on it or on the nearby floor, even if they only vaguely knew the deceased.

Peter remembered an incident years ago when he was a medical student. He'd seen a Puerto Rican patient in the

Emergency Room who had been at a funeral, and who in his moment of grief dove head first into the grave, landing on the casket. The patient spent twenty-four hours under observation for a concussion.

With that in mind, he decided to be quick about paying his respects at the casket. His eyes settled on Roberto. He was so still and peaceful. It was a far cry from the Trauma Room with his chest split wide open and bright red blood pouring onto the tiled floor. Peter shivered and remembered the look of terror in Roberto's eyes. He quickly made his way to the back of the room, where he tried to shake off the sense of foreboding.

"I told you they killed him," a shrill voice erupted behind him.

Peter turned and faced Dusty. He still had that wild-eyed look of fright. The same look he had when he ran out of the hospital the day before.

"Who killed him?" Peter asked.

"He did. Oh—he's coming this way. He sees me talking to you." Dusty turned right, then left, then spun and ran into Peter. "Get out of my way." Dusty flailed at him with his hands. "He knows I know. He'll kill me next." Dusty turned from Peter and found himself face to face with Barbosa. The two stared at each other for a long moment.

"Oh—No!" Dusty spun and again slammed into Peter. "Get out of my way!" He pushed Peter aside and ran with a wide duck stride out the door.

"What the hell was wrong with that little retard?" Barbosa said.

"Beats me." Peter looked at Barbosa for a moment. "I mean no disrespect but I am a little surprised to see you here."

A Cheshire cat grin came to Barbosa's face. He slowly looked around before he answered. "Let's just say I was curious, and leave it at that."

Peter nodded. "It is a unique experience you should have once in your life."

"I want you in my office tomorrow at 10 A.M." Barbosa said coldly.

"Why?"

"Because I said so. That is all you need to know." Barbosa walked away with a smirk and left by the side door.

* * * * *

That evening Barbosa relaxed in his office and reviewed the results of earlier cardiac exams. His private phone rang. The voice was curt and sharp. "Barbosa, what the hell are you doing down there?"

"Solving the problem you've ignored for too long."

"You didn't solve any problem, you're created one. The group is not pleased with your actions. Neither am I. I can't stress enough—"

"I can't stress enough," Barbosa said, "that I helped form the Cartel. I was also instrumental in hiring you. So I'd watch who you lectured, if I were you."

After a momentary silence, the voice on the other end continued. "I can't stress strongly enough that your action has put the organization in jeopardy. The potential repercussions far outweigh any positive gains. We were handling the situation and would have soon resolved the issue at hand. Now, you are exposed, and therefore we are exposed."

"I've taken care of that problem," Barbosa said.

"No you didn't. You dumped it back in our lap."

"Did you do what I asked?" Barbosa said.

"What choice did I have?"

"None. You either cooperate with me or sink."

"No! We all sink. Never forget that," Joshua snapped. "This better work."

"It will. I've a lot of control in this hospital. They make too much money off my procedures to challenge me."

"I'm not pleased, but at the moment, I don't have much choice. It's beyond my control. By the way, for your clarification," Joshua said, "whether you were or were not involved in hiring me is immaterial. I work for the organization and you are not the organization. You are only one of the many cogs on the wheel and until the board removes me, you will cooperate with me and my wishes."

"Don't you ever threaten me."

"First, I never threaten. I just explain options. And second, you may be very powerful at Connecticut General, but in this corporation you are only one vote; a lone vote on this issue. Until fifty-one percent of the board tells me otherwise, you will cooperate. I expect a complete report detailing everything."

"If you have nothing more to tell me, good-bye."

The line went dead.

12 | CHAPTER TWELVE

Dusty pulled his roll cart up to a table that sat outside the lecture hall's side door. Half-eaten donuts and half-drunk soft drinks littered the table. He hated to clean up after lectures, especially medical student lectures. They were such slobs. He picked up a donut and shook his head. It only had a bite taken out of it. What a waste. He dropped it into the garbage can and smiled. It was a crappy donut, not like the ones at the pastry shop.

He continued to clean up the mess when the side door to the auditorium opened. Barbosa walked through and stopped. His presence towered over the cart, blocking Dusty's way. Barbosa didn't say a word. Instead he looked at the cart, then at Dusty. The silence in the hallway was deafening. In a blind panic, Dusty jumped back and dropped a can of opened soda on the floor

"It—it's you! I won't let you kill me like Roberto!"

"What did you say, you little retard?"

"I—I may be retarded but I'm not 'tupid. I know you killed Roberto!"

"What?" Barbosa pushed the cart aside and took a step towards him.

"He told me, he told me you killed the Senator. Told me how. You killed him cause he knew. You won't kill me." Dusty grabbed the table and tipped it over between them. Safe for a moment, he turned and ran like a duck down the hall, a high-pitched wail coming from his open mouth.

* * * * *

At precisely ten o'clock, Peter entered Barbosa's office. He took a seat in front of Barbosa's desk. Barbosa sat back in his chair in silence and stared at him.

"You asked to see me today," Peter said curiously.

"I wanted you to look at something." Barbosa swiveled around in his chair and turned on a TV monitor and VCR that sat on a cart behind him. "I think you will find this interesting." He pushed the play button. On the monitor in the left lower corner of the picture were Senator Demind's full name, medical record number, the date, and time.

Peter watched the video recording of the Senator's fateful angioplasty. He watched it closely in the hope that he might be able to discern what caused the Senator's sudden death. When he did, his reaction couldn't hide his feelings.

"Wait a minute," Peter protested, "That is not what happened."

Barbosa reached over and stopped the tape. "What are you talking about?"

"That tape shows the catheter tip puncturing the coronary artery. That is not what happened."

Barbosa glared. "The name and medical record number is that of the Senator?

"Yes. But that is not what happened." Peter could only repeat himself.

"I don't understand?" Barbosa said.

"I am saying, that is not what happened." Peter's voice rose. "I did the procedure. I would have known if the artery was perforated. That is not something you do without knowing it."

Peter stopped and calmed himself. He rubbed the top of his forehead. "You were there. You know it didn't happen that way."

Barbosa replied. "Well, it's clear to me. You screwed up."

"What?" Peter bolted upright in his chair.

"What do you mean, what?" Barbosa replied. "It's perfectly clear. The tape shows you perforating the Senator's coronary artery. That's what. You screwed up. It shows it plain and clear. I don't see how you can deny it happened."

Peter's mouth hung open. "That's not what happened."

"How can you say that when the tape shows otherwise?"

"I don't know."

"I think it's time to face the facts. Senator Demind is dead and that tape shows the cause of his death. You did the procedure and you need to face it, you perforated the artery, and that was the cause of death."

Peter sat stiff in his chair. He became cold and hard. His mind raced far ahead.

Barbosa continued. "I have a call into Patricia Steward, the hospital lawyer. She's head of risk management. I think she needs to be involved in this."

Peter walked out of Barbosa's office, no sign of emotion showed on him.

Over the next hour Peter walked around the hospital deep in thought, until the beeper at his side interrupted his inner reflection. He looked at it and muttered in a soft voice. "5159, who the hell is at that extension?"

He found a telephone and dialed the extension. "Risk management. May I help you?"

"This is Dr. Pavano. Someone paged me."

"Yes, I did. Patricia Steward, the hospital lawyer and Risk Manager wants to talk to you. She wants to know if you could come to her office?"

"When?"

"Now."

He shrugged his shoulders. "Sure, tell her I'll be there in five minutes."

Peter turned a corner and ran into Dr. Kyle. They both stopped.

"Are you all right?" Kyle asked. "I just heard. In fact, I'm on my way to Barbosa's office to review the tape. Why don't you come with me? We'll look at it together."

"No thanks. I've already seen it. I'm on my way to the Risk Manager's office. She wants to see me. I imagine it's concerning this mess."

"Pat Steward?"

"Yes."

"Watch out for her. She's a typical hospital lawyer. Most of us figure she never could have made it on the outside, so she hides in the hospital and protects it from litigation at anyone's expense. She's thirty something with no man in sight. Not a good combination."

Peter took his time finding Steward's office. It gave him more time to think.

Steward's outer office was plain, devoid of any warmth. Her secretary was on a break and no one greeted him when he walked in. Two doors stood to his left. One was completely open and revealed a small conference room, as bare as the foyer. The second door was partly open. Free-standing bookcases were filled with legal and medical books, two standard chairs in front of a desk held a stack of patients charts, and behind the desk was a plush comfortable swivel chair, empty at the moment.

"It figures. They page me, then they disappear."

"Excuse me?" a voice called from the inner office. The woman was out of his line of sight.

"I'm looking for Patricia Steward."

"You are Dr. Pavano?"

"Yes." He walked in and extended his hand.

She ignored it. "I'm Patricia Steward. Come in and have a seat. I'll be with you in a moment." She turned back to her bookshelf.

"So much for introductions," Peter said in a low voice only he could hear.

He sat down in the chair directly in front of her desk and looked around the office. His eyes finally stopped on Steward. Her buttocks faced him as she bent over in front of a bookshelf. Her modest dress rode up and revealed a pair of well-toned calves. Must be a runner. Probably extremely anal retentive and gets up every morning before sunrise to jog five miles, then eats bran for breakfast.

"OK, let's get down to business." Steward sat behind her desk and opened a file. "We have a couple of problems here. The first is the discrepancy with your dictated version of the angioplasty procedure and the taped version."

"I can't explain that," Peter said.

"I can." She dropped the file onto her desk. "You dictated what didn't happen."

"I did no such thing."

"Don't interrupt me. The fact of the matter is, your word doesn't hold up against the weight of the tape. Hard evidence, indisputable evidence, and your insistence otherwise brings into question your credibility, which you should know is dwindling fast."

"What?"

"Don't use that tone with me. You have exposed this institution to probable litigation by the family. Not to mention a review of how we supervise the residents and fellows. You have opened a big can of worms, Doctor."

Peter looked at Steward, who continued her tirade about the position in which he had placed the hospital. Everything Kyle said about her appeared to be true. She would cut anyone up and use them for shark bait to protect her mighty hospital and her job. The problem was, there was a discrepancy--a major one. For now, he couldn't explain it.

"Look," he interrupted Steward's dissertation, "I didn't perforate the Senator's artery. I don't know how, but the tape is wrong."

"Sorry, Doctor, that tape was removed by Dr. Barbosa immediately after the time of death was called. He gave it to me

100

and I returned it to him only moments before he showed it to you. I don't think anyone will buy your version of the incident. Therefore, I'm going to recommend to Dr. Barbosa that you be released of all obligations and duties. My job is to protect and minimize the exposure of this institution to any litigation. Unless you cooperate and admit your mistake, your career with us is over. Either way, it's fair to say that no matter what you do at this point, my recommendation to the administration will be to cut you loose."

"That is unacceptable." Peter calmly stared at her.

"Too late. Consider it done. Now if you'll excuse me, I have a lot of work to do. That tape isn't public knowledge at present but when it is I will have to do a lot of damage control. I am done with you. You may go." She pointed to the door, swiveled in her chair and pulled a reference book off the shelf.

* * * * *

Barbosa leaned back in his chair, his feet planted firmly on his desk, a big smile on his face. Things couldn't have worked out better, even if he'd planned them himself. He stared at the ceiling and reviewed each turn of events, amazed at what had happened.

Fatigue had caught up with him. It had been a long day. The days of jumping out of bed at four in the morning for an emergency angioplasty, then working until six or seven in the evening were far behind him. He dreaded the occasional emergency call at night the hospital required him to take. He'd have to change the hospital by-laws. Why not retire? He'd amassed a fortune. There was nothing in life he couldn't afford. His wife was happy with her charity commitments. She left him alone most of the time, and that made him happy. He was free to have his little flings with pretty nurses who wanted to tap his power when all he wanted was to tap them. His two children, a son and a daughter, were both married and off on their own. They were as much strangers to him now as when they were growing up. It was better that way.

He looked around the room and came up with his answer. Why the hell should he retire? He had everything he needed here; power and control. He knew the money would be nothing without them.

On the third ring Barbosa dropped his feet to the floor and answered the phone. "Hello, Joshua. So nice of you to call."

"One day your arrogance will catch up with you."

"Maybe. But not today."

"What happened?"

"It appears my Cardiac Fellow killed the Senator all on his own. I didn't have to do a thing. Is he on our payroll?"

"Cut the bullshit!"

"Joshua, when I played the tape it showed my Fellow perforating the coronary artery. What did I tell you? I didn't have to do a God damned thing. The irony is, despite the tape, Pavano still insists it didn't happen."

"Don't get so cocky, Barbosa. We can still get screwed."

"Look, it appears Pavano killed the Senator. We're out of this mess."

"Let's keep it that way. Have a nice evening, Barbosa."

"And you, Joshua."

* * * * *

Peter sat by himself at Murphy's, a popular single's bar. He hadn't been to a place like this in years, due to lack of time and interest. The band played in the corner of the dance floor, while attractive men and women writhed together. Conversation was impossible, so physical appearance and prowess on the dance floor were the only elements that could come into play as each person searched for the perfect mate.

Peter stared straight ahead at the multitude of bottles that lined the back shelves of the bar, nursing his drink. The attractive young lady who sat next to him had lost her patience. She got up and left, but was replaced by a man in his mid fifties. All went unnoticed by Peter, whose thoughts stayed focused.

"I am glad you called," someone yelled in his ear.

The band stopped playing.

"Do you think you could have picked a more secluded place?" Sloan spoke in a more normal voice and looked around.

Peter sipped his drink. "Can I get you one?"

"Bourbon, straight up."

Peter ordered. "Tell me about the Cartel."

"What do you want to know?" Sloan took a slow sip from his drink that had just arrived.

"Everything," Peter said. "If you want my help I want to know everything."

Sloan paused then let out a deep sigh indicating consent. "The Cartel is a group of about five hundred cardiologists who only do angioplasty. They've formed a private little society."

"So? It's not unusual for groups to form societies."

"But most societies don't have an annual combined gross income of fifteen billion dollars. That's thirty million for each member, each year."

"What's wrong with that? Many movie and sports athletes make more than that."

"You're right. Taken individually, that isn't a problem, but fifteen billion dollars buys a lot of power. There's a big scam going on and fifteen billion dollars buys a lot of cover up."

"How far are you willing to go to get the Cartel?" Peter asked.

"However far we need to go."

Sloan tried to react casually but Peter could see by his posture he was salivating.

"First, the investigation into Senator Demind's death is delayed until the Cartel is brought down."

"I can't, that's out of my jurisdiction. That's an automatic investigation. I don't have the authority to even delay it."

06-MUCC

"Then I suggest you speak to someone that does. I need a thirty day delay."

"Why?"

"I have my reasons."

"And second?"

"I'll be in touch." Peter stood to leave, then spun around. "I'll call you. Don't call me." He left Sloan at the bar alone with his drink.

* * * * *

Sloan slid into the passenger seat of a nondescript blue Ford sedan and shut the door.

"How'd it go?" his partner, Thomson, asked. The car accelerated away from the curb.

"He bought it. He will be after the Cartel like a fly to shit."

"If he doesn't get himself killed," Thompson said.

"I hate using him for bait, but that's life." Sloan looked out the window. "With the Senator dead, he's our only hope and this time I don't want to lose."

"Time will tell. Time will tell."

13 | CHAPTER THIRTEEN

Dusty sat on the edge of his bed. His attention focused on his hands. He moved them back and forth, simulating two planes locked in aerial combat. His room was filled with a multitude of model planes. It was his haven. His place where nothing reminded him of his disability.

"Dusty. Are you in there?" his mother called from behind the closed door.

"Yeah." He kept up his aerial dogfight.

The door opened. "What're you doing home? Is anything wrong? Why aren't you at work?"

"I'm not going to work."

"What's wrong?" She sat next to him.

"I'm not going to work."

"Dusty, was someone mean to you again at work?"

"They—they think I'm 'tupid cause I'm retarded. I'm not 'tupid. I'm smart."

"Yes you are. Do you want to tell me what happened? Why won't you go to work?"

"I won't go to work, no." He stood abruptly and walked over to a model F-16 and picked it up. "F-16 is the best plane in the world."

"OK. I won't force you to go. When you're ready to talk about it remember, I'm here."

He ran over and hugged her around the waist. "I love you, Mommy. I'm gonna go for a walk. OK?"

06-MUCC

David Mucci

"What am I going to do with you? Sometimes . . ."

"I know, Mommy. Sometimes I'm a son only a mother could love."

Moments later he waddled down the street and turned onto Franklin Avenue. He loved the Italian section of Hartford. The pastry shops and their fresh treats were his favorite part. He always felt safe walking through Little Italy. After all, a place filled with so many sweet things to eat had to be safe.

La Pastoria was the first shop he came to. It always was. Over time, the staff had come to know him and allowed him whatever he wanted. Once a week, his mother stopped by and settled the bill he'd rung up.

Dusty stood just inside the door. He took a deep breath in through his nostrils. "Ah." He exhaled slowly.

"Hi Dusty," a middle aged woman called from behind the counter.

"Hi," he waved.

"Why aren't you in work? Did they give you the day off?" she asked.

"No!" he replied. "I'm not going to work. No! I'm on a walk."

"OK. Help yourself."

"OK. T'anks." Dusty walked between the racks of cream laden pastries stopping occasionally to pick one up. "I'll take one of these," he'd call out before eating it.

Lost in pastry bliss he paid no attention to customers who came and went. Finally he reached his fill. "I'm full. I'll go now. T'anks."

"Anytime Dusty, come again."

He walked towards the front door between two racks of dessert cakes. He found his way blocked by a customer. He spun and walked the other way. Another customer blocked that exit. Again he spun back to face the first customer who looked up from the cakes and stared directly at him. He was short and stocky, with bulging muscles. His eyes were dark and menacing. Dusty took a step back, turned and faced the other customer, who also looked up at him. Back and forth, right and left he turned, his breathing now rapid, his nostrils flared. Finally, he swatted the air with his hands and ran straight into one of the cake racks, tipping it over.

"No! No! You won't get me!"

The rack crashed to the floor. Cake and frosting splattered in all directions. Dusty stepped dead center into one of the cakes and left cake footprints all the way out the door.

He ran down the sidewalk. "No! You won't kill me! No!"

At the corner, a city bus had just discharged its last customer. Dusty ran as fast as his wide erratic gait would allow, but the door had closed by the time he'd reached it.

"Open! Open! Open! Open!" He pounded on the glass with the palm of his hand.

Before it was half open, he squeezed through and was beside the driver. "Shut it, go! Shut it, go!" He pounded the fare box with his fist. "Go!"

"Go nothing. One dollar. And stop hitting the fare box," the driver replied.

"No! Go now!" He ran down the aisle to the back of the bus and took the last seat. From there, he stared out the rear window intently.

"We're not going!" Dusty yelled to the driver from the back of the bus. "Go now!"

"One dollar," the driver yelled back.

Dusty ran down the aisle with a thud, thud, thud, from his flat-footed gait, and stopped beside the driver.

"Go now!"

"I told you one dollar."

"Hey man, here's a dollar for him. Now will you go?" A longhaired Puerto Rican tossed a crisp one-dollar bill on top of the fare machine.

"T'ank you." Dusty turned and ran down the aisle. Again he took the rear seat.

The bus started down Franklin Avenue. Sweat beaded up on his forehead and he stared out the rear window. At every stop, he

107

would jump up and scrutinize each passenger that boarded. Only when the bus had regained momentum would he return to his seat.

Suddenly, he jumped up and ran down the aisle. "The van, the white van, it's following me. Stop! Let me off!" The bus pulled over for a scheduled stop and Dusty ran down the stairs, pushing aside two elderly women who were boarding.

Once on the street, he started to run. He turned and saw the white van slow down. "Nooo!"

He ran across the street, ignoring the screech of tires and curses from motorists. He took a side street that brought him to a small bridge over a tributary of the Connecticut River. He breathed hard and ran with his head down with small quick steps. He quickly tired, but his panic drove him on.

Halfway across the bridge, he again ran across the road to the other side. He stopped and looked up. Five feet away the white van approached, its side door open.

"Nooo!" Dusty looked right then left, then directly at the van. It stopped abreast of him. In one last desperate act, he pivoted one hundred and eighty degrees. In two strides, he was next to the railing and in desperation he jumped over it, just as two muffled shots rang out from the van. Before his limp body hit the water, the van drove off, side door closed.

Thirty minutes passed before he moved. The current had carried him down river to the next small bridge, where he groped at a pillar with all his strength. When he finally felt it was safe to move, he made his way to shore. Upon rising out of the reeds that dotted the rivers edge he froze, wide eyed with fright as his eyes fell upon the man standing ten feet away, gun at his side.

14 CHAPTER FOURTEEN

"Attorney Small's office," the feminine voice on the other end of the telephone said. Peter glanced at the business card in his hand. "Is Attorney Small available?"

"My I tell him who's calling?"

"Peter Pavano. Dr. Peter Pavano. Please remind him I did the angioplasty on his father a few days ago."

"No need to. He raves about you daily. Please hold. I'll tell him you're on the line."

While he waited, he tried to organize in his mind what he would tell Samuel. The story was so long and convoluted. He quickly decided to approach it like a medical presentation. Short, sweet and to the point.

"Dr. Pavano." Samuel picked up the phone. "Is everything all right with my dad?"

"Yes. He's doing fine."

"That's good news. So tell me, what can I do for you? I'm sure you didn't call just to tell me he's doing fine?"

"The other day in the coffee shop you said if I ever needed help with a legal problem to call you."

"So, is some nurse saying you're the father of her child?"

"No. I've been fired from the Fellowship and thrown off staff at the hospital."

"What? Why?"

"They say I murdered a patient."

"Did you?"

"No sir, I didn't."

"Who was the patient?"

"Senator Demind."

There was a long silent pause. Peter could hear his heart pound.

"I think you better come and see me."

Peter sighed. "When?"

"Now. Come in right away. Also, I want you to bring your contract and any other documentation concerning your employment that you have. Do you have a copy of the hospital by-laws and rules and regulations?"

"I think I do. I think they gave me a set during orientation."

"Fine. Bring those also. I'll see you as soon as you can get here."

* * * * *

The Attorney's office was cozy and warm. The reception area was a soft hunter green, with antique cherry furniture. There were fresh cut flowers on the receptionist's desk and she looked up and greeted him with a smile.

"I'm here to see Attorney Small. I'm Peter Pavano."

"It's a pleasure to meet you, Doctor."

To his surprise, she stood and shook his hand.

"Come with me. Sam is expecting you. He's in the library."

She showed him into a small but functional room that had one wall with a bookshelf from floor to ceiling filled with legal books. On the opposite wall hung copies of Norman Rockwell's four Freedom pictures and next to them hung an original; a much younger Attorney Small at the Woodstock Music Festival with his arm around a very stoned Jimmy Hendrix. Samuel sat on the floor thumbing through an index.

"Dr. Pavano, come in and sit down."

Peter looked at a seat at the small conference table then at the floor. Samuel noticed his hesitation. "You can sit on the floor with me if you want but I'm sure you'll be more comfortable at the table."

A moment later, Samuel sat next to him. His hair was in a small ponytail. He wore comfortable jeans and an open collared shirt. Behind Samuel an expensive dark blue tailored suit, complete with a custom shirt and tie hung from a coat tree on a hanger. Samuel opened a yellow legal note pad and uncapped a pen. "I'm not going to ask you any questions yet. I want you to tell me concisely and with as much detail as you can remember what happened. Don't get side tracked as to the why. We'll deal with that later. I just want to know what happened."

Over the next thirty-five minutes Peter took Samuel from the moment he entered the Emergency Room to see Senator Demind until the moment he picked up Samuel's business card and called him. While Peter talked, Samuel filled sheet after sheet with notes. At times, he underlined words and sentences. At other times, he circled whole blocks of words. When Peter finished, he sat there and watched Samuel peruse his notes back and forth for the next minute or two.

"Tell me about Agent Sloan"

"I met him at Mount Auburn Cemetery just outside of Boston."

"Now I'm even more confused. Back up a bit and fill in the blanks. I want to know the first time you met Agent Sloan."

Samuel's pen raced over the yellow legal pad while he listened to Peter's recanting his meeting with Agent Sloan, which ended with his attempt to blackmail Peter.

Samuel said. "I can't believe the scope of power this Cardiac Cartel could have if it's for real. Holy shit!" He sat back and stared at the ceiling for a moment. "The repercussions. The implications. Talk about tickling the tiger's tail. Sloan said the last person that tried to help them is dead? But that's secondary. At this moment, I need you to tell me everything."

"I thought I had."

"No, you haven't. Sloan attempted to blackmail you because of your past. I need to know everything about your past. Everything. We have to nullify their ability to blackmail you if we can."

Peter sighed. He'd never told anyone about his past. Even Kelsey only got the glossed over details about his dysfunctional family life.

"I grew up in a small town in Pennsylvania." Peter started. "I had a sister two years younger than me, her name's Sasha. I don't know where she is today. I haven't seen her since I ran away. My father worked in the steel mill. Sounds like a soap opera but I guess someone has to work the mills. Anyway, he was obsessed with religion, and used it when it suited him. The more he drank the more it suited him. One day his drinking caught up with his temper and in the name of religion he beat my mother to within an inch of her life. All in the name of God. He felt she was flirting with a guy in his twenties who lived down the street. He threw her out of the house, black and blue and naked for all the neighbors to see. All the while, he stood on the porch and preached from the Bible. It was too much for her, the humiliation that is. The next morning my little sister found her still naked in the back yard. She was dead. She'd taken a piece of rope and hung herself. My dad cursed her dead body and damned her to hell. He made me and my sister stand there and look at her. He said we were to witness what happened to true wickedness."

Peter paused and Samuel jumped in. "Let's stop for a moment. Can I get you any coffee or tea?"

"Coffee would be fine."

"How do you take it?" He got up and walked to the door.

"Cream, one sugar."

When he returned, he had two cups with him. He set one down in front of Peter then took his seat. "What happened when the authorities got involved?"

"What authorities? You're talking about small town America. A . . . God . . . fearing . . . town. This was a private matter. There was no crime. A woman took her own life. She was possessed by the devil."

"What about the bruises."

"Spouse abuse? It hadn't been invented yet. How a man disciplined his wife was his business. No one else's."

Samuel sipped his coffee. He'd stopped taking notes, and just listened and watched Peter while he talked. "OK. What happened after that?"

"The abuse got worse and so did his drinking. It seemed the more he drank the more he used religion to justify his abuse. He'd go on these preaching binges where he'd force us to learn and repeat from memory parts of the bible. It was worse than any military boot camp I've heard of. Finally, I'd had enough. He was molesting my sister and she was helpless. We both ran away the summer I was fourteen and she was twelve. We went to Boston where we lived on the streets. One day she was picked up by the police and placed in protective custody. There was nothing I could do to get her out. Eventually she was placed in a foster home. But me, I was still hiding on the streets."

Peter wiped away a tear from his cheek. He hadn't thought of his sister for a long time. One day he'd track her down. "I guess I rationalized that she was better in a foster home than on the street with me. She was definitely better there than with my dad. So I walked away."

"Do you know where she is?"

"No. Then I met Ethel. Towards the end of the summer I guess I was lonely, and scared, an emotional wreck. I was sitting on a curbstone crying and she stopped. She knew immediately I was a runaway, as if it was hard to tell. Anyway, she took me in, fed me, clothed me and helped me get on with my life."

"So how is the FBI blackmailing you?"

"Ethel was a teacher. She taught high school. She said I could live with her only if I finished my education. I took the name Peter Pavano. Pavano was her last name. Steven, Steven Woods is my real name. She made up false transfer papers and a transcript so the school would allow me in. She didn't want to ask my real school for the information for fear my dad would find out where I was. That's how I'm being blackmailed."

"So the F.B.I is blackmailing you because of phony high school transcripts?"

"Yes. The FBI told me if I didn't help them they'd expose me as a fake and I'd lose my medical license."

Samuel sat back in his seat. "I can't believe how low those bastards can stoop. First of all, there's no way you can get into any trouble. You only need to have verification of equivalent education. If parents teach their children at home and then decide to send them to public school, they only have to produce the core curriculum they taught them. You said Ethel was a teacher?"

"Yes. In high school."

"Well then, it's no problem. She was your legal guardian at that time. It could also be argued, though very loosely, that you were an emancipated minor at the time. So, Ethel vouched for your educational knowledge and categorized you fit to attend the next grade of public school. Though it was wrong of her to make up phony transcripts, you can argue that under the circumstances she had no other choice. Anyway, once you had the chance you proved yourself and held your own."

"So there is no way I could lose my medical license over that?" Peter asked.

"Not over that but this thing with the Senator is another issue. Peter, exactly what is it you want to accomplish? It appears you are in a long term bad situation."

They talked for the next fifteen minutes.

Samuel looked at his watch. "It's ten o'clock now. Give me a moment." He dialed Connecticut General's main number and asked for Patricia Steward's office. After identifying himself she picked up the phone. "Attorney, I have Dr. Pavano in my office and will be his legal council in this problem that has come about."

There was a pause while he listened to her reply. After a moment he said, "Counselor, we have a lot to discuss. Dr. Pavano has been grievously wronged. I think we need to talk today and not over the telephone."

After another pause, he continued, "Well, you may not feel there's any need for us to meet, but I disagree and I think it is in your best interest to meet with me. So, you can either meet with me before or after."

He smiled at Peter. "Oh, before or after we meet with the press to explain that the famous Dr. Barbosa didn't do the angioplasty on Senator Demind. To explain to the press that Dr. Barbosa forced his Fellow, who had only two weeks of formal training, to perform the procedure. That Dr. Barbosa was not even at his side when he did the procedure. I will call for an investigation into gross deviation from the standard of care in medicine with respect to the Senator's care, and with respect to unsupervised procedures done by residents and fellows."

Samuel paused and listened for a moment, then smiled again. "Yes. One o'clock in your office would be fine." He hung up. "OK. Here's the plan. Go and relax, have something to eat. Leave the bylaws, rules and regulations and your contract with me. Meet me outside the hospital at 12:45 and we'll go see that bitch together. I love bucking the establishment."

They shook hands and Samuel walked him to the door.

At one o'clock sharp, Peter and Samuel walked into Patricia Steward's office. Gone were the blue jeans that Samuel had worn in his office, and Peter marveled how that dark blue tailored suit gave him a completely different persona.

"Mr. Small, you didn't mention anything about Pavano being here when we talked." There was raw meanness in her voice.

"I'm sorry Pat, but Doctor Pavano is my client and he is entitled to be present anytime I discuss his case. I know that's alien to many attorneys but that's how I like to do things. Don't worry you'll get over it. Peter, why don't you take the far seat."

Peter did so and watched with anticipation.

Samuel got right down to business. "I have reviewed my client's contract, along with your hospital bylaws and rules and regulations regarding dismissal. If you had also read them, you would know that you have violated my client's rights on numerous counts."

"Dr. Pavano is currently the center of an internal hospital investigation," Steward said. "He lied about the procedure that caused the Senator's death. If you had looked at the bylaws—"

Samuel held up his hand. "Hear me out, then you can have your say."

"Fine. Go ahead." Steward sat back and crossed her arms over her chest.

"First, no charges have been filed so you can't discharge him on supposition or plain speculation. Second, if I still remember basic law, one is innocent until proven guilty."

"We have every right to protect patients from potential harm," Steward said.

"Again," he held up his hand, "I ask you not to interrupt me. You are right, you do have that right and responsibility but you don't have the right to summarily fire my client for a bad patient outcome; that, Ms. Steward, is the Art of medicine. According to your hospital bylaws, Dr. Pavano is entitled to a hearing where formal charges must be presented to a panel of arbitrary physicians. Dr. Pavano has the right to a fair and impartial hearing at which time he can answer any charges. Then, and only then, can the hospital take action against him."

"We have the right to immediate termination if we find gross negligence and do not hold up your hand in my face one more time to stop me from talking."

"Fair enough. However, until the case is formally reviewed, all you can do is place him on probation. You must continue to pay his salary, and allow him to continue on in his studies. If you choose to restrict hospital duties you may but his studies are in angioplasty. You cannot restrict him from observing. He has the right, according to your bylaws, to challenge any termination decision by this hospital by asking for a hearing. Why haven't you apprised my client of any of his rights? You willfully ignored your duties to protect a hospital employee."

"I was hired first and foremost to protect this hospital."

"It seems you have left your hospital more legally exposed by not protecting the rights of my client."

"How is that?"

"Dr. Pavano is a new Invasive Cardiac Fellow. He has all of two full weeks of training. Your hospital, Dr. Barbosa, to be specific, allowed my client to undertake an extremely difficult and dangerous procedure on an unstable patient without adequate supervision."

"Dr. Barbosa was there for the entire procedure," Steward countered.

"Then how do you explain the fact that he was unaware that Dr. Pavano perforated the coronary artery of the Senator? Why wasn't he providing closer supervision? Why didn't he stop the mistake from happening before it happened"

Pat stuttered in an attempt to respond.

"The way I see it," Attorney Small continued, "it was an accident that this terrible event happened. What is more terrible is that my client came to this hospital for training. Instead he was cut loose by the chairman of the department to do a dangerous procedure completely unsupervised."

"He was not left unsupervised. Dr. Barbosa was there."

"Then why didn't Barbosa stop him from making this mistake? That doesn't sound like very close supervision to me. Pavano was unaware he perforated the artery. He can't possibly know everything this early in his training. That's why he's here! No, Counselor, you not only fell down in your responsibilities to my client, you also fell down in your responsibilities to your patient, Senator Demind, by allowing my client such a free hand with so little supervision, that this incident happened and neither of them were aware of it. Oh, I would say you and your institute are very much exposed. And lastly, the way you have grievously treated my client has done him tremendous harm." Samuel leaned back and waited.

After a long staring match Steward blinked. "What is it you want?"

"First Dr. Pavano is immediately reinstated with full salary." She nodded.

"Second, there will be no formal inquiry unless you want what we have just discussed open for public debate. Lastly, my client will be fully reinstated with, of course, close supervision."

"I want your assurance that there will be no press conferences, ever," Steward countered.

"You only have my assurance that there won't be one this week. Have a good day." Without any further discussion Samuel rose and Peter left the room.

15 | CHAPTER FIFTEEN

It had been only fifteen minutes since Peter and Samuel walked out of Patricia Steward's office. Peter stood in Barbosa's outer office. "Where is the good doctor?" Peter asked.

"He's giving a lecture to the medical students." Beth had a slight grin on her face.

"When he returns tell him I want to see him."

"No need to. He's heard already. I would say he got the call thirty seconds after you left Steward's office."

Peter raised an eyebrow. "And?"

"And what? Was he angry? Did he rant and rage? Did he storm out of here? What do you think? But, not before he gave me explicit instructions for you." Beth looked at him.

"And what were those?"

"It was simple. You are not to see any of his patients. You will only see patients of Dr. Kyle's and Dr. Clayton's, that is, only if they say it's alright."

"That's fine with me." Peter turned to leave.

"Peter . . . I mean Dr. Pavano."

He turned back towards her.

"You need to be careful. Dr. Barbosa is a very dangerous and vindictive person." She glanced at the empty doorway then wrote something on a piece of paper. "If you really want to find out what is going on talk with this person." She handed it to him.

Peter read the name but didn't recognize it.

119

"It all started with him." Beth continued. "He may help you. He may not. It all depends on how much danger you want to be in and how much he is willing to put you in. Either way, you are dealing with very dangerous men, and Barbosa is as bad as they get."

"Why are you telling me this?"

"Do you remember Dr. Collas?"

"Yes. He was the fellow here before me. He showed me around when I interviewed."

"That's right and he wasn't careful enough. He ended up dead but it wasn't a suicide."

"How do you know?"

"I knew him. He had no reason to kill himself. He got too close. I told him to be careful but he wouldn't listen to me."

Peter thought for a moment. "Why are you telling me this?"

"Dr. Collas dated my fraternity sister. I introduced them. The name on that paper I gave you. He's my step-uncle."

"Does Barbosa know that?"

"No. Do you think I would have given his name to you if he did?"

Peter looked at the floor for a moment, then back at Beth. "I don't understand. If you think Barbosa was involved in his death why are you still working here?"

"Trust me, I won't be here much longer. Two more credits at night school and I have my degree, then, I'm history." She stared at him hard and long. "You be careful, Dr. Pavano."

"And you." Peter tipped his head to her and left.

Peter found Clayton deeply focused on the monitor in Angiosuite #1. The sixty-three year old patient's heart jumped rhythmically as the low radiation bathed it and highlighted it on the screen. Peter didn't announce his presence. He quietly stood behind Clayton and observed. The dye shot through the arteries and vanished as quickly as Clayton injected it through the tip of the catheter. In that instant, Peter could see her arteries were open and clean. She had no coronary artery disease.

"Mrs. Pullman," Clayton leaned over towards the head of the table, "though we won't know until we completely review the pictures I just took, it does appear that you have a blockage of one of your arteries. The dye barely squeaked through. As soon as I look at it more closely, we will sit down and discuss your options."

Peter shifted which caused Clayton to catch him in his peripheral vision. He spun around. "Dr. Pavano. How long have you been standing behind me in silence?"

"I just walked in. How did her angio look?" He stepped forward.

"Unfortunately, it appears she has a blockage and is in need of our expertise. Of course, we have to formally review the tapes before we make a final recommendation to this lovely patient."

Peter kept his silence.

"Dr. Pavano," Clayton continued, "I have heard interesting news about you. It seems you have fallen into Daniel's den of lions. As the hand of God kept the lions from devouring him, so has that same hand kept the lions from you. I am sure just as they circled Daniel, they will continue to circle you. Keep your faith, young doctor, keep your faith."

"If I remember," Peter replied, "it was Daniel's faith and that long arm of God that crushed his enemies eventually." Peter's eyes drilled into Clayton's.

A short time later, Peter picked up a phone in the hospital lobby and dialed the number off of Sloan's business card. Eventually Sloan answered. "Sloan, it's Pavano. Did you do what I asked in delaying the investigation?"

"Aren't I supposed to be the one asking you questions?"

"No games, Sloan. And while we're talking about games, you can forget your pitiful blackmail plot. If you want to expose my past, go ahead. There isn't a damned thing in my past that can be used against me but I gather you've known that all along."

"Can't blame me for trying, can you?"

"Actually, I can. So I'll ask you one last time before I hang up, what about the delay in the investigation of the Senator's death?"

Sloan's voice became very business like. "The director has approved the thirty days you requested. After that, it's a public matter."

"Thirty days is fine. If I can't finish this in thirty days, I'm out of here anyway." Peter looked around. "This isn't going to be free Sloan. It's going to cost you."

The pause was long and heavy.

"After that bullshit attempt to blackmail me, trust me, it's going to be a lot."

"I doubt the director will approve very much, though I'm sure we can get you something." Peter heard Sloan's heavy breath over the phone.

"Then you and your director are fools and I am history."

"No! No! Pavano, don't hang up . . . come on, be reasonable. Work with us. How much are we talking about?"

"Five million dollars."

"You expect me to say, 'OK, sure, where do you want it deposited?' I need something to work with. I need some hard evidence to take to the director. Call it a down payment. We need to see what you want us to pay for. Then we'll negotiate."

"Sloan, there will be no negotiation. It is all or nothing."

Again, there was a long pause. Only Sloan's heavy breathing could be heard. "For that much, and I am not saying that much will be approved, you can bet we want to see what you want us to pay for. We look first, then if we feel it is worth the price, that is the price we are willing to pay, then we will talk finances."

"So you want a taste," Peter said sarcastically.

"That's correct," Sloan recovered. "We will deal with you after we have . . . a taste. But I'm going to tell you, you will not get five million. We've waited this long. We can wait a little longer for someone who is more reasonable."

"I'll give you your taste, Sloan, but for the main course it is five million dollars now and always will be. That, my blackmailing friend, is not negotiable." He hung up and walked down the hall to meet Clayton.

Peter found Clayton writing notes on a patient's angiogram. He sat in front of the monitor and watched the tape in slow motion.

"Dr. Pavano. It is nice of you to join me. I am already halfway through them."

Peter didn't reply. He sat and for the next thirty minutes watched the monitor and listened to his teacher expound on each case and the planned procedure. One by one they reviewed each tape. Always the same: first, they saw the dye injected into the arteries, and then they slowed the tape, reversed it, and reviewed it one or more times. So it went over and over again until all the cases had been reviewed and recommendations made.

"Dr. Pavano, our work is done. Shall we?" Clayton stood.

"Would you mind if I looked at this one?" Before Clayton could object, Peter popped in Mrs. Pullman's tape and pressed start. "This was the nice woman you were finishing up with when I caught up with you earlier today."

Peter watched and saw the blockage Clayton had mentioned to the patient.

"Oh, yes," Peter said. "Plain as day. This is a bread and butter case." He turned to Clayton. "A milk run, as Dr. Kyle likes to refer to them. She'll do fine." Peter shut off the tape and ejected it. With a slight flick he tossed it on the table. "This one you almost didn't need to review. You could have seen it clearly during the procedure."

"That, Dr. Pavano," Clayton stuttered for a second, "is not acceptable. You must take the time and review each one carefully. You would be surprised what you could miss."

"So true, Dr. Clayton. One's eyes can be deceived very easily."

Shortly before four in the afternoon, Peter slipped into Barbosa's office. Beth looked up.

"Is he here?" Peter asked.

06-MUCC

"No."

"I'll be quick. I need a favor." He watched her eyes and knew he could trust her.

"OK."

He handed her a piece of paper. "I need you to pull this list."

She glanced at it. Peter saw her gaze into empty space for a moment.

"If you think it is too dangerous, I want you to say no," Peter said.

She looked at him. "When do you need it by?"

"Noon tomorrow."

She looked at the list again, then at him. "Come by at 11:30. Barbosa has a Chief's meeting from eleven to noon. We'll split the difference just in case."

16 | CHAPTER SIXTEEN

O ne of the most chaotic times in the Emergency Room at Connecticut General is between 11:30 a.m. and noon. At that time, the morning blood work of most of the E.R. patients returns and is evaluated by the physicians. Inevitably that review prompts more blood work to be drawn, for further tests. Other patients, lost all morning in the black hole otherwise known as the Radiology Department, miraculously return to the E. R., their stretchers pushed by transportation aides, x-rays in hand. The closer the clock gets to lunch time, the faster other departments worked to move patients and test results back to the Emergency Room. Then they could go to lunch while the inundated E.R. staff coped with the onslaught.

Kelsey timed her entrance accordingly. She wore Peter's lab coat, and his stethoscope dangled around her neck. Peter's hospital identification badge hung clipped on the coat's left breast pocket. It faced backwards so no one could see the picture. For the moment she felt safe from recognition. The Emergency Room hadn't been part of her territory as a sales representative. She only hoped she wouldn't run into a physician she'd dealt with.

Kelsey strode boldly to the main board that held the patient charts. Without hesitation, she reached up and grabbed one that had been flagged for admission. With it tucked under her arm, she walked into the crowded nurses' station and sat down in front of one of the three computer screens.

She opened the chart and leafed through. "This can't be right," she said making a show of her disgust.

She typed Peter's password on the keyboard. When she pressed return, she had access to the system.

Kelsey glanced around. No one paid any attention to her. She took a piece of paper from her left breast pocket and got started. Written on it were patient names and medical records numbers that Peter had just received from Beth. She typed in the first one. On the monitor, the file opened up. After she scrolled to the appropriate admission, the printer four feet away churned out the specific segments of each chart she'd highlighted. Chart after chart, patient after patient, the printer spit them out.

After eight to ten pages had printed, she reached over and retrieved them. Those pages were neatly placed in her briefcase on top of the others.

She was on her fourteenth chart when a nurse ran up to her.

"Doctor! Come with me, I need your help!"

Kelsey looked up. "Excuse me?"

"Mr. Shilo in Room Four. That's his chart you have. He's not doing well: I need you to take a look at him."

"I'm sorry but—"

"Don't 'but' me. You can look at his chart later. Now, Doctor!"

Kelsey hesitated, then stood and hurried after the anxious nurse.

The patient was ashen in color. Beads of perspiration pooled on his forehead, and his breathing labored as she watched. Kelsey saw he was in trouble. "What's wrong?" she asked.

"What's wrong?" the nurse snapped back. "Doctor, you were just looking at his chart. I told the other resident this patient should go to the Cardiac Care Unit. But no, he wouldn't listen to me. I'm only a nurse. He said a monitored floor was good enough. Well, look at him." She pointed to the patient. "His blood pressure is only eighty systolic. You can't send a patient in congestive heart failure with a blood pressure of only eighty to the floor."

"I agree with you," she said. Beads of sweat formed on her forehead too.

"Well? What do you want to do?"

Kelsey looked at her, then at the patient.

"Doctor! If you don't do something about his blood pressure soon he's going to arrest."

The back of her hand involuntarily went up to her mouth. Her eyes met the patient's just as he gasped and rolled his eyes back.

"He stopped breathing!" Kelsey blurted out.

"Code Blue! Room four!" the nurse yelled out. "The monitor's flat line. Start CPR. I'll bag him."

The nurse ran to the head of the bed, grabbed an AMBU Bag, placed the mask over the patient's face and pumped the flexible plastic oxygen reservoir in a repetitive manner.

Kelsey stood there, paralyzed with fear.

"Doctor! Start CPR. He's flat lined!"

The heart monitor showed a straight line. His heart had stopped.

"Doctor!" she yelled, but Kelsey continued to stand there, frozen.

Three other nurses ran in. One pushed Kelsey aside, placed the palms of her hands on the patient's chest and pushed up and down in an attempt to compress the heart.

"Get me a doctor that knows what to do!" the nurse at the head of the bed yelled.

One of the nurses ran out of the room only to return moments later. "Dr. Kline is here with his resident."

Kelsey knew him, but when he rushed in his eyes fixed on the patient. To Kelsey's relief a nurse moved between her and Dr. Kline. That was fine with her. She backed up and inched towards the curtain.

"What's going on?" Dr. Kline asked.

"He's in congestive heart failure, hypotensive, has emphysema and arrived with an asthmatic attack. He arrested and that doctor there panicked and hasn't been able to help us at all."

Dr. Kline turned, but Kelsey was gone. She'd slipped out of the room, her only thought to grab her briefcase and get out. Once outside the E.R., she brushed tears from her eyes and looked both ways down the hallway. She saw a ladies room. She ran in and locked the door behind her. With her back pressed against the door, her emotions took over. Tears rolled down her face and she shook uncontrollably. The image of that terrified patient's look moments before he arrested haunted her.

Ten minutes later, dry-eyed and composed, Kelsey emerged from the ladies room. She still had eleven charts to copy, but she couldn't go back to the E.R. That was out of the question. Her backup plan would have to do. It was more dangerous and she had a greater chance of being caught.

A quick elevator ride brought her to Medical Records. Peter had briefed her on where to go.

After an agonizingly long walk, she found herself in a cubicle. She sat for a long time and waited for the pounding in her chest to subside. When her breathing slowed, she typed in the access number and again logged onto the system.

There was one major problem with the plan: the printers in Medical Records were all within the confines of the Medial Records Director's office. Nothing got printed or even left the office without her approval. She'd been known to rip copies of charts out of residents' hands if she thought they'd copied material not pertinent to their research projects. Attending physicians avoided her like poison. She was in great shape for her early fifties, and she had a look that threw daggers.

Kelsey knew she would have one chance, if she were lucky. Over the next few minutes, she worked within her own computer. She copied the fragments of charts she needed into a side file she'd created. When she finished, all she could do was wait. There were about forty pages to print. That would take almost ten minutes. Kelsey turned and peered into the Director's office. The wall was all glass, so she could look out and watch her staff.

The Director sat behind her desk and read a report. Kelsey stared at the five printers and waited. Eventually, one started to spit out paper. That was it. She pressed the print key and held her breath.

Finally, the third printer came to life. Page after page rolled slowly into the collecting tray. She counted each page with heightened anxiety. A wave of nausea rolled over her when the Director cast a gaze at the printer. Her heart raced when a resident walked into the office and picked up her pages off the third printer. She could only bite her lip and watch.

The resident leafed through the pages. When he realized they were not his, he placed them back into the tray where more pages had collected. He picked up his pages and moved over to the Director. Without a word, she took them from him and went through each page and checked them against his request and release form. One page she confiscated. Kelsey watched her reprimand him for copying a wrong page.

Seconds before her printer finished the resident left the office, copies in hand.

"Shit," she muttered.

She had to wait a little longer. It wasn't long before another printer came to life. A few sheets slid into the tray, then stopped. A female resident entered and picked them up. She started through the same routine with the Director.

"OK, Kelsey," she said to herself. "It's now or never."

She walked into the office, scooped up the forty plus pages, turned, and started to leave.

"One moment, Doctor!" the Director called out. She was not distracted easily. "Nothing leaves this office unless I approve it. Bring those copies here." She held out her hand. The resident moved to the side.

Kelsey stopped, her back to the woman. Her palms felt clammy. "I have to get you my release. It's in my bag." She started to take a step out of the office.

"That's fine. But leave those copies with me."

129

"I'll be back in a second."

"No!" the Director raised her voice. "Leave those copies with me now!"

Kelsey, not hesitating, walked out of the office, with the copies.

The Director jumped up. "Doctor! Get back here! Don't you walk away from me when I'm talking to you!"

Kelsey reached her cubicle, shoved the copies into her case and headed for the door.

"Stop right there! Now!" the Director yelled, starting after her. "Someone call security!"

Kelsey broke into a run. She dashed out the side door, rounded the corner and entered the stairwell. She heard the Director yelling behind her. She ran two steps at a time up one flight. At that landing, she tore off the lab coat and stethoscope and dropped them into her bag. The door one flight down crashed open. The Director gave chase.

Kelsey entered the hallway, then turned and calmly walked to the bank of elevators. There stood a group of people in obvious mourning. A family member had just died. She shouldered her way to the front of them and buried her face in her hands. She knew hospital personnel learned quickly to leave grieving family members alone.

Kelsey felt the eyes of the Director, who was only feet away, scan the group. The elevator doors opened and she slid in with them. She lost herself amongst the weeping mourners when the doors closed before the Director got a close look.

Once on the ground floor, Kelsey stayed with the family all the way out the front door. The instant she was outside, she ran.

17 | CHAPTER SEVENTEEN

Barbosa listened to the shrill on the other end of the phone. It was close to four in the afternoon. The day had been long and problematic for him and this was the last thing he needed to deal with before he went home. Finally, he slammed the phone down on the cradle and yelled. "Beth, get your ass in here now!"

"Yes Dr. Barbosa, you yelled?" Beth smiled as she stuck her head into his office.

"Don't get smart with me or you'll find your ass booted out of here onto the street. Get Pavano up here now!"

Fifteen minutes later, Peter sat in Barbosa's office, in the now familiar chair that sat in front of his desk. This was Peter's first face-to-face encounter since Barbosa showed him the Senator's angioplasty tape.

"Dr. Pavano. I had a very distressing phone call from the head of the Medical Records Department a few minutes ago. Do you have any idea why she was so upset?"

Peter looked at him with a blank stare then shrugged his shoulders. "No, sir. I do not have a clue." He leaned forward in anticipation.

Barbosa leaned back in his chair and smiled. His voice was soft and calm. "Peter, it appears the hospital has had a security breach. Someone, a female to be precise, has used your security password to access some medical charts. She used the terminal

06-MUCC

in the Emergency Room. She also had the balls to use one of the terminals in the Medical Records Department. She stole copies of charts off the printer right in front of the Medical Director herself. Then she ran out of the hospital before anyone could stop her."

Peter frowned. "You said she used my password?"

"Yes I did. I don't suppose you know anything about this?" Barbosa now sat forward, his stare fixed on Peter.

"No. I don't." Peter rubbed the back of his neck. "What records were taken?"

"That is none of your concern. What is, is that your password has been deleted."

"Then how can I do my work? I need access to old records."

"Medical records has a new password for you. Technology is a wonderful thing Peter. It can giveth and it can taketh. Your new password will only allow you access to charts on patients that are actively in the Emergency Room at the time you see them. Also only selective patients of Dr's Kyle and Clayton, of course, none of mine will be included in that list."

"Of course."

"And those consults that Beth gives you will also be included. Otherwise everything else is off limits."

"That is fine with me Dr. Barbosa. I have no need for anyone else's charts. And if someone else has my password, as it appears someone does, I want that breach of security stopped." Peter smiled at Barbosa.

Barbosa pointed his finger at Peter. "I'm watching you Pavano. I am watching you. One mistake and I will take you down." He dismissed him with the wave of his hand.

Out in Barbosa's outer office, Peter smiled and winked at Beth as he left.

"Dr. Pavano." She handed him a sheet of paper. "Here are the requested consults from last night."

Peter looked at the sheet. A paper clip held a small piece of paper to the top of the sheet. Peter read that small-added note, removed it and placed it in his pocket. "Thank you Beth. I have a lot of work to do."

"I would say you do."

* * * * *

Barbosa paced for a moment in front of his desk. If he handled it himself and things went wrong, he would alienate too many members of the council. It was better to make the call and drop it in Joshua's lap. With acid building in his stomach, he sat behind his desk and dialed.

"Joshua, I think it is time we coordinated our efforts."

Joshua sat silently behind his desk while Barbosa informed him of Peter's unproven, but almost certain duplicity.

"I think," Joshua replied, "what you have done limits him the best you can within the hospital. I think we need to bug his car, his apartment, and have constant around the clock visual surveillance when he is out of the hospital."

"Though it pains me, I have to agree with you. I just don't trust him."

18 | CHAPTER EIGHTEEN

It was one of those summer days that shrouded the sun in a mist of haze. Samuel walked lazily across the bridge and stopped midway across the span. He glanced at the sky and knew that by sunset the thunderheads that were now forming far over the horizon would deluge the streets with water and turn the area into a Turkish steam bath by late afternoon. He leaned against the warm wooden railing and gazed around. The water of the Connecticut River flowing below was cool and inviting. How far was it? He asked himself. Twenty? Twenty-five feet below?

His hand ran along the railing and stopped at a gouge in the wood. That in of itself held little meaning to Samuel. It was the perfectly formed hole seven inches away that drew his eyes. His hands ran over the backside of the railing. There was no exit hole. There was, though, a bulge in the wood. With a fishing pocketknife in hand he leaned over the railing and unroofed the hole. A small piece of lead fell into his hand. He placed it, along with his knife, into his pocket and continued his walk, again looking at the sky in anticipation of the thunderheads.

* * * * *

It was three in the afternoon. It was shift change in the Emergency Room. Between three and three-thirty, the nurses are too busy signing out patients to the evening shift and tidying up loose ends on their charts to care about much else. Their sole mission during that time was signing out and going home.

At two minutes after three, Kelsey walked into the department. She walked over to the computer station. Her eyes stayed focused on the floor in front of her as she walked. She refused to make eye contact with anyone. The moment she sat down at the second computer she pulled out a small note pad that held the medical numbers of the needed charts. On the inner flap of the notepad cover three passwords were written. They were Drs. Clayton, Kline, and Barbosa's. Beth had given them to Peter. They were clipped onto a list of consults she gave him on the day Barbosa had yanked his password.

She typed in Barbosa's password, gained access, and in less than five minutes was gone with the printout of four charts. Hit and run. That was her tactic over the next three days. She was in and out during shift change, trauma emergencies, and code blue cardiac arrests. At any moment of confusion amongst the staff, Kelsey was present. Peter would page her on an independent beeper and keep her informed. For Kelsey, the fleeting moments of anxiety and terror of being discovered in the Emergency Room, like a cornered animal, were replaced by the tension of turning the next corner and running head on into someone she knew. She was a sales representative, a job that required she be highly visible. She avoided the cafeteria. Instead, she attempted to sequester herself in the library, her nose in a book, at the far booth in the coffee shop. It made for long and stressful days with no time to let her guard down.

On the third day, she walked to her car, placed the last of the charts into the trunk along with the ninety-seven others and drove away.

* * * * *

Late that afternoon, Peter answered his page at one of the many hospital phones. It was the operator with an outside call for him.

16-MUCC

"Peter, it's Samuel. Can you talk?"

"Sure. I'm in a hallway. What's up?"

"I think you are in more danger than we thought earlier."

"Why?"

"I was talking to a friend of mine on the Hartford Police Department. I was doing a little snooping. He told me the other day they fished a kid with Downs Syndrome out of the Connecticut River. He was alive but pretty shaken up. He kept ranting about being chased and shot at. He said he jumped off a bridge into the river. He also said they killed his friend because he knew how the Senator was killed, and they were trying to kill him because they knew his friend had told him how they did it. The police blew him off. They said he was retarded."

"His name is Dusty."

"That's right. And there's more. I took a walk. I went to the bridge he said he jumped from. I pulled a bullet out of the wooden railing and had my friend look at it. Despite being smashed, one side still had some markings and the ballistics matched the gun that killed that hospital technician the other day. That kid knows more than anyone is giving him credit for."

Peter looked down the still empty hall and rubbed the back of his neck. "I'll call you tomorrow. I want to pay a visit to Dusty. I haven't seen him around the hospital for a few days. I hope he isn't hiding someplace."

"If I was him," Samuel said. "I'd be hiding someplace far away."

19 | CHAPTER NINETEEN

Finding Dusty's address had been easy for Peter. Using Barbosa's entry code, he simply entered Dusty's name. It was inevitable that at one time or another Dusty had visited the Emergency Room for a fall or a cut. To Peter's relief, an ER visit one and a half years ago for a laceration popped up on the screen. Peter scrolled to Dusty's database and copied down the address. He exited the system, then the hospital.

A half hour later, Peter climbed the aged, cracked brick steps to Dusty's house. The steps led to the inner stairs of an old wooden three-family apartment building, one of many that lined both sides of the street. On the second floor landing, he knocked on the door of Dusty's apartment. There was no response. He was about to leave when he heard movement inside. It was the quick shuffle of feet. He knocked again. This time with more force.

"Dusty. Hey Dusty. It's Dr. Pavano. I wanted to see if you were all right. Could you open up please?"

The door opened slowly. Once Dusty saw it was Peter, he threw it wide open. "Come in. Fast!"

Dusty grabbed him by the arm and pulled him into the small entrance way. Then he stuck his head back out the door and looked in all directions before he slammed it shut, and locked it.

"They tried to kill me!" He quickly paced back and forth.

"Yes. I know."

"They tried to kill me. They chased me down the street but I was smart, I took a bus. When they chased the bus, I ran off it

137

and jumped off a bridge into the water." He stopped pacing and stood in front of Peter proudly. "They shot at me but missed."

"Why would someone want to kill you?" Peter asked.

"Because I know. I know he killed the Senator. I know how. Roberto told me before they killed him and now they want to kill me before I tell anyone." He started to pace again.

Peter grabbed the opportunity. "That's one of the reasons I'm here. I need to know what Roberto told you."

"No, no. I can't tell you. Then they'll try to kill you, too, and it will be my fault. No, no, no!"

"I'll take the chance. They are trying to blame me for the Senator's death. Dusty, you know I didn't kill him."

"That's right, that's right. I know. That doctor, the bad one, Barbosa. He killed him. Roberto told me." Dusty stopped pacing and stood still. His arms fell to his side, his head hung, and he started to cry.

Peter put his arm around him. "It will be all right. No one is going to hurt either of us but I need to know exactly what Roberto said."

Dusty wiped a tear from his check with the back of his hand and sat down in the nearest chair. He spoke in sobs. "He tried to tell Barbosa . . . but he only got in trouble . . . he got yelled at . . . then they killed him." Dusty became quiet and hung his head. Then his head snapped up. "No. You are a friend. It's not safe to tell you. You are in danger around me. I have to go, to protect you."

Before Peter could reply Dusty had opened the front door and started down the inner hall stairs. When Peter started after him he heard heavy footsteps running up the wooden steps towards him.

"Help! Help! They're here! They'll kill us!"

Dusty violently pulled Peter back into the apartment by his arm, slammed the door and dead bolted it. He ran and hid behind the living room sofa, burying his head in his lap.

Suddenly hard knocks resonated from the front door.

"Don't answer!" Dusty yelled.

The knocks became heavy slams in an attempt to break the door down.

Dusty jumped up, spun in a circle and yelled. "We gotta run! We gotta run!"

When an extra loud crash slammed the door, Peter grabbed Dusty by the arm. "Is there another way out of here?"

"Yeah, yeah." Dusty suddenly focused on a task and not the danger.

The front door let out a mournful crack as the wood started to give way to the weight of the body behind it.

"Let's go now!" Peter said.

"Follow me."

They ran into Dusty's room and he shut and locked the door behind them. Just them they heard the front door shatter and fall apart.

"Dusty! We are not safe here! We have to get out!"

"I know. Follow me."

They heard heavy footsteps running through the apartment. Dusty jumped to the window and opened it. "We go out the window."

The doorknob rattled. Peter looked at the door then the window. The ground was over twenty feet below. A loud thump came from the door, then a loud bang.

Peter knew the door wouldn't hold half as long as the front door did. "OK. We'll jump," Peter said.

"No. That's 'tupid. You'll get hurt." Dusty opened a footlocker at the base of the windowsill and pulled out a rope and wooden ladder. He tossed it out the window. It uncoiled to the ground.

"It's a fire ladder," Dusty said. "Climb down."

The door cracked but held by a splinter.

"Go!" Peter yelled.

Dusty didn't have to be told twice. This time the door split down the grain and the top hinge flew off. But it still held. The next blow would be its last. Peter saw Dusty scamper down the ladder. Suddenly, like an explosion, the door shattered. A huge man

)6-MUCC

powered through the splintered wood, tripped and rolled onto the floor. In a desperate act, Peter picked up Dusty's wooden chair and slammed it down onto the man's head before he could get up.

With the attacker momentarily stunned Peter dove out the window and threw himself down the ladder headfirst. His hands holding onto the wooden rungs only long enough to slow him from a freefall. Before he reached the ground, the attacker, still dazed, appeared in the window gun in hand. The first shot hit the wooden rung Peter's hand was wrapped around and split it. Peter shrieked as he fell the last ten feet. He let out a groan when he hit the ground. His shoulder absorbed most of the fall. Stunned, but still aware of the danger, he rolled to his left. The ground near his head kicked up dirt from the impact of the second bullet.

"Peter! Peter!" Dusty called from behind an open metal basement bulkhead door.

In an instant, Peter dove behind it. The pings of metal resonated from the third and fourth bullets blindly slamming through it. Peter slid down the musty cobwebbed stairs and Dusty pulled the door shut. He had no sooner locked it than someone tried to pull it open.

They heard muffled yells. "Go around the front. They're trapped in the basement."

Dusty pulled Peter to his feet. "Hurry, there are two of them. Come on, follow me."

"We're trapped again!" Peter said. "One's outside the bulkhead and the other will be coming down the stairs."

"Hurry, follow me." Dusty said again.

Without any other option, Peter found himself again having to rely on Dusty for his life.

"Hurry up." Dusty called back to him from the corner of the basement.

Peter jumped when he heard the front door slam and heavy quick steps on the dry wooded floor above them. Dusty climbed up onto some wooden crates and opened a small side window. "Shh," he said, fingers to lips.

Dusty stuck his head out the window then crawled onto the side driveway. "Hurry," he whispered.

Peter squeezed his way out at the same time one of the killers ran down the basement stairs.

"They went out the side window!" the voice from inside the basement yelled.

"Hurry!" Dusty called to Peter. He had the basement window to the house next door opened.

They both dove through it just as the attacker who stayed in the backyard ran around the corner. The killer unleashed a half dozen shots from his automatic weapon. The bullets flew through the window. Glass shattered in all directions and showered them both with sharp bits, superficially cutting them on their hands and faces, but the bullets missed. They jumped to their feet amongst the slivers of glass and ran to the steps. There they had to duck more blind shots fired through the open window.

"Go around front," the killer at the window yelled. "I'll cover the back door."

Dusty ran up the stairs with Peter a half step behind. At the top Dusty pulled Peter into the hallway, then into a closet. The door had barely shut when the second killer burst through the front door and ran towards the stairs. Dusty threw the door open and slammed it into the attackers face.

"Hurry!" Dusty yelled as he stepped over the body strewn and stunned on the floor. Peter gave him a kick to the head as he passed.

They ran out the front door and onto the street. Peter again a half-step behind.

"Where's your car?" Dusty demanded.

"Across the street. Let's go." They ran to the five year old tan Mercury Sable. Peter had his keys in his hands before he was halfway to the car. His hands were precise, the keys slid into the lock. The door flew open.

"Hurry! Hurry!" Dusty pounded on the roof. "Let me in!"

Peter punched the unlock button. Dusty had his door closed before he had settled into his seat.

"Go! Go!" Dusty yelled.

Peter turned the ignition and threw the car into drive before the engine fully started. The screech of tires replaced the grinding of gears as the car raced down the street. Smoke streamed off the spinning rubber. In the rear view mirror Peter saw the two killers emerge and run for their car.

"They're chasing us!" Peter said.

"Go left at the light. Don't stop," Dusty said with confidence as he looked over his shoulder.

Peter had momentary doubts. His life depended on following a mildly retarded person but Dusty had saved his life more than once in the last few minutes. "Where are we going?"

"Go left! Go faster. I have a plan."

Peter looked at the speedometer reading fifty mph, then down the road. The light at the intersection was green but he couldn't turn left. There was traffic coming in the opposite direction. He had no choice. He jammed on the brakes. Dusty flew forward into the dash. The line of cars in the opposite direction blocked them from turning left, at least momentarily. The moment the car swerved and slid to a stop Peter stomped the gas pedal and at the last moment his car, tires spinning, barely jumped between two cars without being hit. They accelerated down the street as Dusty wildly grabbed for anything to hold on to.

The killers followed them. They spun left, their passenger door careened off the front grill of the next car in line but they bounced clear and continued the pursuit.

"Faster! Faster!" Dusty called out. His head spun back and forth from the front window to the rear. "Go right at the stop sign. Then take your second left."

"That's Frog Hollow. We won't be safe there. We're close to the hospital. Let's go there."

"No! He's there. He killed the Senator and Roberto. Can't go there. He's there. They work for him. Trust me. Go faster. I have a plan."

Peter knew what Dusty said made sense and that bothered him. With little choice, he followed Dusty's directions and swerved the car around the corner into Frog Hollow.

"What now?" Peter asked.

"Go faster. Him! Him!" Dusty pointed to a lone Puerto Rican leaning against the corner of a building. "Stop there."

Peter stepped on the brake pedal and locked up the brakes. The car slid to a stop. He glanced in the rearview mirror and saw the killer's car round the corner in pursuit.

"Now what?"

"Get out. Hurry."

Dusty jumped out and ran to the Puerto Rican and said something. He then turned to Peter. "Follow me."

The two ran around the corner and into the building by way of a side entrance. Once in the hallway, Dusty stopped.

"It's OK now." Dusty said.

"OK? What do you mean OK? This isn't safe. They'll kill him and then get us."

"Watch," Dusty said. "This will be fun." He cracked the door open just wide enough for them to hear.

The killers ran into the alley and stopped. There were four doors between the two opposite buildings. The Puerto Rican stayed at the corner, leaning casually against the building. He watched with detachment as the two men tried to decide which door to take.

One turned. "Hey, Spic. What door did they go in?" He walked up to him. His muscle bound body towered over the thin lanky Puerto Rican.

"Hey, white boy. You comin' to my hood, dis me, then try to jack me for info?"

The burly guy pulled a gun and shoved it into the Puerto Rican's face. "I don't give a fuck if I offended you. This fuckin' gun will offend your face a lot more if you don't tell me what fuckin' door that retard and his friend went into."

The Puerto Rican stayed calm. "Bro, you white people just don't learn. Do you? You think we afraid to die?" His hands moved in a rhythmic fashion as he talked. It was nonsense rap movements to most, but they were actually hand signals known as stacking to his lieutenants and foot soldiers. "We ain't afraid o' nothin'. I been capped three times so far. I been down for mine, white boy. You understan' "down for mine"?" He shook his head. "No you don't. It mean loyalty. Loyalty's what it's about. Loyal to mine; that something you white people don't understand."

The attacker pressed him hard into the brick wall, one hand on his throat, the other on the gun pressed into his left check. "One more time. Then I do freestyle wall painting with your puny brain. Where did the retard and his friend go?"

The second killer pulled his gun and nervously looked around. "Come on John, pop him. Let's go. You take one building; I'll take the other. They're getting away."

"Chill, white boy," the Puerto Rican said. "I understan' you gotta take care of business. I didn't see which door they went into. But my four friends did. Go ahead, axe um." He looked up. "Hey Carlos, Ramon. They wanna know which door a retard an' his friend went in. You know?"

"Yeah." came the reply from the roof.

The three in the alley looked up and saw Carlos with a M-16 military automatic assault weapon aimed at them from the roof.

"Yo, ax me. I seen them, too."

They looked at the opposite roof. Ramon was there with his assault weapon, also aimed at them.

"Your two Spic friends won't do you any good. If they miss even by a inch, they'll hit you."

"You must think you're a fuckin' genius, bro, but you're not. I said four friends, not two."

The two killers turned around, but not fast enough. Each had the barrel of a nine-millimeter Glock pressed against the back of their heads in an instant.

"Now motherfucker, it's my turn." The Puerto Rican calmly took both guns out of the killers' hands. Then they were thrown face first into the wall. "You see motherfuckers, that retard's my friend and he tells me you tried to do him. Now, I gotta take care of business. I gotta make sure you won't try again. He also thinks one of you's the motherfucker that did our friend Roberto. We're gonna jack you up till you tells us. Then we gonna fade ya. We gonna cap y'a ass. Welcome to the catch wreck." With a hand jerk to the rear of the alley, the killers were pushed at gunpoint and taken through a basement door.

Peter turned to Dusty. "How did you know they'd help us?"

"Juan's my friend." Dusty smiled. "I helped his sister get a job at the hospital in Housekeeping. This is his corner. He's my friend. I told you to trust me. I'm not 'tupid.'"

"No, you are not. Right about now you are one of the smartest persons I know."

"Got that right." Dusty beamed a smile.

Dusty and Peter stood back when the door opened. Juan walked into the hallway. "Dust, you OK?"

"Yeah. This is my friend Peter. He's a Doctor. He was Roberto's friend too. He's OK?"

"Doc, welcome to the Hollow. You can chill; you're safe here. Come up, we'll talk."

Despite the dilapidated appearance of the outside of the building, Juan's apartment was relatively clean and orderly. Peter was sure there were rats and roaches in the building. There was no way to avoid that given the surrounding conditions but he saw no evidence of filth that he'd expected.

"Take a seat. Want some coke?"

"Excuse me?" Peter said. He'd just been chased and shot at. Now he was sitting in an apartment of a drug dealing gang member being offered drugs.

"Coke, Doc." Juan looked at him. "Doc, you thirsty, you want some Coke or just water?"

"Oh, a coke is OK."

"Diet or Regular?"

"Regular. Thank you." Peter shook his head.

"Enjoy Doc." He handed him a can of Coca-Cola. "So Dust, what's the poop?"

For the next ten minutes, Juan and Peter sat and listened to Dusty recant everything that had happened to him. When he stopped, Peter leaned forward. "Dusty, I need you to tell me what Roberto said. What did he say about the Senator's death?"

Five minutes later, Peter stood up. "I've got to get back."

"Anytime, Doc. You is a friend of the Hollow. Come anytime. Just remember which side of the street to park on. Don't want your wheels stripped by another gang. Turf's turf. It's gotta be respected."

Peter shook Juan's hand then turned to Dusty. "Do you want a ride home?"

"I think the Dust is gonna stay here for a day or two. It'll be safer that way. Don't worry Dust, you'll call your ma and tell her you're sleepin' over."

Peter walked up to Dusty. "I can't tell you how thankful I am that you were there to save my life. If it wasn't for you, I'd be dead. You are one very smart person, and you should be proud of yourself." He gave Dusty a big hug then left.

Less then five minutes after Peter left Juan's apartment, Carlos ran in, blood dripping down his face. His nose was definitely broken. "They slipped us!"

"What! Where are they? What happened?" Juan barked.

"We were working them. You know, real hard. And the big one, the one that was in your face. He just laughed and snapped the wood his hands were tied to. Before I could do anything, he slammed me. I got off a shot. I hit him in the leg. It didn't even slow him down. By the time we got to the street, they were in their ride and halfway outta the Hollow."

"Shit. The Doc just left. No way to warn him." He turned to Dusty. "Sorry Dust, not much we can do now."

20 | CHAPTER TWENTY

"Well Joshua, it seems you are more of a bumbling fool than I gave you credit for. Your best men can't even get a half-wit retard with Downs. I am more impressed with you everyday. So, what do you have planned next?" Barbosa scanned the ceiling in disgust.

"They'll find him. I'm not concerned about him. I'm more concerned about Pavano. He was with the kid yesterday."

Barbosa laughed in the receiver. "I thought you had a twenty-four hour watch on him."

"He wasn't seen leaving the hospital. He was supposed to be inundated with work from you. May I remind you?"

"No, no, no, Joshua. Let us not sidestep blame," Barbosa said. "Have you found the leak on the council?"

"I think so. Blotnick is a good friend of Rosenthal. He said he briefed him on our meeting."

"Now you're suggesting Rosenthal was the leak to the Senator. That makes no sense," Barbosa said.

"When you have all the information, it does. Collas did rotations as a medical student at Connecticut General. One of his rotations was with Rosenthal, just before he retired. During that time, Collas also was dating a girl from University of Connecticut. That girl happened to be Rosenthal's nieces fraternity sister. Figure it out, Barobsa. We had no idea where Collas kept getting his information. It was from Rosenthal. It's obvious he had a change of heart."

147

"I hope that change will be dealt with."

"It will be and Blotnick will be admonished for his lapse in security."

"Do you think he knew and is part of this?"

Joshua paused for a moment. "No, I don't think so. I think they were good friends and when Rosenthal retired from the council, Blotnick felt an obligation to keep him informed."

21 | CHAPTER TWENTY-ONE

Peter dialed Sloan's number from a hospital phone. Sloan picked up his cellular phone on the fourth ring. "Sloan. It's Pavano." Peter leaned casually against the wall. "Peter, good to hear from you."

"Thing's are getting a lot more dangerous here. Since yesterday, I've been shot at, involved in a high speed car chase through the city, and had my neck saved by drug dealing gang members." He looked over his shoulder making sure no one was listening. "I have ninety-seven charts for you."

"I hope they'll be of substance to us."

"You'll find them of some interest. I've categorized them and written notes on all of them. It should be self-explanatory."

Sloan's cellular phone was crystal clear, free of any static. "When can I have them?"

"Tomorrow at noon. Park your car at Bushnel Park, under the arch and sit on the nearest park bench. They'll be brought to you." Peter hung up and went to round on some patients.

* * * * *

The following day was another spectacular summer day in central Connecticut. The air was warm but there was just enough cloud cover to stop the sun from overheating the city. Sloan sat on his designated bench at the designated time. Lunchtime walkers and

06-MUCC

joggers passed back and forth in their attempts to hang onto their health.

Five minutes later a voice addressed him. "Agent Sloan." Kelsey approached.

"You have me at a disadvantage. You know who I am but I have no idea who you are."

"That isn't important. I have what you want." She handed him a key. "Union Station locker number 43. Both suitcases are yours. Peter said it's all self-explanatory and even you should be able to figure it out. He will contact you tomorrow. He wanted you to have a chance to look through them. He also said he expected a final answer on a five million dollar question." She started to walk away. "Have a good day."

Sloan placed the key into his pocket and walked to his car.

22 | CHAPTER TWENTY-TWO

The next day after rounds, Peter took a piece of paper out of his pocket and dialed the number. He had decided that it was time to use Beth's connection. He'd looked at the name and number many times since she gave it to him. Only now did he feel he had enough questions to ask to make the contact useful. On the third ring, a man answered the phone.

"Hello."

"Hello. My name is Peter Pavano. I am a doctor at Connecticut General Hospital. I am currently doing an Invasive Cardiology Fellowship."

"Well Dr. Pavano, how may I help you?" The reply was pleasant.

"I've been involved in a few problems with the hospital. I was told you could help me." Peter was uncertain how much to say over the phone.

"Well then Doctor, could you tell me who you are involved with in this controversy?"

"Actually, it's my Chief, Dr. Barbosa."

"Ah. So, I assume you want to know about the Cartel?"

Peter was startled by his directness. "Yes, I have a lot of questions that need to be answered and I was told you could answer them."

"That is very interesting," said the voice. "Who told you that?"

"A friend of mine. I would rather not say at this moment."

"I wonder." There was a pause. "Is this person your friend or enemy?"

"Why do you say that?"

"The last Fellow I spoke to about the Cartel ended up dead. They said it was suicide, but I have my doubts. Are you sure you want to take the risk?"

"Risk! Let me tell you, in the last couple of days I've gone from being a Cardiac Fellow to being accused of murdering a Senator, being thrown out of the hospital with my privileges revoked, and involved in a high speed car chase through Hartford with more bullets then I care to count shot at me."

"In that case, I would say you should come over."

After listening to directions Peter replied, "I'll be there in an hour."

Peter hung up the phone and paged Clayton. "Dr. Clayton, I have to leave the hospital for about two hours. I have to meet with my lawyer about that very unpleasant situation with the Senator's death."

Peter pulled to a stop, checked the number on the mailbox to make sure he was at the right house. He was on a wide, well traveled street in a wealthy, tree lined neighborhood of West Hartford. It was a far cry from Frog Hollow, he thought. He pulled into the driveway and stopped.

The house was a prewar Tudor, with real stucco on one side and fieldstone stacked like a mosaic puzzle on the other. He rang the doorbell. Soon, a fashionably dressed woman in her late seventies answered.

"May I help you?" she asked.

"Hello. I am Dr. Peter Pavano. I called less than an hour ago. I assume it was your husband I spoke to. He asked me to come over to talk with him."

"Could you wait a moment?" She shut the door, but not completely. He could hear her yell to another room in the house. "Henry, were you expecting anyone?"

Peter heard an indecipherably muffled reply. The door reopened. "Dr. Pavano, please come in. Henry is in the library. He is expecting you."

Peter followed her through an elegantly decorated living room and into an old English styled library. The walls were paneled in cherry wood, with built in bookcases. The room was accented in burgundy and sage green. The floor was a worn oak.

"Dr. Pavano, come in. Have a seat."

Peter walked over to a deep cushioned wing-backed chair and sat. He let out a sigh the moment his body hit the seat. His muscles, tensed for the last few days, gave way to exhaustion. He looked on the kind face of the gentleman seated next to him. He guessed he was in his early eighties. His name was Dr. Henry Rosenthal. He was a retired cardiologist.

"From the little you told me over the phone, it sounds like we need to talk." The man reminded Peter of Kris Kringle. His shape could be generously described as rotund, though he wore his weight with elderly grace. His hair was white and his beard was fluffy, giving his face extra fullness.

"So you want to know about the Cardiac Cartel?" Henry asked outright. "What can I tell you?"

"Everything. What it is. Who's involved? Why would they want to kill me? How's that for a start?"

Henry smiled calmly. "I think those are valid questions. Who is the Cartel and what is the Cartel? Let me take you through it my way. You see I am getting old. I'm eighty-three. So, I need to tell a story from start to finish, otherwise I get a little off the beaten path. My wife says I get sidetracked easily."

"That's fine. Anyway you want to tell it is fine with me." Peter sat forward in anticipation.

"Well, let's see. The Cartel. What is it? And who is it? Basically, I am the Cartel."

"What?"

"That's right. I am the Cartel. I thought of it. It was my brainchild but you can relax. I assure you, you are safe here with

06-MUCC

me. Though I am the Cartel you are in no danger with or from me."

"I don't understand." Peter felt a small twinge of discomfort.

"Years ago, I was one of the first Invasive Cardiologists in the Hartford area. I was full of vim and vigor. Unfortunately, I was very naïve. I thought you could do things for the good of mankind without the process becoming corrupt. That was my mistake."

Peter sat back in the chair. Henry's tone intrigued him.

Henry continued, "Invasive Cardiology was in its infancy. It was very expensive and, for some time, not well standardized. A patient at hospital A would be charged twice as much for the same procedure as a patient at hospital B and just because they paid more it didn't guarantee them getting better care. In fact more cases were the opposite: the higher the cost, the less efficient the hospital was and the less experienced. So I thought, let's standardize it for the good of the patient."

Henry's wife entered with some tea. She placed it on the small table between them, then left with a gracious smile.

"Where was I? Oh, yes. I wanted to create a nationwide network with complete standardization of fees, and levels of competency. We'd be like the Good Housekeeping Seal of approval. If a program was approved by the Cartel, the patient knew they were getting the best care at the lowest price. We were to set a minimal level of procedures an institution had to do yearly to get their accreditation. You see, if an institution did only a few procedures, they wouldn't be proficient in it. They also wouldn't be cost effective. They'd be weeded out."

"That sounds like a great idea." Peter said while Henry poured the tea. "But, what happened? It seems your plan would have had great public awareness. But the Cartel is a secret organization."

"Have some tea." He handed Peter a cup. "What happened? First, I was a little too naïve. Secondly, Barbosa happened. He is a dangerous and vicious man."

Peter sipped his tea.

"Before my plan could be implemented, a tremendous amount of planning had to be done. In my naiveté, I started with a small group. Then, I figured I'd expand it and after big institutions throughout the country bought into it, it would be announced and implemented. But, Barbosa had different plans. The meetings were already secret. They had to be. We wanted to prevent small hospitals from being able to politic, and thus water down, the standards. Barbosa used that secrecy to push me out and create an empire. An empire of greed and deceit."

"Why didn't you fight them?"

"I was weak. I was threatened. My wife's health wasn't the greatest. I was demoralized. The fight had been taken out of me. To this day I regret that more than anything else. The Cartel as I perceived it, could have been a wonderful thing for the public. Instead, it was turned into the medical world's equivalent to a Colombian drug cartel. In Colombia the cartel peddles drugs and kill people that get in their way. The Cardiac Cartel peddles medicine and they kill people that get in their way. It is truly frightening."

"That's an interesting story," Peter said. "But I don't think you understand. I am being accused of murder and there are people chasing me, trying to kill me. I need something tangible; something I can take to the authorities to clear myself and implicate them. I need something more than a history lesson."

"Dr. Pavano, the history is where you start. You have to understand, you are dealing with a fanatically paranoid group. They don't have one ounce of trust for each other. So, early on they kept files on each other. They all bought into it. The files implicate each and every one of them. They all swim or sink together. Everything they do is reported and filed. You get those files and there is your hard evidence."

"Where are they kept?"

"First, I have to tell you, you are not the first to try. I've helped two others. Both are dead and you are being blamed for one of them."

06-MUCC

"Senator Demind?" Peter said.

"That's correct. I am old. I don't have much longer to live. Nothing terminal," he added raising his hand, "just old age catching up with me and before I meet the Almighty, I want to set right what I allowed to get out of hand. I wanted good, and it ended up bad. A young Cardiac Fellow just like yourself caught wind of the Cartel. He had dated my niece years ago when he was a medical student at the University of Connecticut. So, he came to me for information. He met privately with the Senator. Even though I am old, I am not out of the loop. I still have my spies and contacts at C.G.H. I fed both the Fellow and the Senator enough information to guide them on their way to discovery. The Fellow ended up dead. Suicide or so they say, and we both know what happened to the Senator. So, if you move forward, you will be in grave danger."

"I'm already ducking bullets. How much more danger could I get into?" Peter said. "I need to find those files."

"That is simple. The headquarters of the Cartel is in Massachusetts on the eleventh floor of the American Standard Catheter Company."

"The Cartel is involved with the Cardiac Institute also?" Peter asked.

"Owns it. Runs it. That also was my idea. An institute for the higher education and training of all cardiologists at any level of their career."

Peter stood and extended his hand. "Doctor, thank you."

"Be careful Peter. They are a powerful group. They don't like being threatened. They have deep pockets and strong support. From this moment on, you are not a safe man to be around."

"When I walked into this house, I wasn't a safe man. Thank you again."

The occupants in the car at the end of the street watched as Peter backed out of the driveway. The passenger spoke on a cellular phone. "That's right Pavano is just leaving. Do you want us to continue as planned? Or follow him?"

He listened to the reply and hung up.

"He said to let Pavano go and continue as planned. He'll take care of the rest."

They drove around the block and parked in the side yard of some people they knew were away for a few days.

06-MUCC

| **CHAPTER TWENTY-THREE**

"No Kelsey! Absolutely not, I want you back in Massachusetts, away from here."

"I'll be in no more danger than you," she replied.

Peter leaned against the wall in a corridor of the hospital. He massaged the tense muscles in his temple. The phone was pressed tight against the side of his face and he talked in a low firm voice into the receiver. "I told you no. The Rosenthals were discovered dead less than an hour after I left there. Those bastards had to have followed me there. I'm sure they're watching my every move. The only place I feel safe is in the hospital. I'm on call tonight and I think I'll stay in one of the on call rooms. I don't want you staying in my apartment alone. I want you in Boston. It's only a two-hour drive. Tomorrow, I have a meeting set up with Sloan. I have a few issues to go over with him."

After Peter hung up the phone, he leaned all his weight against the wall and thought for a moment. He ran through what Dr. Rosenthal had told him and that solidified what Dusty had told him. Very quickly, he finalized his plan. He just needed to stay alive long enough to complete it.

* * * * *

The doors that surrounded the carousel house had been retracted, exposing the carousel to the heat of the day. Gone was the slight breeze that had made lunch in the park tolerable. The carousel was large, old, and refurbished. Its solid wooden ponies that ushered in the turn of the twentieth century flowed up and down with a jerky grace that caused little kids to have to hold on with two hands. Despite the heat of the noonday sun, the carousel was crowded with people on their lunch break who took refuge under the expansive wooden umbrella roof.

Peter climbed onto the platform moments after it started. With the circus rhythm of the musical pipes tooting in the background, he mounted an inside horse. He had only turned his head for a moment. When he turned back, a disheveled homeless man was riding the pony next to him.

"Is that the best you can do Sloan?" Peter asked.

Sloans eyes widened. "How did you know it was me? I thought the disguise was pretty good."

"First of all, you don't have any dirt under your nails. And most of all, you don't have the stench of someone who has been in the same clothes for at least a week or two. In this heat, your smell should be able to keep even flies away."

"You are very observant."

"You forget I lived on the street years ago, and being observant is what keeps me alive." Peter didn't look directly at Sloan when he talked.

Sloan talked through the side of his mouth, not wanting to look at Peter either. "I looked through the charts you gave me."

"And?"

"They're useless to me. They raise questions about Barbosa's judgment and practice: with whom he did angioplasty on and whom he sent out. So what? It allows us to raise a few proprietary issues about him. Maybe even get him sanctioned but in no way can we go after the Cartel with that stuff."

"I told you Sloan, that was just a taste. The important stuff will cost five million."

"Now, that's an entirely different problem."

)6-MUCC

"That problem is one you better solve if you want anything else from me." Peter bobbed up and down. His eyes casually looked around.

"I wouldn't be so bold if I were you. Yesterday, Dr. Henry Rosenthal and his wife were killed. Actually, they were butchered with a knife. But, I'm sure you are well aware of that." Sloan turned and looked at Peter for the first time. "Your fingerprints were all over the room where the bodies were found. They had been stabbed and slashed multiple times."

Peter remained calm on the outside but his stomach burned with the instant release of hot acid. "You know I didn't kill them. I had no motive, no reason. He was helping me. If anything, I wanted him alive to testify against the Cartel."

"I guess that makes it your problem, not mine. The five million dollar issue is dead. If I were you, I'd hope just to get out of this mess in one piece. In a very short time not only will the Cartel want you dead, the local police will be after you for murder." Sloan's tone was simple and matter-of-fact.

Peter thought for a moment as he bobbed up and down. "I need you to suppress the release of my fingerprints to the local police." This time Peter looked directly at Sloan.

"I'd say that can be done for 48 hours, if that, but I can't even guarantee it and beyond that would be nothing but a gift." Sloan looked around the perimeter of the carousel and when he glanced over to Peter's horse he was surprised to see it was empty.

24 | CHAPTER TWENTY-FOUR

Twenty minutes after leaving the carousel, Peter slowed his car and pulled to a stop two hundred feet from his apartment. He stared at it and a shiver ran down his spine. His mind raced back to his near escape from Dusty's apartment and he realized he had no escape from his third floor room; he'd be trapped. There was only one door in and that meant one door out. No, he thought, he wasn't safe there. He stepped on the gas and his apartment quickly disappeared in the rearview mirror.

For the next hour, he drove around aimlessly and thought. He soon came to the conclusion that he had 48 hours at best, and any time spent in the hospital as a Fellow was wasted time. He had a plan but to set it in motion he had to be safe. He knew only one place to find sanctuary, however unlikely it was. Ten minutes later he entered Frog Hollow and parked. If someone had told him one week ago—no, just yesterday—that he'd be turning to one of the most dangerous and violent gangs in the state for help and protection, he'd have dismissed them as delusional.

Peter stepped out of his car and looked up and down the street; it was deserted. A queasy, nauseous feeling grew in the pit of his stomach. The buildings of the neighborhood were in tremendous decay with more windows broken than not. Taking a closer look he saw what appeared to be pockmarks on some buildings but realized they were bullet holes. The plywood that covered the broken windows was covered with graffiti.

06-MUCC

It was dead quiet on the street, devoid of any life or movement. It was so quiet it screamed out at him. After a moment he noticed two lone people down the street walking in his direction. A car slowly inched out of a side alley. He watched the two approach it, lean in and talk to the occupants. The car then took off and disappeared down the opposite alleyway at a quick pace.

Peter stood on Juan's corner, unsure what to do. He couldn't help feeling eyes were watching him. He remembered how quickly, and out of nowhere, the gang members had appeared and surrounded the killers earlier. That thought made him feel very nervous and exposed so he ducked into the alleyway, which looked empty.

"Don't move. Don't turn your lily white, mother fuckin' ass around."

Peter instantly knew the tubular piece of metal pressed against the nape of his neck was the barrel of a gun.

"I'm—"

"Shut the fuck up."

The pressure on his neck increased.

"Hands on top of your head, white boy."

Peter complied and his eyes drifted down the empty alley. From behind and out of his sight, he felt two separate hands pat him down from head to toes while the gun remained pressed against his neck. Nothing was left untouched.

"He's clean."

A third gang member appeared from the shadows and stepped into Peter's peripheral vision. Peter started to turn toward him.

"Look straight ahead." His head was forcibly twisted back and the gun pressed harder into the nape of his neck.

Peter felt the warm breath of one of them exhale next to his ear. The malodorous air streamed over his neck and into his nostrils. "Doc," the voice said in his ear, "you returned to the Hollow so soon. I hope we didn't frighten you?" Juan walked around and faced him.

"Actually, you did." Peter replied, weak with relief.

"It's security, Doc. We're on a 186."

"A what?"

"A 186. You know Doc, a high alert. It's a little gang war we're in. You noticed the streets are empty. You stand out here long enough during a 186 and you might get shot."

"But, I'm not dangerous."

"You never know who has a gat in his back pocket."

"A gat?"

"A gun, Doc, a gun. We're in a dangerous line of business, and we live in a dangerous part of town. We can't be too cautious. You understand, I'm sure?"

Peter just nodded. The lump in his throat slowly receded.

"So, what brings you back to the Hollow?"

"I didn't feel safe at my apartment. The fact is, I don't feel safe anywhere at the moment."

"'cept the Hollow. Now that's funny!" Juan grabbed his shoulder and gave it a squeeze.

"Well . . ."

"Hey, it's good you came back. Those two that chased you and the Dust, well they got away. With them after you, I doubt you *are* safe anywhere but here. Come on up. The Dust and I were about to have something to eat."

Peter followed Juan up the back stairs, shocked at the thought of what would have happened to him if he'd gone to his apartment with those two thugs loose again.

"Hi, Peter." Dusty greeted him with a wave of his arm the moment he entered the apartment. "You come for dinner?"

Peter walked over and sat next to Dusty. "I thought it would be safer here with you and Juan for a few days. I didn't feel safe in my apartment. Is that all right?"

"Great. We'll have fun." Dusty had put the prior day's trauma out of his conscious thoughts. "Maria, Maria," he called out. "My friend Peter is gonna eat with us. OK?" He jumped up and ran into the other room.

)6-MUCC

A moment later, a pretty young woman came out of the kitchen. She was in her mid-thirties with a dark olive skin complexion and naturally deep black hair. Peter stood out of habit.

"I'm Maria, Juan's sister. So, you are the famous Dr. Peter that Dusty constantly talks about?"

"Well, I wouldn't say I'm famous for anything much."

"Wrong, muchacho." A new voice came from the door. "You are famous, very famous." A young Hispanic male Peter had not seen before entered. "Word is you been gang banging—take a look." He walked to the television and turned it on. The news had started and they were airing a special report.

Peter stared in disbelief at a picture of himself that hung in mid air over the left shoulder of the television news reporter. It was the picture the hospital had on file. Peter listened in shock and anger as the reporter droned on, something about being wanted in the stabbing deaths of Dr. Rosenthal and his wife. The words blended into one another. There was something said about being a suspect in the death of Senator Demind, something about, do not approach, he should be considered dangerous.

"If you really didn't kill those people," Juan replied, "I'd say you're getting it up the bottom dry. You sure you're not Rican?"

"That's OK, Peter." Dusty walked over and put his hand on Peter's shoulder. "You'll be safe with me and my friends."

Despite Peter's anger, he marveled at Dusty's innocence. He'd been chased and shot at, almost killed more than once, yet now he was safe, and that's all that mattered to him. The big picture was beyond the scope of Dusty's intellect. At the moment, Peter envied him. "Thank you, but I'm in a lot of trouble that needs to be cleared up. I need to make a phone call."

"OK." Dusty eagerly turned to Juan. "Juan give him your phone."

"Sure. Anything you want, Dust." He reached into his pocket and pulled out a cellular phone.

Peter dialed Samuel's number but was put on hold by the secretary. It seemed like an eternity until Samuel picked up. "Peter, what the hell did you get yourself into?"

"I don't know. Every day, no, every hour, it gets worse. I didn't kill anyone." His voice was calm. "You have to believe me."

"If I thought you killed anyone, I wouldn't be talking to you. Where are you? No . . . no! Don't tell me. That way I won't have to lie when I'm asked again."

"What do you mean "again"?" Peter asked.

"Your friends have already been here."

"What friends?"

"The State Police."

"How did they know to contact you?" Peter leaned forward in his chair.

"Most likely that psycho hospital lawyer. By the way, I don't think we should be too concerned about your hospital privileges at this point."

Peter stood and started to pace with the phone pressed hard against his ear. Juan and Dusty watched and listened to one side of the conversation.

"OK," Samuel continued. "Tell me what you did after we split up at the hospital. The last I knew, you were going to find that housekeeper."

"I found him. In fact, he's here with me."

"That's good. OK. Take me from the time you left the hospital."

Over the next 45 minutes, Peter talked. His story was specific and full of detail. Samuel interrupted only occasionally with a question. When Peter got to the meeting with Dr. Rosenthal, the questions increased. Finally, Samuel had the entire story, and so did Juan. Dusty had listened, but who knew how much he understood.

There was silence on both ends of the phone. "Well?" Peter finally said.

"Give me a moment. I'm thinking," came the reply.

After a long silence, Samuel started. "The conspiracy of power that you've described within the Cartel isn't anything new. The money they control opens up the ability to manipulate almost anything and anyone. It's obvious, at least to me, that you're innocent. We know you're their patsy, their pawn. We also have to accept the reality that a fair outcome, i.e., in the courts, is not probable or possible. We've got to accept their ability to manipulate the system and any evidence you'd use to acquit yourself."

"That's great. So what's your suggestion?"

"For starters, cheer up. All is not lost or as hopeless as it seems. The Cartel's power and strength is also its weakness."

"Explain."

"You forget, you're talking to a displaced hippie from the sixties. Back then individuals took down governments. Songs that we sang galvanized a generation."

"You want me to sing a song? Great."

"Peter. Quiet and listen. Individuals single handedly changed the course of history," Samuel said. "You forget Watergate, the Pentagon Papers, the bombing of Cambodia. In each case, Big Brother had dirty secrets to hide; secrets that showed abuse of power. The protests and demonstrations were ignored until an individual produced hard evidence. All the standing on the corner and finger pointing, the chanting slogans and waving protest signs ended. It all came down to, 'hey you've got a dirty secret and have broken the law, and I have the proof'."

Peter smiled, Samuel was thinking along the same lines as he was. "But, I don't have any proof."

"That's right. No one will believe anything you have to say about the Cartel until you have hardcore evidence. You need to implicate those bastards. You need to get into the Cartel's headquarters and get the evidence to implicate them and exonerate yourself. Isn't that what Rosenthal told you to do? What do you have to lose? What are they going to do, put you in jail?

They're already chasing you for two, maybe three, murders. What the hell's a break-in?"

"That's what I've been thinking also. I'm working on a plan." He turned and eyed Juan.

"The bottom line is this: until you have hard indisputable evidence acquitting you and implicating them, there is nothing I can do to help you. You're on your own; a fugitive. I want you to keep in touch, but not too often. Good luck Peter."

"Thanks . . . bye." Peter looked up at Juan, who'd sat quietly listening to the conversation.

"Deep shit, Bro. You're in deep shit."

Peter took out a business card from his wallet and dialed the number on it. On the third ring, Sloan answered. "Sloan, I thought you were going to give me two days before releasing the fingerprint results."

"Peter, it was a clerical mistake. I'm just as angry as you are."

"Somehow I tend to doubt it." Peter's tone was more than sarcastic.

"Peter, I have to tell you the prospect of getting you any sort of deal with the agency at this point is beyond slim."

"I find that very convenient. You know, Sloan, I gotta tell you I just don't believe you anymore."

"Peter . . ."

"Don't Peter me. I'll be in touch. And you can keep your damn five million dollars. I don't think I'll need it from this point on. I have other plans." Peter punched the end button and cut Sloan off mid sentence. He made one more call.

"Kelsey, where are you?"

She looked at the road and realized it didn't matter. "Basically nowhere in general. I was praying you'd call."

"Are you ok?"

"For the moment, I think so. My apartment was ransacked; it was like a tornado went through it. I've been driving around for the last two hours hoping you'd call. I know I'm being followed.

06-MUCC

I've seen the same car in my rearview mirror over and over. It's more than a coincidence."

"OK, I want you to come to Connecticut. It's obviously not safe where you are. I want you to go to Capitol Avenue and Main Street. On the corner is a bar called Spencer's. I'll meet you there at five. It'll be during happy hour so it will be crowded. I'll find you."

Kelsey's line went dead.

Juan stood up and started to walk towards the kitchen. "Before you save yourself bro, you need to eat. The world can wait an hour or two. Then we'll talk; it sounds like you need my help. Come on Dust, food's on. Did you tell your mom you'd be staying with us for a few days?"

"Yeah. She said OK." Dusty turned to Peter. "Mom lets me stay here every now and then. She likes my friends."

The three of them walked into the kitchen.

* * * * *

Several hours after she'd hung up the phone with Peter, Kelsey walked past the doorman at Spencer's and entered the world of Happy Hour. A world where singles hustled other singles and middle managers with one too many drinks in them openly badmouthed their bosses.

Spencer's was enormous; it took up one entire block from corner to corner. It was multi-leveled with a different theme for each room. One part even held a restaurant with a dance floor where patrons could ballroom dance. At one time, in the not to distant past, the restaurant was noted for its fine cuisine and elegant dancers who glided around the crowded dance floor in a counter-clockwise rotation. But the neighborhood had changed and the elegance was gone. Frog Hollow and the threat of gang violence had taken its toll, the fine wines replaced by beer, the gourmet food by Buffalo wings and nachos. The dance floor remained, but the music, once waltzes and fox trots, had been replaced by MTV's top Hit list.

Kelsey bypassed the restaurant and the crowded next room that held four pool tables, multiple dartboards and drunken patrons, and proceeded to the far end of the building. She felt more comfortable at the sports bar where each table had a small television that was tuned to any number of sporting events. The tables were filled with a crowd she felt safe around: jocks, armchair quarterbacks and sports fans.

She found an empty stool at the far corner of the bar, ordered a gin and tonic with a twist of lime, and waited to see what would happen next. She fidgeted on the stool, and felt uneasy. She knew she had been followed all the way from Massachusetts but there was nothing she could do about it. She could only assume whoever had followed her was by now in the bar watching over her.

"Why are you all alone, young one?"

Kelsey turned her head and found herself facing a Jamaican Rastafarian, his hair in dreadlocks.

"I'm waiting for someone." Using the rudest body language she could muster she spun on the stool and placed her back to him, but she found herself face to face with a Puerto Rican no better looking than the Jamaican.

"I see you don't care for my friend." His hair was black and naturally curled in tight loops. His face was hard.

Kelsey tensed slightly and wondered if they were the ones who had followed her. Uncertain, she replied. "No, I don't like your friend, and I don't care too much for you either." She started to get off her stool to leave.

"Your friend Doctor Peter Pavano didn't tell us you were prejudiced towards Jamaicans and Puerto Ricans."

"You know Peter?"

"We are his friends." A smug smile came upon his face. "And if you want, we will take you to him."

Kelsey felt a chill run down her spine. The Puerto Rican's eyes were two beady slits. "Where is he?" she asked, having made up her mind she wasn't about to leave Spencer's with either of them, even to meet Peter.

"Close by. In fact, he's in the next room. Why don't you take your drink and follow us. Join the Rican and the Rasta for a drink."

Kelsey looked around. She got off her stool and walked, drink in hand, a few paces behind her two new acquaintances. She stopped at the doorway and looked around the room again. Not seeing Peter, she followed the two repugnant looking men into the poolroom.

The room was filled with smoke and loud chatter. The occasional clack of pool balls striking one another came in between curses due to missed shots. On the far wall hung a multitude of dartboards, all taken by teams of coed players who flung darts through the air at the target a few feet away.

Kelsey still didn't see Peter, nor had anyone followed her from the other room, yet. The two she'd followed now milled around a dartboard where three other greasy haired Puerto Ricans stood throwing darts. She approached them, feeling somewhat safe amongst the masses.

"I thought you were going to show me where Peter is?"

"They did," one of the men throwing darts replied. He tossed the last one in his hand and turned to face her.

She stared at him in disbelief. "Peter?"

He had dark curly hair, slicked down with grease. His exposed skin was darkened with make-up. He wore loose army fatigues and was a dead ringer for a Puerto Rican gang member.

Peter smiled at her. "Are you alright?"

She nodded. "I'm sure the people who followed me are here also."

"That's OK, we're covered. Let's go over to a table so we can talk."

She looked at him, then at the gang members. Her mouth hung open. "Peter, what is—"

He cut her off with a wave of his hand. "Let's sit. It's a long complicated story."

She followed him to a small pedestal table and sat on a barstool. To her dismay, two of the gang members joined them.

Carlos suddenly grabbed Juan on the arm. "186, Bro. We got visitors."

Juan looked across the room. At the far wall leaned the two men his gang had tried and failed to kill; the ones who had chased Peter and Dusty. They stared over at Peter with smug smiles.

"This time we're gonna take care of business," Carlos said.

"No. We gotta stay cool. They can wait. First we gotta look out for the Doc and his lady here. We gotta get them back to the Hollow. We'll deal with them later."

"What's going on?" Kelsey asked.

"You see those two gorillas standing under the 'Bud Lite' sign?" Peter said.

"Yes."

"They're the two that chased Dusty and me and tried to kill us."

"What are we going to do?" she asked.

Juan answered. "You're gonna leave with the Doc and go back to the Hollow. You'll be safe there."

"But if I walk out with him they'll know, if they already don't, that it's him, disguise or not. They'll kill him and most likely us, too."

"Don't worry," Juan replied. "Me and my homies will take care of business. Carlos, you take the Doc and his squeeze back to the Hollow." Juan made a few jerking signs with his fingers in the air, got off his stool and blended into the crowd.

* * * * *

John Butterman was in his early thirties. He was a martial arts specialist; tonight he was dressed in casual but nice attire. He'd

171

blend with most crowds on a Friday night out on the town. But this wasn't a casual night out for him. He was a highly paid mercenary for the Cartel. With the many bungled attempts to silence Peter, he'd been called in by Joshua to assist in his disposal.

Butterman, who had just left Spencer's, climbed into the van that was parked on the side of the road. "What is she doing?" asked one of the men who appeared very uncomfortable with this group.

"She was approached by two Spics. They talked for a short time then she followed them into the poolroom. She's still there at a table talking to a group of them. One, in particular, Frank and Bob identified as one who tried to kill them in the projects. The two of them are in there along with Sal and his three friends. They're keeping an eye on things. I hope those two fools have enough sense to not be recognized. The one the bitch is talking to is Pavano. We knew that was him a long time ago, actually the moment they walked into the club. We were almost able to take him out earlier but the crowd blocked us. That's OK. He can't take a piss without being escorted." He pressed a finger against his ear and listened to the report being transmitted from one of his team inside the club. "You stay here. Something's going down inside."

Butterman left the van as fast as he had entered.

* * * * *

"What are we going to do? Those two guys are next to the door. How are we going to get by them?" Kelsey asked the Jamaican.

"You just watch little lady. They be too busy to worry about you. Be ready we have to move fast," he replied with a Jamaican drawl.

Kelsey stared at the two killers. Her eyes locked on one of them for a little too long and the killer stared back. She shivered involuntarily as the killer smirked at her and with a slight nod of his head acknowledged the recognition.

Suddenly Juan stepped into her line of vision along with five other gang members who stood next to him in a straight line. It looked like a shoot out at high noon, but instead of guns they held darts. The killers tried to protect their heads and face, but there was no time, and the method of attack was so strange, so out of the ordinary, they were completely caught off guard. Six darts flew fast, straight and true. All six struck and lodged deep into the two ugly faces of the killers. They shrieked and attempted to pull the darts out, but to no avail. In an instant a second wave of darts struck them. One or two missed their faces but stuck in their necks.

"I think we can leave now," the Jamaican calmly said.

He slid off his stool and started to walk into the crowd. But before Kelsey could follow, a man in his thirties sat on the now empty stool. A light jacket was slung over his left arm and his right arm was under it.

He leaned close to Peter and whispered loud enough for her to hear. "John Butterman, at your service. Under this jacket is a gun. It has a silencer so no one will hear if I blow you away right here and I will if you don't cooperate. Then I'll kill her."

Kelsey looked at the man. His left hand rested openly on the table, the other stayed under the coat. She felt an adrenaline surge and instinct took over. "Hey you!" she shouted at him. "Hey, I'm talking to you!"

"Don't be a hero, lady. You can die first if you want to."

Her hand had touched a beer bottle, but left it where it was. She badly misjudged the time she'd need to smash it into his face. She seethed with anger.

Suddenly his face contorted with pain. He looked down at his hand and found it impaled onto the wooden table. A dart had been rammed through it and a small pool of blood was forming under his palm. Kelsey looked up and saw the Jamaican with fire in his eyes. This time with no hesitation she picked up the beer bottle and smashed it as hard as she could into his face. They all heard the sickening sound of facial bones smashing

173

into smaller pieces as he fell to the floor unconscious; his left hand still attached to the table top, his gun lifted by the Jamaican as he slumped.

"Now," the Jamaican said, "would you two please follow me."

Kelsey and Peter fled as more darts were hurled at the two killers against the wall. The crowd reacted with shouts of disbelief but no one approached to stop Juan and his gang. With the last round of darts gone, they followed right behind the others.

"We can't go out the front door." Juan stopped and shouted at them. "Use the fire exits. We'll split up,"

The group ran down the hall and split into two groups. Kelsey, Peter and the Jamaican pushed through a door and entered an empty room, which was obviously being remodeled. They ran to the fire exit but were blocked by a large stack of sheet rock piled against the door.

"Don't they know this is a fire hazard?" the Jamaican said. "Let's go, we will find another way."

They ran into the hallway and went left but ran head on into Butterman. He pulled out another gun but before he could aim it the Jamaican raised his foot and planted it firmly into his abdomen. Butterman fell back and let out a loud grunt.

"Back into the room!" The Jamaican dove through the archway with the others moments before a bullet slammed into the wooden doorframe. The Jamaican returned the fire but Butterman jumped behind a cigarette machine.

"Are you both all right?" Even under fire, the Jamaican's voice was calm.

"Yes," Peter said. "But we're trapped."

"For the moment, yes."

Kelsey crawled over and found momentary safety next to Peter.

"We're trapped, mon," the Jamaican said. "We need to find a way out. I don't know how long we'll be safe here." They hadn't traded a shot since the initial volley, but that would certainly change soon.

Peter looked around the room. "I have an idea." He ran to the far side of the room, grabbed a handful of greasy rags, then stuffed them into an empty paint can and ran back next to the Jamaican. "I need a match."

"Here." He gave him his lighter. "What if I didn't have one?"

"All Jamaicans do. How else could a good Rasta smoke his ganga?"

Peter lit the rags, which instantly flared up and produced a thick black smoke from the grease and paint residue. "Keep him pinned down while I toss this."

The Jamaican complied by squeezing off a few rounds. Butterman ducked farther behind the cigarette machine. With a tremendous effort Peter tossed the smoke belching can far down the hall toward an open door in the opposite direction. In no time, the hallway filled with smoke and it filtered into the nearby crowded room. Then Peter reached up and pulled the fire alarm. Red lights flashed and horns instantly sounded. That, along with the heavy smell of smoke, sent the mildly intoxicated crowd into survival frenzy. Instead of taking the fire exits they ran en masse into the hallway and headed for the front door.

When the hallway was jammed with pushing, shoving patrons Peter yelled. "Let's go!"

The three of them jumped into the crowd and surged past the killer and out the front door. The crowd spilled out onto the street in a mass of confusion. In the chaos, Peter and Kelsey followed the Jamaican around the corner and into a car with dark tinted glass.

The door of the van flew open as Butterman stormed inside. At that moment, the Jamaican had spun his car around and Peter glanced out the dark tinted side window and into the van. His eyes locked onto one person inside it and his anger reached new heights. At that moment he knew what he had planned was the correct method of dealing with everything.

Moments later they were in Frog Hollow.

| ## CHAPTER TWENTY-FIVE

The morning sun filtered through the shades into the extra bedroom of Juan's apartment in Frog Hollow. Kelsey lay naked in Peter's arms. The fright of the evening had given their lovemaking an added thrill. Now she rested her head softly on Peter's chest and slept. It was different for Peter; he'd been awake for some time. He stared up at the ceiling, his mind going over and over the course of events. He picked each piece apart, analyzing it, trying to see how it fit into the big picture. As it came together, his plan took on its final form. Finally, he could sleep.

After a few hours, he awoke to Kelsey's warm naked breast pressed tightly against his side. Her right arm was draped over his abdomen and her head was still nestled on his chest.

Prompted by Peter, she slowly opened her eyes "Hi." She smiled at him.

"Hi. How'd you sleep?"

"I really don't remember so I guess I slept well. How about you?" She propped herself up onto her elbows, but Peter, too preoccupied at the moment with his plan, couldn't fully appreciate her provocative posture.

"Not so hot," he said. He slid out of bed and started to get dressed. "I couldn't stop thinking, trying to piece everything together. I've been trying to figure out which parts of this mess are connected."

"And what did you come up with?" She rolled out of bed and also got dressed, not in the least upset with his momentary disinterest in her.

"First, I need to start at the beginning: the Senator's angioplasty. They have a tape that shows me killing the Senator by perforating the artery. I know it didn't happen that way, and I know Barbosa had a hand in it. I think he gave me a faulty catheter and the balloon tip blew off during the procedure. I never checked it afterwards and Barbosa must have switched it for a good one, gambling no one would notice in all the confusion. Unfortunately, Roberto did, and was killed."

"How are you going to prove it?" Kelsey asked.

"I'm not. I have a better plan. It's kind of like an eye for an eye. Sit down and I'll explain."

Over a light breakfast of coffee and toast, Kelsey met Dusty. He stared at her a lot and smiled. She took it in stride and occasionally smiled back. At nine o'clock, Peter dialed Samuel, and was connected to him without delay.

"Peter, I thought you'd be interested in knowing that Agent Sloan is sitting in my waiting room, he wants to talk to me about you."

* * * * *

After listening to Peter for a short time Samuel hung up. A moment later he buzzed his secretary and Agent Sloan entered. He left the door open.

"Agent Sloan, what can I do for you today?" Samuel asked.

"I'm here to give you all the reasons why you should cooperate with me."

"You don't waste any time, do you? Right to the point. Nice and direct, but you sound like you're about to threaten me. Are you?" He sat back in his chair and placed his hands behind his head and looked at Sloan.

177

"No, Attorney, I want to go over just facts and reasons, no threats. Shall I take you from A through Z for starters?"

"How about A through C. We can stop there for 'Cartel'." He stared at Sloan and rocked in his chair.

"I have a better idea." Sloan stood and shut the door. "Why don't we just start and stop at C."

"For Cartel."

"Yes, that's right. For Cartel." Sloan returned to his seat.

| **CHAPTER TWENTY-SIX**

It was a simple plan but it had its flaws; one of which was the need for expert help in one area. Peter sat with them at the kitchen table and presented his plan and the issues that needed to be solved.

Dusty, who'd continued to eye Kelsey all morning, spoke up. "I can get you into the hospital."

"OK," Juan said. "Let's listen to the Dust."

All eyes fell upon him. He gave Kelsey a big smile and after a moment's hesitation puffed out his chest, stood and presented his plan. "I can go anywhere in the hospital. I can go into any room. That's cause they all need to be cleaned. We have the keys to every place."

"But you won't know what to look for," Peter said.

"No!" Dusty threw his hands into the air in disgust. "'top talking. Let me finish. I'm not 'tupid, remember."

"Sorry." Peter cracked a small smile. "Go ahead."

"'cause the housekeepers have all the keys we can get into anyplace. I can open the special trash doors that only unlock and open from the inside. They do that for security. They don't want people breaking into the hospital and running around." He nodded at Kelsey. "I go to work and open it. Peter can sneak into the hospital." He sat down, proud of his plan.

"You thought of that, Dust?" Juan asked.

"Yeah. Nice plan, huh?"

"Yes it is," Peter said. "We'll sneak in tonight."

"No!" Dusty again threw his hands into the air. "I only work days. If I go to work at night someone will know somet'ing's wrong."

"That will increase the danger," Kelsey said. "There are a lot of people there during the day. You stand a higher chance of being spotted."

"No!" Dusty again threw his hands into the air but immediately pulled them down when he realized he'd contradicted Kelsey.

"Why do you say no?" Kelsey asked.

"Well," He looked at her then nervously stared at his feet. "When I go to the mall with my mother and there are not too many people there I get a lot of people staring at me, but when there are a lot of people there nobody sees me. I'm just like them, one of the many."

"You know, you're pretty smart," Kelsey said to him with a smile that made him blush.

"It could work," Peter said. "But I'll need some things before I can blend in and roam the hospital. I can't go back to my apartment. I have a locker with a few things in it that could help me. Do you think you can get them for me?" he asked Dusty, who nodded.

"The last problem," Peter continued, "is that we need the help of someone who has a high level of skill with computer."

"You mean illegal computer skills, don't you Doc?" Juan had a grin on his face.

"Yes, I do. Do you know anyone that can help?" Peter asked.

"Actually, I do. One of my boys has a brother that's a computer geek. He did a small amount of time in the can for hacking a web site. I think he's got the brains and the goods to help you. I'll call and see where he is."

* * * * *

Dusty arrived at work at 11:00 A.M., many hours late for the day's work that started at 7:30, and a few days late all together.

Jan, Dusty's boss, was a pleasant woman in her sixties. He decided to act as if this was just another workday.

"Dusty, are you all right?" she asked when he arrived.

"Yes. I'm OK," he said. "I'm here to work."

"That's OK, you can work. Your job is safe, no one's going to fire you," she said. "You're one of our hardest workers and these last few days were the first you've ever missed. It's OK if you're not feeling well. We were worried about you, though, next time call just to let us know you'll be out sick. If you still feel ill, you can take a few more days off." She was more than kind to her employees and they returned the kindness with loyalty.

"No! I'm here to work." With that he rushed out of the office.

Ten minutes later, he wheeled his garbage can into the Doctor's Locker Room. He looked at the first few numbers on the tops of the lockers, then at the piece of tape hidden under his left shirt-sleeve. On it was written #317 and the combination of the lock.

He looked around and saw that for the moment, he was alone. With jerky jumps he shuffled between the fixed wooden benches and the standard, full-sized, gym lockers that ran up and down both walls.

"Two, zero, zero," he mumbled to himself. He moved down a few feet then looked up again at the number on top of a locker. "Two, six, seven. Getting closer." He had a nervous smile on his face. He moved on. "Three, one, seven." He checked it against the number on his arm. "That's it."

He looked around and was pleased he was still alone. He stared at the three rows of numbers written under the locker number on his arm. They confused him. Right, left, right. Juan had made him practice over and over until he got it correct. It was three to the right, one to the left, and two to the right. He was so bad with combination locks they'd had to replace his with a key lock, which he always wore around his neck on a chain.

The side door to the locker room flew open and two enraged surgeons entered. Dusty jumped back and froze.

"Son of a bitch! God damn-it!" one of them bellowed.

Dusty's hands flapped up and down. He turned left then right. There in the near corner, he saw what he needed. He ran and picked it up.

"Son of a bitch!" the other surgeon replied. They both had blood down the front of their surgical scrubs. "Those God damn surgical gowns are supposed to be waterproof."

"I hope that son of a bitch doesn't have A.I.D.S.!"

"I doubt it. That bastard was eighty-six years old. He probably couldn't get it up to stick it in a whore if he tried and I doubt he was an intravenous drug user. I'm more concerned about hepatitis."

"That God damn aorta blew up in my face. I'm amazed we're not totally soaked with blood."

"'cuse me, 'cuse me. I'm from housekeeping." Dusty pushed by them, wastebasket in hand. Beads of sweat covered his forehead.

"Fuckin' twit," one of the surgeons said as Dusty pushed him aside.

"No fuckin' manners. That's why he's cleaning up garbage for a living."

The two stripped off their blood soaked scrubs and walked into the showers. Dusty trembled and breathed fast but without stopping he emptied the wastebasket and quickly returned it to the corner. He had to do it now! He had no choice. He looked around. The locker room was empty again and from the other room he could hear the sound of the showers. He moved in front of Peter's locker and pulled up his sleeve.

"Two-three, right." He spun the knob three turns to the right and stopped on twenty-three.

"One-four, left." He spun the knob two turns to the left and stopped on fourteen.

"Three-zero, right." He spun the knob once to the right and stopped on thirty.

He lifted the handle but it wouldn't open. He shook it up and down and it still wouldn't open. "No! No! No!" he cried as he pulled up on the handle.

"T'ink! You're smart, not 'tupid." He looked at the numbers on his arm. In front of the numbers was three, one, and two. "Three, one, two . . . three, one, two." He thought about Juan. He said three turns to the right, one to the left and two to the right. That was it; he'd done it wrong.

Suddenly there was silence. The water in the shower had stopped. He knew it would only be a few seconds before they emerged and he'd be caught. His hands visibly shook while he spun the knob. He spoke the numbers out loud to force himself to concentrate.

"Two-three, three turns to the right. One-four, one turn to the left. Three-zero, two turns to the right." He lifted the knob. It opened. He quickly reached in and grabbed Peter's white lab coat, and the stethoscope that hung on a hook. Then he rifled his hand through the top cubby area and found Peter' extra identification badge but when he pulled it out everything else in the cubby area fell onto the floor. At that moment, the two naked surgeons walked around the corner, talking while they toweled the water off their bodies.

Dusty turned. "Oh no!" He slammed the locker shut and with the lab coat rolled in a ball under one arm and the stethoscope gripped tightly in the other hand he ran towards his cart. One of the surgeons blocked his path so he gave him a push. The towel went into the air and the naked surgeon flopped onto the tile floor.

"Hey, you fuckin' asshole!" he yelled.

Dusty threw the gear into the cart and started to leave but he remembered Peter's last words. 'Don't forget a pair of medium sized scrubs. They're on the far wall stacked on a shelf next to the door'. Dusty turned and saw them but they were by the door three feet from the yelling surgeons. He had no choice so he pulled the broom out of his cart and turned to faced them. With a tense grimace on his face he held the broom above his head and let out a yell. "Aughh!" He ran at them and swung the broom up and down in front of him. The two naked surgeons bolted through the side door into the nurse filled lounge just as Dusty hit the door with the broom. He then grabbed a pair of scrubs, ran back to his cart, and stuffed them on top of the lab coat and was out the other side door before anyone from the lounge had dared enter.

He felt proud of himself as he wheeled his cart down the hall. "That was easy," he said aloud, but when he turned the corner he came to an abrupt stop. Coming towards him was Barbosa, with three medical students in tow.

Barbosa stopped and they stared at each other. Dusty saw him glance at the students, then back at him. For the moment, Dusty knew he was safe. Barbosa was loath to do anything to him with that many witnesses. In a bold move, Dusty moved on and walked calmly past them with a wide Cheshire cat grin on his face. Once around the corner, he broke into a spastic run until he reached the elevator. Then he pushed the cart onto an open elevator and pressed himself against the far wall until the door closed.

* * * * *

The door to the trash loading dock flew open. Dusty stood in the doorway, agitated and fidgety, near panic. The door hadn't been open ten seconds when he started to jump up and down and yelled. "Peter! Peter!"

He lunged for the door when he heard no reply and started to shut it but threw it open again when he saw Juan's car pull into view. It stopped for a moment then drove off. He saw someone run from the car and duck behind the trash bin. Dusty froze with terror when that person vaulted onto the dock. It was a gang member instead of Peter.

"Sorry I'm late."

Dusty recognized the voice as Peters' but it took a moment for him to realize that it was Peter in disguise. "Where were you?" Dusty demanded. "I was scared. I almost shut the door."

Peter pulled the door shut behind him then pulled Dusty into a small room filled with trashcans.

"I almost got caught," Dusty said. "First by the doctors in the locker room. But I chased them with a broom—"

"You did what?"

"Yeah—yeah. Then I walked into Barbosa. He didn't chase me 'cause he was with young doctors. I walked right by him and came here." Dusty pointed to the cart. "There are your things."

Peter took the lab coat along with his stethoscope, badge and scrubs, and changed into them. He stacked his clothes behind a bin and then turned to Dusty. "How do I look?"

"Like a gang member who's dressed like a doctor."

"Good, I'll see you back at Juan's. You be careful."

"No." Dusty pointed a finger at him. "You be careful. I won't be there to protect you."

"No, you won't be." Peter put a hand onto his shoulder and gave him a squeeze.

Peter stayed off the elevator and kept to the stairwells. He knew his disguise was modest at best. He'd dyed his hair black and had Maria style it in a Latino way; and once again had applied a mild dark base pancake to his skin. That alone changed his appearance enough that he felt instant recognition would be avoided; despite that, he moved with caution. He exited the stairwell on the third floor where Radiology, and specifically Cardiac Radiology, was around the corner. When he stepped into the hallway he felt exposed, but when a group of secretaries walked by him and didn't give him any notice he breathed a slight sigh of relief.

He turned the corner and stopped in front of the x-ray file room door. After a deep breath, he opened it and entered, then walked by two secretaries who also ignored him. Residents and Fellows file by them to review x-rays a hundred times a day.

Peter sat in front of a computer screen and typed in the Senator's name and medical record number. A few seconds later, it listed all the x-rays and angiograms that had been performed

185

on him. More specifically, it listed the file number of those x-rays and angiograms so they could be retrieved and reviewed. Peter scanned the file and saw what he wanted. The Senator had been admitted a few times for chest pains. That didn't surprise Peter, given the Senator's large girth. He scrolled to the Senator's prior admission; he was in luck: the Senator had had an angiogram done. Moments later he walked between the rows of tall file cabinets that held the packets of x-rays and stopped where the angiograms were stored. When he found the number of the cassette he needed he pulled it off the shelf. Casually he looked up and down the aisle and saw he was alone. Just as casually, he slipped the cassette into the inner pocket of his lab coat.

Peter walked towards the exit when one of the secretaries turned towards him. "Did you find everything you were looking for Doctor?" She stared at his badge to find his name, but the picture on his hospital tag caught her attention. It was obviously not a picture of the person standing in front of her. She looked at the picture closer and realized it was Dr. Pavano. A quick glance at his face made her see right through his disguise. In a panic, she jumped up from her chair and ran to the exit, where moments ealier a guard had been flirting with one of the x-ray technicians.

Peter heard her cry for help and a moment later a guard ran into the file room. "Pavano, stop right there!"

Peter spun and ran through the side door with the guard in pursuit twenty feet behind. Across and slightly down the hall he charged through the fire escape and down a flight of stairs, three steps at a time. When he reached the next landing he heard the door above him bang open and slam against the wall. The guard was still twenty feet behind but Peter knew he had to get off the stairs or it'd just be a foot race, one he'd eventually lose. At that landing he opened the door and ran onto the floor where he found himself in the hall outside the east wing patients' ward on the second floor. He sprinted down the hall past two nurses.

Overhead Peter heard the page system announce 'Security Code Red'; that was for him. The guards all had two-way radios and it was only a matter of time before he was cornered, so he had to create a diversion. He turned to three other nurses and yelled, "Get the crash cart. There's a Code Blue in the end room!"

That's all it took. The call, 'Code Blue', rang out down the hall and nurses and carts filled with resuscitation gear instantly appeared.

The guard entered the hallway and hesitated, he wasn't sure which way Peter had gone. When he looked down the hallway, though, he saw him among the sea of bodies running towards the end room. The guard resumed his pursuit but was held up and pushed aside by the staff responding to the Code Blue.

Peter turned and saw him and quickly realized he had few choices, so he ran through the fire exit that led into the center stairwell. Lucky for Peter, the floor wrapped around the stairwell and also had an entrance on the other side of the floor. Instead of going up or down, he ran through the opposite door and re-entered the floor on the opposite side. The guard entered the stairwell after Peter and instinctively ran down it.

Confident of human nature, he felt he had thrown the guard off so he quickly walked down the corridor and left the ward. Once in the hallway, he slowed to a stroll and turned onto a walkway between buildings. He glanced out a big bay window and saw a slew of police cars skid to the front entrance, and several policemen ran into the hospital. His chances of escape were disappearing fast.

He thought for a second then picked up a wall phone and dialed 5111, the hospital-wide emergency number. When the operator answered Peter shouted, "Call a Code Blue on C-304!" Then he hung up.

Overhead the call rang out. "Code Blue room C-304. Code Blue room C-304."

Now there would be interns and residents running throughout the hospital. He jogged down the hall, then stopped. Hell, if one was good, more were better.

At the next phone, he again dialed 5111. "Call a pediatric Code Blue for the nursery!"

A pediatric cardiac arrest always sent a hospital into a panic; no matter how large the hospital was, no one wanted a baby to die, so everyone responded.

One last thing caught his eye; he reached up and pulled the fire alarm box. In medical school, he was taught confusion was a bad thing but for today confusion was good; very good.

All hell broke loose throughout the hospital. The fire alarms rang; the operators paged 'Code Blues' for adult and pediatric floor along with the 'Dr. Firestone' pages that notified people where the fire was.

Peter ran down the hall and jumped into a service elevator that had just opened up. For the moment, he felt safe since everyone knew not to use elevators in the event of a fire. Once in, he pressed B for basement and held his breath, hoping it wouldn't stop and put him face to face with a security guard or policeman.

The ride down was agonizingly slow. When the elevator finally stopped at the basement and opened, Peter still held his breath and was ready to charge whoever opposed him. Thankfully, he was alone. He exited onto a dungeon corridor at the loading dock where, just outside, he heard a police car with its siren on pull up and, in the background, the air horns blast from approaching fire engines.

He quickly made his way deeper into the bowels of the hospital where he hoped to find a way out. He rounded a corner and stopped as two voices approached from the opposite direction. Unable to retreat because he assumed the police were on the loading dock, he ducked through the only door there was and found himself in the morgue. In the middle of the room lay an open, empty casket resting on a dolly, and off to one side was the bank of refrigerated drawers that held the bodies. Through another archway were the autopsy tables, all empty at the moment.

Peter only had seconds to duck behind a small desk when the door flew open and the two men from the hall entered.

"Sign this paper, sign that paper. That's all they care about," one of them said. "I swear paperwork is what's killing this country."

"Damn straight. Come on, I'll give you a hand with the body."

They opened one of the body cabinets, reached in and pulled out a black body bag, then hoisted it into the coffin and closed the lid.

"I hope your pathologist left us something to work with cause the last one he cut up was a mess. We had to have a closed casket. Our mortician was pretty pissed off, so was the family."

"Bill, that kid was shot in the face at close range, so there wasn't much to start with. Anyway, it was a medical legal case, the police needed the bullet fragments for evidence."

"Explain that to the family."

"Go back up the hearse and I'll open the loading bay for you."

They had barely left when Peter realized what he had to do. It was his only way out. He stepped from behind the desk, opened the casket and with great difficulty hauled out the bagged body. It fell to the floor with a thud, the head striking the tiled floor with a sickening crack. Next he dragged the body bag to the bottom storage bin and opened it. It already had a body in it. With no choice he rolled the body bag onto the other body and shut it. Lastly, he climbed into the casket, closed the lid and waited for them to return.

The coffin was unbearable. A metal bar formed the middle rib of it and dug into his back. He always thought they'd be comfortable; a final resting place filled with comfortable pillows and soft satin sheets. He was wrong. The lid touched the top of his nose, giving him the sensation that he was about to suffocate, which he slowly was. Coffins are airtight.

Without warning he felt the coffin vibrate. The two had returned and were wheeling him down the hallway where they loaded the coffin into the hearse. Peter heard their muffled voices

189

but was unable to make out what they where saying. Inside the coffin, it had quickly become stifling hot and Peter was quickly drenched in sweat. He wanted to throw the lid open and get some fresh air. He realized the irony of his situation. For the last few day's people had been trying to put him in a coffin, now it was the only place he could stay alive.

At the point he thought he couldn't take it anymore, he felt a slight sense of motion as the hearse pulled away from the landing. From that point on, it was a matter of being patient. He had to wait for the right moment. He visualized in the dark the route they took. He felt them stop, most likely a traffic light, then he felt them turn a corner.

One more light, he calculated would be enough. When he felt them slow he threw open the coffin. "Hey!" he yelled. "What are you doing? I'm not dead! Who put me in here?"

"What the hell!" The color in the driver's face drained to ghost white as he screamed and reacted by pressing the gas pedal to the floor. The hearse jumped across the intersection and hit a light pole.

Peter crawled out of the coffin, opened the rear door, and was down the street before the driver could stop hyperventilating and let out his first scream.

27 | CHAPTER TWENTY-SEVEN

Later that evening, the doors to the West Farms Brokerage Firm were opened at the normal hour of eleven o'clock. The cleaning crew was prompt and very efficient; they had four other office firms to clean that evening. On a normal night, they would sweep through the building and be gone in two hours. Juan followed the crew in; he was dressed like everyone else in the company's jumpsuit. It hadn't taken long to make the calls needed to put him in uniform. It was amazing all the dirty little secrets he had accumulated on people. It seemed they would do anything to protect the fact that their son or daughter. In this case, the woman the owner was having an affair with behind his wife's back, was a drug addict. The owner wanted to keep both indiscretions very quiet, so if Juan wanted to follow his cleaning crew for the evening, what issue was it of his? Everyone turned a blind eye to Juan being there; it was the way of the street.

Juan opened the door to the computer room and slipped in. The cleaning crew had informed Juan this room would be the last cleaned. He slipped behind the small walkway that ran behind the firm's main computers and knelt down. Next, he pulled a laptop computer from his bag and attached a cable from it to the brokerage firm's main computer. Then, he booted up both systems. Once they were up and running, he accessed the main disc drive and opened the firm's client list. Finding Dr. Barbosa's name, he highlighted the information and downloaded it to his laptop. That done, he shut down both systems and slipped out as quickly as he had entered.

28 | CHAPTER TWENTY-EIGHT

The next day Peter stood outside the Cardiac Insti tute in Boston. It amazed him that less than a month had gone by since he'd stood in the atrium waiting for his first lecture on angioplasty. It seemed like ancient history—a moment that was barely on the edge of his memory.

"I'd feel better if you'd let me come with you," Kelsey said as she held his arm tightly.

"No," Peter replied. "It'll be safer alone." He looked into her eyes. "Just in case something happens."

"Nothing is going to happen."

He gave her a kiss then walked up the front walkway and entered the atrium. The warm sun was starting its descent over the city skyline. He looked at his watch. It was 2:15 in the afternoon. The crowd milled around for another 10 minutes then they rushed back to their seats for the next lecture. That was when Peter left his spot and walked with one group down the corridor, following some of them down a flight of stairs. He was now on the lab level where he'd practiced on "Dilate-Me-Bill".

Peter lagged behind the others and let the four he'd followed enter their labs. He had to find one that was unoccupied. At the sixth lab, he stopped and turned the knob. The door opened slowly and he peeked in. There were two voices, an instructor and a student so he shut it with care and moved on down the hall. Only after rounding the corner did he find one that was empty. He walked in and went directly to the main computer console and sat down. It took him a precious minute to find the power switch. When he switched it on, every monitor in the room came alive.

He took the VCR tape of Senator Demind's angiogram out of his jacket pocket and placed it on the counter. Though computer literate, he had no idea how the system in front of him worked but knew he only had thirty minutes, at best, to figure it out. That's when a new group would arrive and this room to be assigned again.

Peter needed to find the instruction book, and fast. He rifled through a few drawers. At the bottom of the third one he found the operating manual. With no time to read it for content he scanned the index and found the section on VCR downloads. He opened to that section and quickly scanned the instructions. They were too detailed and he didn't have time. With his index finger, he ran line by line and followed what minuscule directions he'd gleaned out of it. He inserted the tape into the machine and pressed the play button and the Senator's angiogram was displayed on a small monitor.

From what he had read, the download from the Senator's tape had to be timed precisely to start a fraction of a second before the dye was injected into the coronary arteries. Then immediately after the dye washed out of the picture the download had to be stopped. Only then would the computer have a complete sequence of heartbeats, and, a complete picture of the coronary arteries. The computer would then reconstruct a computer-generated image for "Dilate-Me-Bill".

He pressed the play button and watched the monitor, then hit stop. "Damn." He'd pressed the stop button too late; the heart had started a new sequence of beats. His finger pushed the rewind button for a second. He'd have to do it again. This time when he pressed Play he saw the tip of the catheter already in place. "Son of a bitch!" he muttered to himself, he hadn't rewound it far enough. Time appeared to fly by while he jockeyed the tape back and forth until it was at the beginning. His right index finger hit play and his left index finger depressed the enter button not a moment too soon. The monitor showed the dye wash through the pulsating artery and wash out until it was gone. Peter pressed the stop button and the download stopped. This time the timing had been exact. The download had been perfect.

Time was running out. His watch showed five minutes gone.

He had to pick up the pace. He flipped the pages to the next part of the manual and quickly followed the set up. It told him he had to make the computer reconfigure the image of the Senator's heart and coronary arteries in "Dilate-Me-Bill".

He again glanced at his watch. Ten minutes gone.

Peter stood and hurried to "Dilate-Me-Bill". From a side table, he picked up the angioplasty catheter and with a small pocketknife he incised the rubber around the tip of the catheter. It had to be precise, just scored, not perforated. The last inner ring of rubber fibers had to hold until it was inflated, so that the tip would blow off the outer balloon and the inner one would remain intact. Just the way he assumed it had in the Senator's case. Someone would have to specifically watch the tip of the catheter at exactly the right moment or he would miss the disaster, as had Peter during the real procedure.

Everything was set. All that was left for him to do was to recreate the ill-fated procedure and record it.

"Hey! What are you doing?"

Peter spun around. A lab instructor stood in the open doorway.

"Actually, I'm doing nothing. That's the problem," Peter replied calmly. "My instructor went off to check on something five minutes ago and I've been standing here doing nothing since then."

"This room was unassigned."

"I know. The lab we were originally in had a monitor problem so we came in here."

"Who's your instructor?"

"Dr. Citrullo." He remembered his instructor's name from last month.

"That's who I'm looking for. He's not supposed to be assigned to teach this afternoon. Tell him Lou's looking for him, I'll be back in ten minutes." He turned and the door shut behind him.

"Ten minutes. Shit!" He didn't know if he could finish in ten minutes. He sprinted to the main console and started the program. "Dilate-Me-Bill" came to life: its chest heaved up and down with simulated respirations and the cardiac monitor bounced with every simulated heartbeat.

Peter returned to the side of the table and quickly inserted the angioplasty catheter into the dummy's groin, threading it up the plastic tubes to the simulated heart. He had at best one chance to get it right. Time would not allow a repeat. He reached up and turned on the simulated fluoroscopic x-ray machine. It was completely computer generated with no radiation exposure. With his left hand on the catheter and his right on the syringe he advanced the catheter. His thumb squeezed the plunger on the syringe causing dye to course through the artificial heart and highlighted the arteries. Peter was amazed how these arteries exactly replicated those of the Senator's. The download had worked.

The heart jumped with every beat and over and over he attempted and failed to thread the guide wire into the coronary arteries. To Peter, it was like trying to thread the eye of a needle, but with that needle attached to a vibrator.

He looked at the clock on the wall; two more minutes gone.

Sweat formed on his forehead and the muscles in the back of his neck tightened in a tense spasm. He stopped and took a slow deep breath, then tried again. Finally, the guide wire slid into place. He advanced the catheter over it and placed the balloon at the site of the computer generated arterial constriction. With anxiety and anticipation, he inflated the balloon and held his breath.

"There!" The tip popped off and in an instant it was gone.

He took his foot off the pedal and the pump quickly bled off the pressure deflating the balloon. He removed it from the dummy and looked at the clock; five more minutes gone.

06-MUCC

Back at the main console, Peter pushed Play, then Pause. To make the tape authentic, it needed the Senator's name, hospital identification number, and date the procedure was done. By manipulating the curser with the mouse and doing cut and paste, Peter had the computer copy the hospital logo along with the other information and transferred it to the new tape. In a microsecond, it had overlaid the needed information. Peter inserted a new tape and pressed the record button at the same time he pressed replay on the computer. A new tape of the Senator's procedure right down to the hospital identification was made and no one would be able to tell it was a fake. Only one thing was missing: Peter had to add the Senator's cardiac arrest. He scrolled through the computers options and found Sinus Tachycardia, Ventricular Tachycardia and Ventricular Fibrillation. He logged them in the correct order and the computer simulated the Senator's quick demise after the balloon tip dislodged in the tape. Peter counted the seconds as the computer recorded, in agonizing real time, the procedure onto the tape.

"Has Dr. Citrullo returned yet?" The lab instructor asked as he stood in the doorway. "Hey," he said, "you're not supposed to be touching anything on that console." He walked over to Peter. "What are you doing? And where's Dr. Citrullo?"

"He went to find a replacement catheter. We had a problem with that one." Peter pointed to it. "The balloon tip ruptured. Before he left, he set up the training tape for me to watch."

Peter looked down. Thirty seconds left to record.

The instructor walked over to the table and picked up the catheter. "Damn, I can't remember one of these ever breaking."

Peter glanced down. The recording had finished. He pushed the stop button then the eject button. A moment later the tape was in his fanny pack.

"Hey Lou, I heard you were looking for me." Dr. Citrullo walked into the lab.

"I was. Your student told me what happened with this catheter. I've never seen this happen before."

"What are you talking about? I'm not teaching this afternoon."

"Isn't he your student?"

They both turned to Peter.

"No."

Before they could react, Peter was out the door and up the steps. It was now the top of the hour and the hallway and atrium were crowded once again. Peter melted into the crowd and headed towards the front door, but thirty feet from it he stopped. The entrance guard must have been alerted because he stood closer to the front door. Peter turned around and saw Dr. Citrullo and the other lab instructor standing on a rise with two other security guards scanning the crowd. Just before they looked his way, he stepped behind a statue.

The seconds ticked by. Peter had to know what they were doing so he peered around the statue in time to see them break into two groups. An instructor and a guard went one way; the other two went the opposite way. They hadn't spotted him, but it was only a matter of time before they did. There was nowhere to go and to make matters worse the crowd was thinning out. The next round of classes was about to start.

Peter was trapped. One of the guards was now only ten feet to his right when suddenly a hand grabbed him on the shoulder. He spun around and threw his hands up ready to protect himself. Defenseless, he found himself pressed firmly against the statue with a baseball cap thrown on his head and sweet tender lips pressed firmly against his. It was Kelsey. Her quick move shielded him from the guard and instructor, who only gave them a momentary glance when they walked by. They were too busy to be bothered with two people kissing.

"The atrium's clearing out," the instructor said within earshot of Peter. "Let's make sure he doesn't go down any hallway and use a door."

Kelsey released her grip. "I hope you're not mad I didn't stay outside?"

'06-MUCC

"Not at all, you just saved my butt. Come on we should get out of here."

"Put this on." She opened her rucksack and took out Juan's gang leather jacket. The two cuddled and lightly kissed all the way out the door.

29 | CHAPTER TWENTY-NINE

The following morning Kelsey pulled her Toyota Celica to a stop beside the security booth at American Catheter. The guard smiled but appeared anxious. He'd greeted her every morning during her short tenure at the company, but today her picture hung on his bulletin board.

Kelsey saw him glance down and read something then look up. "I'm sorry, Kelsey. I have a notice that we're not to let you into the building. It says you don't work for American Catheter anymore."

She smiled at him. "That's OK, Wayne. I guess they fired me. They must not have liked my friends. You gotta take the good with the bad."

"The good with the bad?"

"The good is I don't have to work for those jerks any more and I leave with my integrity. The bad is you still have to work for them." She waited for a laugh; none came.

"I still can't let you in. In fact, I have to confiscate your company identification badge. You're not to have access to the building."

"It's all yours, with pleasure." She tossed it out the car window. It floated through the air and landed on the counter in front of him. She stared at him and smiled, which made him fidget. "I have a desk filled with personal things. I do have a right to retrieve them."

706-MUCC

"Yes, I guess you do. One moment." He picked up the phone spoke for a moment then hung up. "You can go in and park. Another guard will meet you at the door and escort you to your desk, then back to your car. I'm sorry but that's company policy."

"I'd expect nothing more. Thanks, Wayne." She drove off into the garage and parked one level up.

Normally, at the door to the building, she would have slid her security badge through a slot and the door would have automatically opened. With her badge at the security post, she had to wait for a guard to appear.

"Are you Kelsey?" the guard asked, opening the door from the inside.

"Yes."

"I'm to accompany you to your desk, then back to your car."

"Then let's go. The sooner I get my things the sooner I can move on with my life."

The door shut and locked behind them.

Peter and Dusty lay crammed in the trunk of Kelsey's car. Peter lifted the trunk a crack and listened. It was quiet. He stuck his head out and peered around, still nothing. He climbed out and helped Dusty, who jumped out and ducked behind the car. Peter gently closed the trunk and joined Dusty.

"I think I hear something," Dusty whispered.

Peter cocked an ear to one side. "You're right. It's a car. Remember when it's time, we'll have to move fast."

"I know, you already told me."

The car rounded the bend and drove up the ramp, then parked a short distance from them. A middle-aged man got out and headed for the door. When he was ten feet beyond Peter and Dusty, they stood and casually walked behind him. The man swiped his badge through the slot and the door opened. It was inches from closing when Peter' foot wedged between it and the doorframe. He and Dusty gave each other a smile.

"So far, so good," Peter said.

They waited a minute before entering and when they did the hallway was empty.

They entered the first elevator at the elevator bank and took it to the basement. A few moments later they found themselves at the maintenance locker room. Dusty entered first. They'd agreed he'd be the point man. It was Dusty's idea, "Mostly people look at me with pity, I don't scare them." They'd use that to their benefit.

Dusty poked his head out the door. "It's empty. Come on."

Dusty immediately riffled through the batch of protective coveralls and tossed one to Peter. "Here, put this one on. It should fit you."

Peter climbed in it and zipped up the front, which covered his street clothes.

"Hurry," Dusty said. Peter saw that the longer they were in the locker room the more agitated Dusty was becoming. He hoped Dusty would keep it together.

At the equipment locker, Dusty pulled out a carpet shampoo machine and the necessary chemicals. "Here." Dusty pointed. "You take the machine, I'll take the chemicals."

Peter grabbed the handle and rolled it into the hallway. Dusty was right behind him with a pail filled with spray bottles. He moved quickly past Peter and waddled to the elevator. "Hurry."

The next problem they faced was how to gain access to the eleventh floor. The elevator had an eleventh floor button but it could only be activated with a security key. To Peter's surprise Dusty had a plan; all things considered, it was a very good plan.

The elevator door opened on the ground floor lobby. Dusty rushed out and ran up to the guard desk. "'cuse me, 'cuse me I need help."

He grabbed one of the guards by his sleeve and gave a tug. "Come wit' me."

The guard hesitated and looked at the other who smiled and motioned for him to follow.

06-MUCC

Dusty's speech was fast and staccato. "I don't wanna be fired. I'm new here. My boss will yell at me."

He led the guard into the elevator.

"Look! It doesn't work!" Dusty pushed the eleventh floor button over and over again. "It won't light up. It won't work!"

"I told him we need the key," Peter said with a disgusted look, "but you can see what we're dealing with here." He eyed Dusty.

Dusty threw his hands into the air. "I know we need a key. I know we need a key." He pulled at his locker key from C.G.H. that he always wore around his neck and held it up. His speech was louder now. "This was the key my boss gave me. It doesn't work!" He tried to place it into the slot but of course it didn't fit.

"You gotta help me. If I don't get the carpet cleaned on floor eleven, my boss will t'ink I'm 'tupid and can't do what he tells me to. I'm not 'tupid. He gave me the wrong key!"

Dusty was panting and saliva dribbled down his chin. "Help me. You have to have the key. You're Security. You have all the keys!"

"OK, OK." The guard held up his hands. "Just calm down." He pulled out his key chain and inserted the proper key and pushed the eleventh floor button, it lit up. "Go. Clean your carpets. Knock yourself out." He stepped back and the elevator doors closed.

Dusty turned to Peter with a big grin on his face. "I'm not 'tupid, I'm smart."

Peter looked at him wide eyed with amazement. "Damn straight Dusty, I think you're brilliant."

"T'anks. Nobody ever told me that before."

Moments later, the elevator opened on the eleventh floor. Dusty and Peter walked out, equipment in hand. They were met by a stern stare from Joshua's secretary. Her desk was off to the side but it faced the bank of elevators.

"May I help you?" She spoke as if that was the last thing she wanted to do.

Dusty trotted right up to her and stood very close to her chair. He'd learned long ago that invading someone's personal space would make them very uncomfortable, especially if it was him doing the invading.

"We're from maintenance." His saliva spewed onto her blouse. She immediately slid her chair back. "We're here to shampoo the rugs. My boss said do it now. Then we're to report back to him for our next job."

"You can't do it now. It's the middle of the day. Come back after regular business hours."

"Nooo! Now!" He moved closer. "I'll get fired!" He wailed. "He'll say I'm 'tupid and can't do what I'm told to do!"

"I'm not going to walk on wet rugs all day," she said.

"No! We don't use water. We spray this dry chemical on then rub it in with that machine that picks up the chemical and the dirt."

She put her hands up to keep him at arm's length. "Fine. Just stay out of my way."

The express elevator from the private garage sounded and then opened. Peter heard two voices and recognized one of them. He spun around with his back to them and bent over the machine, fiddling with nothing in particular. Barbosa and a colleague walked onto the floor deep in conversation.

The secretary smiled. "Please go right in. Joshua and the others are in the conference room."

Dusty walked away from the secretary and stood right in front of them. Barbosa gave him a noncommittal look, obviously too preoccupied to make the connection. They entered the conference room and shut the door behind them.

"It will take us a few moments to set up. We have to move this furniture," Dusty said.

* * * * *

Barbosa walked around to the far side of the conference table and sat down. The room was only half full but five television monitors were on rolling carts around the room. The five missing members from the west coast were present on the screens via secured hookups.

"Now that we're all here, we can get started," Joshua said. "You all know by now that actions taken on by our Connecticut chapter have put us in deep trouble."

"Bullshit!" Barbosa said. "I was forced to take certain actions because of your indecision and weakness."

"Stop this fighting," demanded one of the TV screens. "That's how we got into this mess. I really don't care what animosity the two of you have for each other. If you want to fight, take it outside and do it like real men. We're here because we have a problem. We'll deal with the causes later. Right now we need solutions."

"Agreed." Joshua nodded.

"That's fine with me," Barbosa added and turned to Joshua. "You want to handle it? Fine, tell us how."

* * * * *

Outside in the hallway Peter plugged in the shampoo machine and switched it on. It gave off a low hum and vibrated over the rug. Dusty continued to bother the secretary.

"You have to move. We have to clean around your desk," he said while he sprayed the cleaning powder around her desk and chair.

"Be careful!" She stood up and brushed powder off her skirt. "How long will it take you?"

"Twenty minutes to do this area and around your desk," Dusty replied. He continued to spray the powder making sure some got on her shoes.

"You have ten minutes. I'll be gone for that long. When I return, I expect the both of you to be gone. If you're not, I'll call the guards and have you thrown out. And yes little man," she looked directly at Dusty, "you will be fired then."

"No . . . no! We'll be gone in ten minutes. I promise," Dusty said with a sputter.

She walked around the corner and Dusty rushed over to Peter and took the rug cleaner from him. "Go," he said. "She'll be back in ten minutes."

"Something tells me she'll be back in less than that." He walked without hesitation to the door directly behind her desk, opened it a crack and peered in. The room was empty and the door to the adjoining conference room was shut.

He entered the office and shut the door behind him. To his relief the lights were already on. The office was plush with elaborate furniture and paintings. A large solid mahogany desk faced the door but he ignored it. It was the smaller desk, also solid mahogany, to his right that he walked to. A computer terminal, its monitor filled with changing patterns from a screen saver, was what he wanted. He touched on the mouse, which shut off the changing geometric patterns and opened up Joshua's home screen.

"Thank God," he mumbled. He'd been correct. Joshua's arrogance with the Cartel predisposed him to be lax about security. He wouldn't inconvenience himself with computer passwords during the day. The building was safe. Who would dare break in during broad daylight?

Peter double clicked on the file named 'Cartel Charter'. That opened to a sub file that listed everything including the founding members and the members of the Board of Directors who had ruled through the years. Everything he needed to sink all of them was there and it was just a click away.

He took out a laptop computer and attached a cable into the appropriate slot in the rear of the Joshua's computer then into his laptop. With a few clicks, he copied the files he had opened onto the laptop's hard drive.

The next file was even more damaging to the Cartel. It contained the list of every patient who in the last ten years had

205

undergone unnecessary procedures. Even more damaging to the Cartel was that each note had an addendum added to it that explained how the first procedure had been modified. After reading three notes, he realized how simple it had been.

With no time to read anymore he initiated the files transfer with a push of a button. From that point on he skipped opening and browsing any of the files. Time now worked against him. It seemed he couldn't download the files to the computer fast enough; he just wanted to get out of there. He felt himself getting warm and perspiration built up under his armpits. When the last file was copied he shut down his computer and stored it in his chest pouch again.

* * * * *

"This morning," Joshua continued, "the insurance companies announced they had received approximately thirty charts of patients who had repeat procedures at Connecticut General. How they received them we don't know."

Barbosa jumped in. "They were riffed from our Medical Record Department by one of your employees, Kelsey Depucci."

"That's unfortunate, but as we agreed we'll deal with those matters at another time."

"That's fine," Barbosa said with a sharp tongue. "I just mentioned it as a point of reference. Go on."

Joshua nodded his contempt. "All major insurance companies have announced an immediate suspension of payment for any repeat angioplasties. It appears that the charts came to them by way of Pavano's private lawyer, and one of the insurance companies plans an immediate investigation. They intend to review all repeat procedures to see if any were done fraudulently."

A voice came from one of the monitors. "What's our exposure at best?"

"Very little," Joshua replied. "All hospital records, angioplasty records and tapes will support the need for each and every procedure."

"What do you want to do then?" another voice asked.

"I think we should take the offensive."

"Explain," Barbosa demanded.

"We announce that there is indeed a loose group of invasive cardiologists who have been quietly talking to each other about forming a public corporation that will supply inexpensive angioplasty to the American public. We claim that over the last two years we, as a group, have been reviewing guidelines for quality control. Of course, we deny that any organization like the Cartel exists. We make the public believe that their over inflated sense of conspiracy has gotten the best of them. We go public as I recommended at our last meeting. We even offer to meticulously review each and every chart that they have doubts about and if they find that any procedures were unnecessary the hospitals and the cardiologists will fully reimburse them."

"Again, what is our exposure?" Barbosa asked.

"Zero," Joshua said. "The records are iron clad. The only way anyone could dispute those charts and angio records is to get into the records we keep here. They're secure. They can't be accessed from the outside. They're stored on a closed system that isn't connected to any outside line."

One of the members in the room asked, "Should we keep those records?"

"No. They need to be destroyed and when that's done, there'll be no hard data to support their review. It will be just supposition and difference of opinion."

"I want the backup tape destroyed too," Barbosa said. His eyes bore in on Joshua.

"Agreed. We wouldn't want anyone blackmailing anyone, would we?" He glared back.

"Get the tape," Barbosa demanded.

"Now?"

"Yes. Now," Barbosa replied. "And after we burn it, we'll erase the main databank."

"You are a paranoid group." Joshua stood and walked to his office.

* * * * *

The office room door flew open and Joshua was poised to enter, looking over his shoulder into the conference room. In that moment of misdirection, Peter crawled under the desk and into the leg well. He hoped he hadn't been seen.

Peter heard Joshua move around the room and stop. Peter's curiosity got the best of him so he very carefully he peered out from behind the desk. He saw Joshua grab at some books that appeared to be bonded together. They rotated on a hinge and revealed a wall safe. Joshua opened it and pulled out a computer backup tape. He shut the door and spun around. Peter ducked back under the desk just in time. His heart pounded. He hadn't been seen. He could hear Barbosa in the other room belligerently blaming American Catheter for all the problems. After a moment, he heard Joshua walk back into the conference room and start to defend himself.

Peter inched out from under the desk and peeked around the corner. The door had been left open and he had a clear view into the conference room. That meant they also had a clear view of him. A shiver ran down his spine. Thirty feet away was Barbosa who, by the grace of God, had his gaze towards a different part of the room. It was only a matter of time before that changed and when it did his window of escape would be slammed shut. Anxiety, and tightness, welled up in his throat. The sensation of not being able to breathe took over, but Peter fought it the best he could and crawled along the floor to the front door. Very slowly and with deliberate care, he opened it and slipped into the secretarial area.

* * * * *

"Here's the tape," Joshua said. "How do you want to destroy it?"

"Burn it," Barbosa replied. He picked up a trashcan and threw some papers into it. "Give me it."

Joshua did.

"Anyone have a lighter?"

Joshua handed him his.

Barbosa lit the papers and threw the tape onto the flame. They all watched it in silence.

* * * * *

Joshua's secretary caught Peter coming out of the office. "There you are. What the hell were you doing in there?" There was fire in her eyes and her hand reached for the phone. "I'm calling security."

"You're calling no one, lady. I've had enough of this." Peter yanked the phone out of her hand and placed it back onto the cradle.

She opened her mouth to yell. The conference room was only feet away.

Peter clamped his hand over her mouth. "Shut up and you won't get hurt. Dusty, give me your overalls."

Without hesitation Dusty unzipped his coveralls.

"Sit down." Peter forced her into her chair. He kept his hand clamped over her mouth. Her eyes were wide with fear.

"I don't want to hurt you," Peter whispered, "but scream and I'll break your fucking neck. Understand?"

He let up slightly on her mouth and heard a soft 'yes'.

"Open your mouth wide," he said.

She hesitated for a moment so with his free hand he grabbed a handful of hair and pulled it hard. She complied and opened. Peter slid a sleeve from Dusty's coveralls into her mouth. Then he wrapped the cuff end around the back of her neck and tied to the other side sleeve. He'd created a makeshift gag.

"Don't move."

He took off his own coveralls and with the sleeves and pant legs bound her hands and feet together. "Dusty get the elevator."

* * * * *

The flames died out and the tape was destroyed. Barbosa turned to the group. "Now we only need to erase the files in his personal computer. Then we're all safe." He motioned at the computer terminal in the corner. "If you wouldn't mind."

"Not at all." Joshua walked over and turned on the monitor. It had a direct link to the one in his office. "What the hell!" He peered at the screen. "Did anyone access the files while I was in my office?"

"No." Barbosa walked over. "Why?"

"Look! The files are open. I never leave them open." Joshua spun the monitor around so everyone could see. In Peter's haste to leave, he had forgotten to close the last file he had opened.

"So what's the problem?" Barbosa asked.

"Open your eyes Barbosa. Someone has been in this system and if they were they could have copied the files. They'd have everything."

"The retard! Shit! It was him," Barbosa said.

"What are you talking about?" Joshua asked.

"Out in the hall. When I came off the elevator, there were two maintenance workers. One looked like the retard that's caused me so much trouble at the hospital. He's a friend of Pavano. I wouldn't doubt it if the other one was Pavano."

* * * * *

When the elevator door finally opened Peter and Dusty rushed inside. Peter pushed the button for the garage but nothing happened. Suddenly, the door to the conference room burst open and Joshua and Barbosa stormed out. They ran head on into the tied up secretary.

"What kind of bullshit security it this?" Barbosa hollered.

Peter stood in the open elevator and jabbed the 'door close' button again and again. His eyes locked onto Barbosa's. Then before anyone could react the elevator the doors began to shut. Peter smiled, pointed his right index finger at Barbosa and pretended to shoot, then he blew smoke away from the tip of his finger just as the door slid shut. The last thing Peter saw was Barbosa red-faced and in a rage.

* * * * *

Before the doors were half open, Peter and Dusty were down the hall and out into the garage.

"Her car's gone!" Dusty said.

Just then horns sounded and over the loud speaker blared, "Security Code Red!"

"Follow me," Peter said.

They ducked behind the row of cars and hid between the wall and the front bumpers. Peter crouched down and ran bent over. Dusty copied him. They made their way around the corner and down the ramp towards the security gate, hidden from view by the cars. At the guard station, the metal security gate to the street was shut.

"We're trapped!" Dusty said with a shrill. "How we gonna get out?"

"There." Peter pointed to an oncoming car. It rounded the bend and stopped at the guard booth.

The guard stepped out and they watched him validate the man's identification. Then he looked in the front seat, the back seat, and even the trunk to make sure there weren't any unwanted passengers.

"When I say go, we run," Peter whispered.

"OK."

The guard stepped back into his booth and raised the metal gate; but only far enough to clear the roof of the car. When the car started up Peter yelled to Dusty. "Run."

The two of them dashed past the car and were out onto the street before the guard could react.

"Where is she?" Dusty jumped up and down.

"Over there! Come on."

"Hey! You two stop!" The guard gave chase.

The rear tires of Kelsey's Toyota smoked and spun wildly then stopped with a skid beside Peter and Dusty. They jumped in and were gone before the guard had made it to the middle of the street. The last thing the guard saw was Dusty sticking his tongue out at him from the rear window.

30 | CHAPTER THIRTY

It had been an extremely long day and they were exhausted. They decided to overnight in a motel on the outskirts of Boston, but before they settled in for the night Peter had one more place to visit. It was two hours before sundown and he didn't want to miss the chance to go there one last time.

Juan, who met them at the motel, Kelsey, and Dusty, drove him there, but they stood off to one side and let Peter go in alone. They thought he'd prefer it that way but Dusty didn't understand. He wanted to go too but Juan simply said, "No".

After Peter walked out of sight, Kelsey had second thoughts and started after him. She wanted to be with him, to give him some moral support. He'd been alone far too long for such a short life.

When she caught up with him, he was already there so she stopped a few feet from him. He sat on the grass in front of a gravestone and looked up at her.

"I hope you're not angry with me," she said. "I thought you might like some company."

He smiled back and patted the grass next to him. After she sat down she read the gravestone. "This is the Ethel who took care of you."

"Yes. She was a good woman."

"And she raised a good son." She touched his arm lightly.

213

"I only wish I really were her son. Then my life wouldn't be such a mess."

"I'm sure she always thought of you as her son, and you treat her memory with great respect. She did well with you. I'm sure she'd be proud."

"There were times in the last few days I thought I'd have the chance to ask her face to face."

"That's for sure. The thing is, if we tried to tell anyone what we've been through these last few days they'd say we were crazy. Can you believe Juan's gang used those guys as dart boards at Spencer's?" She laughed and was relieved to see a smile on Peter's face.

"Yeah," he replied.

"And you, Mr. Smoky-the-Bear, I think you made the biggest smoke bomb Spencer's has ever seen." Peter finally laughed.

She felt overcome by the urge to embrace him but before she could she found his arms around her. He gently leaned her back onto the grass and kissed her with tremendous passion.

After a long embrace, she stood up. "Come. I think it's time to leave." ·

Peter stood and looked at Ethel's grave in silence. Kelsey grabbed him by the arm and stood beside him. "Ethel," she said. "you did good. You should be proud of what you did for Peter and what he's become." She turned to him and smiled. They started to leave Mount Auburn Cemetery arm in arm but only got a few feet from Ethel's grave when Juan's car whipped over the small rise and screeched to a stop.

"Get in!" he yelled. "They tracked us here."

Peter saw a second car fly over the rise not far behind them. Both he and Kelsey dove into the back seat next to Dusty, and Juan took off before the doors were shut. Within seconds, they tore through the Cemetery with the killers in close pursuit. Juan rounded a corner and had to swerve off the cemetery road and onto the walkway to avoid a funeral procession, sending mourners diving for cover as they dropped the casket. Shooting up over a rise, Juan again found himself on the road with the killers not far behind.

Following the signs, Juan exited the cemetery and turned right onto the main road, then swung left, cutting through traffic amidst the screech of tires and the wail of horns. The chase was on and now it was simply a matter of speed and driving skills.

Peter climbed over into the passenger seat beside Juan. "Everyone buckle up nice and tight"

The killer's car had a turbocharged engine and was capable of keeping up with Juan's, but they couldn't overtake him. Juan's car looked old and beat up but under the hood was a pristine highly tuned engine.

Speeds exceeded one hundred and ten M.P.H. Peter knew they had to lose them, and soon. A chase like this would very soon attract the police and they were the last people Peter wanted to see.

Juan swung right and they found themselves driving up the on ramp for the Massachusetts Turnpike.

"No, we don't want to get on the turnpike. If they don't catch us, the State Police will."

"Not much choice now, bro," Juan replied.

Up ahead, they saw a line of cars backed up at the tollbooth getting their tickets for the turnpike.

"Shit!" Looking around Juan saw their only shot and knew he had to time it perfectly. With his speed still eighty M.P.H., he closed in on the line of traffic. A few feet from the last car in line was the end of the median divider, after that a line of red plastic traffic cones. At the last moment, Juan swung his car into the opposite oncoming traffic and towards the exit side of the east bound tollbooth. Two cars were leaving their booths, having paid the toll. Picking the first booth, Juan steered for its opening only to see the front of a car pull into it. He jammed his foot on the brake and the tires locked up and the car skidded sideways as he turned the wheel in the opposite direction. Moments from a broadside impact against the tollbooth, Juan released the brake and pressed on the accelerator, swinging the car straight again. This time he was aligned with the second tollbooth. No time for calculations, he just needed luck now. The second car had cleared the booth and Juan shot through it in the opposite direction as another car was approaching. The other driver panicked and spun his wheel, locking his brakes and sliding into the tollbooth sideways. Juan then swung the car around in a 180 and shot back through the toll both going in the right direction this time.

Peter looked back and saw the car that was chasing them swing around the traffic cones and follow them at high speed. "Juan you've got to lose them. This chase can't last much longer, we've already drawn too much attention. The police will be all over us."

"Leave it to me, bro." Juan pushed the accelerator to the floor as they turned right off the exit ramp. They paralleled the turnpike for a half-mile then curved away from it. A mile down the road Juan saw a turn off to the right. "Hold on."

He swung the car onto the dirt. Dust blinded the car behind them but they knew it was still there. Up ahead, they all saw at the same time that the road ended in a dirt cull-de-sac and then rose into a grassy knoll to meet the turnpike.

"No Juan don't do it," Peter cried.

"Hold on, my friends, this will be better than any amusement ride you've ever been on."

Peter held tightly as the car rose up the knoll and shot across the turnpike. There was no gauging, no judgment, just a blind shot through traffic. Miraculously, they missed a car and a sixteen wheeler and crossed the turnpike. The pursuing car wasn't as lucky. It got broad sided by a dump-truck and exploded into flames, setting off a chain reaction that littered the highway in both directions with smashed twisted cars and trucks.

Juan shot through the field on the opposite side of the turnpike and bounced up and down all the way to a dirt road. The rest of their ride back to Hartford was slow and easy via back roads, all the way back to the Hollow.

31 | CHAPTER THIRTY-ONE

Peter tossed back and forth in bed most of the night. He had revised his plan in his mind over and over, second-guessing himself and problem solving until he felt comfortable that all bases would be covered. Sleep had come in fitful spasms. With the sun barely over the horizon, he gave up on sleep and sat at Juan's small kitchen table, writing up his list. Soon, Maria stood at the stove cooking breakfast. The aroma of bacon and eggs floated through the small apartment, gently waking everyone else who soon joined Peter around the table where they relived yesterday's adventure.

"Ok, bro." Juan said, "What are we gonna do today to top yesterday?"

Peter smiled and scanned his list, then he looked up. "Today we finish it. We put an end to the Cartel, to Barbosa and to this entire foolishness and then we get on with our lives." He handed the list and a diagram to Juan. "Can you get these things and do what I described on the diagram?"

Juan scanned the list for a few seconds. "Yeah, but this one will cost." He pointed to the last item on the list.

"Kelsey can rent it for the day. There's a marina on the river just south of Portland. She can put it on a credit card."

"That's fine with me," Juan replied.

"You need to follow the plans on the diagram exactly."

"No problem, bro."

"What about me?" Dusty asked.

"Today you get the day off. I want you to stay in the apartment. Juan and Kelsey have to take care of their task, to make the plan work. You have been more help than one could have ever asked for. I think a day of rest is called for."

Dusty didn't like that answer; he sat and pouted. Kelsey stood, walked around to him and put her arms around him from behind. "Dusty, what Peter is trying to say is that we would not be this far alone if it hadn't been for you. You have saved the day so many times. We each have our task and today it's our turn to help Peter. Believe me there is still a lot of work to be done and a lot will rest on your shoulders."

"OK, I guess," he said begrudgingly.

* * * * *

At 8:00 A.M., Peter dialed Barbosa's office. Beth answered. "Beth, I need to know if you are still a friend?"

"Yes." The answer was without hesitation. "What do you need?"

"A half hour alone in Barbosa's office."

"At noon, I go to lunch and the great doctor has a meeting with administration from 12:00 to 1:00."

"Thank you." He hung up. Then he dialed another number. "Sloan, it's Pavano. I have everything you need to put the Cartel and everyone in it away. This also is your lucky day, you can keep your five million, you can have it free of charge; it's my gift to you."

"What's the catch?" Sloan asked.

"Simple, you let us get away. I guarantee the material I'll give you will exonerate me and my friends and put the Cartel away for good."

"What's to stop me from arresting you and getting the evidence?"

"My plan won't allow it. Here's the deal, you will meet us tonight at three in the morning. There is a small pier at the end of

Maxium Road; you'll find it off Brainard Road. There will be a thirty-foot cabin cruiser docked there. When we arrive, I'll give you a laptop computer. My friends and I then leave on the boat. Once we are far enough off shore, I'll call you on your cell phone and give you a number to dial up on the computer. There will be an attachment for your phone to give you Internet access. I'll also give you an access code. Then, and only then, will you be able to download the information into the laptop. So, if you arrest us no number, no code."

"Why the boat?"

"That's simple. Across the river there will be a car waiting, also a small plane will be waiting at Brainard Airport a mile down river. The boat will stop at all places and then proceed down the river, making lots more stops. All of us, or some of us will get off at any of these places or continue down river to Long Island Sound. Only we will know for sure. It's a little precaution I worked out for our protection. No offense."

"None taken."

"Do you accept?"

"Yes."

"I'll see you at 3:00 am." Peter hung up.

* * * * *

It was two minutes past noon when Peter approached Barbosa's office. His disguise was a simple one, casual dress with a baseball cap pulled low. He wore a delivery uniform that Juan had gotten for him and he looked like any other courier delivery outfit that visited businesses daily. He took a deep breath and opened Barbosa's office, ready to turn and run. To his relief, he entered and found it empty. Without delay, he sat down at his computer and pulled a laptop computer out of his carrying bag and set about attaching a cable between the two of them. After they were connected, he booted them up. He logged into Barbosa's brokerage account, when it asked for the username and password he opened a file on the laptop and downloaded the file Juan had stolen the night before from the brokerage firm. The username and password were encrypted but that didn't matter, he didn't have to read them; he only had to send them electronically through Barbosa's computer to the brokerage firm's computer. There the encrypted file was read and confirmed by the brokerage firm's computer and Barbosa's account opened and appeared before Peter. Next, he opened another file on his laptop. This file had the Cartel's financial accounts and routing numbers listed. This information Juan had gotten from the Cartel's computers when he downloaded everything from Joshua's computer at Cartel headquarters. Once that was open it was a matter of finding the right accounts and transferring the money. This would take a few minutes and he looked at his watch; fifteen minutes had passed. Peter wanted to be finished and on his way in a half-hour. It would be close but he was still on schedule.

* * * * *

Out in the hallway, unknown to Peter, Dusty stood guard. He had ignored their request for him to stay in Juan's apartment. He figured Peter needed a lookout. His intuition again proved correct when he heard the booming voice of Barbosa from around the corner talking to someone.

"Next time they cancel a meeting I want to be notified. I don't have time to sit around waiting for them to appear. I'll talk to you later."

Dusty opened Barbosa's outer office door and waited until he saw Barbosa turn the corner then stepped back into the hall and shut the outer door making sure Barbosa had seen him.

Barbosa stopped. "You little shit, what are you doing in my office?"

Dusty held up a VCR tape. He had come prepared with a plan. "You are through, done, finished. I got the evidence here to put you away. I'm gonna give it to the police and you're gonna go to jail, you killer."

"You little shit, come back here," Barbosa yelled.

Dusty was halfway down the hall before Barbosa started after him. He ran, but with every other step he looked over his shoulder.

"Drop that tape, you little shit!" Barbosa yelled.

"No I won't," Dusty yelled back. With every waddled step he took, the distance between them shortened. He felt his chest pounding and his breath burned in his throat. At the corner, he turned left and stopped. He found himself in a dead end with no exit. He wasn't trapped though; he knew the hospital inside and out. He'd beaten them in the past because he was smarter than them and today would be no different.

Barbosa rounded the corner and stop. "OK you little shit, drop the tape. You're trapped. You have no where to go."

With defiance, Dusty clutched the tape in his left hand and raised the middle finger of his right hand high in the air towards them. "This is for you. You are the s'it-head, not me."

Dusty spun ninety degrees and dove towards the wall and disappeared from view.

Barbosa ran forward. "What the fuck! A laundry chute?" He turned and ran towards the stairs.

One flight below, Dusty bounced head first onto the bundles of dirty laundry that had poured down from the floors above. He rolled off the soft bundles onto the floor.

"Hey Dusty what are you doing sliding down the chute?" a laundry worker asked.

He didn't answer, he just ran out the door. In the corridor, he started towards the stairwell but that door flew open and Barbosa burst through.

"Drop that tape you little shit," he yelled again.

"No I won't!" Dusty turned and ran in the opposite direction. By the far wall he slid open a grilled door and jumped onto a service elevator. He pulled the grill shut only to have it bounce open before he could latch it. Barbosa threw the gate open the

'06-MUCC

rest of the way but Dusty raised his foot and kicked him dead center in the groin. Dusty pushed him back and in that split second pulled the grate shut and locked it. Barbosa rose just as the bottom of the elevator left his view. Barbosa turned and ran down the hallway and painfully bounded up the stairs two at a time with a visible limp. On the next floor, he exited only to see the elevator continue its upward climb. He started up the stairs when he came face to face with a guard on his way down.

"Is everything alright?" the guard asked, seeing Barbosa obviously stressed.

"That little shit retard from housekeeping stole a patient's tape from my office and he kicked me. He's in the service elevator."

"Let's go." The guard turned and led him up to the next landing. "There are two more floors. I'll take this one."

Barbosa ran to the top floor and when he entered the hallway he saw Dusty run out and go down the corridor.

Dusty saw Barbosa and doubled his pace. Up ahead, he opened a door that led into the surgical wing of the hospital. He saw a broom against the wall and picked it up and wedged it into the door latch; which immediately rattled in an attempt to be opened. A sharp bang resounded against the door and Dusty jumped back startled. He turned and ran down the hall. Once through the next door he found himself in the Surgical Suite. Barbosa knew where the hall led to and ran around, entering by another entrance. Dusty rounded the corner only to face Barbosa again. He spun and fled with Barbosa in quick pursuit.

They ran down the hall that separated the many operating rooms. When Dusty reached the third room Barbosa caught him and pushed him to the floor. Dusty rolled when he fell and accidentally rolled through a door into an operating room where there was an exploratory operation being performed.

"What was that?" one of the surgeons asked.

Dusty didn't answer; he kept rolling until he was covered by the operating room table's drapes. Moments later Barbosa burst in.

"What is going on here?" the head surgeon asked.

Barbosa ignored him and went from one side of the operating room table to the other. Then he looked on the floor.

"I asked you what is going on? Get out of my operating room!"

"Shut up," Barbosa replied, and bent down pushing the surgeon to one side.

"Will someone call security?" The surgeon kicked at Barbosa with his foot but Barbosa simply fended it off with a hand. He again pushed the surgeon aside causing him to drop the scalpel, which fell onto the floor.

"There you are you little shit." Barbosa reached under the operating room table and grabbed Dusty by a leg and pulled.

"Help! Help me! He's gonna kill me!" Dusty was pulled from under the table, his free leg and arms flailing at Barbosa. The two rolled around the floor under the feet of the surgeon.

"I've had enough of this." The surgeon reached down and grabbed Barbosa in a headlock, lost his balance and toppled onto him.

The operating room echoed with shouts and screams along with profanities as half the staff tended to the patient, whose abdomen was split wide open and his guts exposed, and the rest tried in vain to get control of the rumble that now involved one of the nurses.

Dusty kicked and kicked until he broke free, then he got to his feet and ran out the door. Down the hall he turned the corner only to find himself face to face with the guard. He spun around and headed back down the hall, going straight until he crashed through a set of swinging doors with Barbosa again in pursuit. He was now in the Labor and Delivery Suite. In the background, screams and cries resounded from the collection of women in active labor.

Dusty ran to the end and turned with Barbosa and the guard only feet behind him. With no options left, he pushed open a door and ran into one of the birthing rooms. It wasn't empty. A woman lay on the table with her legs in stirrups, exposed from the waist down. She panted and cried with pain through a contraction while her husband tried in vain to soothe her discomfort. The obstetrician coached her on with calls of 'push, push'. Dusty slipped unnoticed to the opposite side of the room where he was in full view of the delivery.

"Oh no!" He put his hands to his mouth. He'd never seen a naked woman. Not even in a picture. He backed against the wall and froze.

Barbosa charged in but the guard stayed outside. "You little retarded piece of shit, come here!"

The obstetrician turned his head. "Get out of my delivery room. Now!" He turned back to his patient. "Push, push."

"Fuck you, asshole. You," he pointed to Dusty whose stare was frozen on the naked woman's bottom. "Get your ass over here now."

The husband who was only feet from Barbosa spun around. "Hey! You, get out of here. Now!"

"Shut the fuck up," Barbosa replied.

"You son of a bitch." The husband grabbed for Barbosa's throat and the two locked in a death grip. They rolled forward and fell to the floor.

"Ohhh!" The woman gave out one final cry and delivered her child.

"Oh no!" Dusty said. The spell now broken, he ran past Barbosa, who hit the husband a few times in the chest and face then rolled off and gave chase out the side door.

Dusty ran down the hall and out of the Birthing Suite, then back through the operating room corridor. When he reached the door to the stairwell he turned and saw that Barbosa and the guard weren't far behind. Dusty jumped into the stairwell and ran up instead of down. At the top of the stairs, he faced the door to the roof. Realizing he'd made a mistake, he turned but instantly stopped.

"He went up. He's trapped now." Barbosa's voice came from below.

"Noo!" Dusty pushed the door open and ran onto the roof. There he ran from one corner to the other. Quickly he realized there was no ladder or exit. He jumped up and down searching for an idea.

Barbosa and the guard burst onto the roof. "You go around that way, I'll go this way," Barbosa barked.

The door to the roof slowly shut and Dusty, who had climbed onto the small roof above the door, dropped down into the stairwell. With a small two by four he had picked up he jammed it into the door latch, effectively locking Barbosa and the guard on the roof. He laughed as he skipped down the stairs hearing the clanging of the door in an unsuccessful attempt to open it from the outside.

Meanwhile, Peter had finished his downlinks and after logging off, exited Barbosa office at 12:35 and headed back to Juan's apartment, oblivious to how Dusty had again saved him.

A little before four in the afternoon, Barbosa's private line rang. "What do you want, Joshua? Didn't we see enough of each other yesterday?" Barbosa reclined in his chair and waited impatiently for a reply.

"How did you think you'd get away with it?"

"Get away with what? I don't have time for games. Get to the point or leave me alone."

"Get to the point. I'll get to the point. Forty million points."

"Tell me what you want or goodbye."

"It's simple, at noon today 40 million dollars were wire transferred from the Cartel's private account into your personal brokerage account."

"What?"

"That's what I said. I'm curious as to how you thought you'd get away with it?"

"Get real, you little shit, I don't need to steal 40 million dollars."

"Bullshit. You are an opportunist of the first degree. You obviously had access and the ability. You and the Cartel are fighting over your inept handling of this whole affair, and with Pavano stealing the files that had our account information you figured you could move the money and blame it on him. But you made one mistake, a stupid one."

"What was that?"

"You transferred the money into your brokerage account. I know they are encoded and password protected, so I know only you could have moved the money."

"Are you stupid? Pavano must have stolen my password the same way he stole the Cartel's."

"We figured you'd use that excuse. Sorry, we're not buying it."

"Joshua, I'm tired of you and your accusations . . ."

"And we are tired of you. You're through Barbosa, *You're* out."

"What? You're throwing me out of the Cartel? That will be interesting, I hope you have a lot of support."

"I'm not throwing you out of the Cartel, the Cartel's throwing you out of this life. The vote, by the way, was unanimous. Enjoy your last moments with us."

The line went dead. Barbosa slammed the receiver down, picked up the phone and threw it against the far wall. He turned and stared out his window for a short moment. He was not one to dwell on decisions too long. He opened his wallet, pulled out a business card, and dialed the number on his other phone. A moment later he was connected. "Sloan, this is Dr. Barbosa. Here's the deal, you want to know about the Cartel, I'll tell you everything you want and need to know."

"What's the deal?"

"I want a signed document from the Justice Department that I get complete immunity and protection from prosecution. In return, you get everything you need to put them away."

"I am a little shocked, to say the least."

"I want immediate protection from physical harm from the Cartel."

"So, you've fallen out of favor with them."

"That is none of your concern. I need protection, take it or leave it."

"Oh, we will take it. I'll have a car pick you up at the hospital in one hour. Bring everything you need, you won't be coming back."

Barbosa hung up the phone and went to his safe. "Those bastards think they were the only ones that kept files. They'll rue the day they fucked with me."

An hour later, Barbosa's phone rang. "What."

"Dr. Barbosa, agent Sloan sent us, we will wait for you in the lobby."

"Fine, I'll be right there." He hung up, gathered his files, and left the office, walking straight to the elevator and never looking back.

33 | CHAPTER THIRTY-THREE

The night was dark and overcast, the moon only a quarter full. For the fleeting moments that it shone from behind the clouds, it cast little to no light on the ground. Even with his eyes adjusted to the night, Agent Sloan had difficulty discerning shadows from true objects. At first he ignored the movement off in the distance until it continued to move directly towards him. He placed his hand on his shoulder holster and felt reassured that his service revolver was in easy reach. The water lapped against the pier behind him and the mooring line on the deserted boat snapped back and forth.

The movement stopped and a voice cut through the darkness. "Sloan, it's me, Pavano, and my friends."

Sloan leaned against one of the first pillars on the pier and visibly relaxed. He watched as Peter, Kelsey, Juan and Dusty stepped out of the darkness and approached him. Juan was on guard, his head turning and twisting in all directions, peering into the darkness, making sure they were alone.

They stopped next to Sloan. Peter opened his backpack and took out a laptop computer and cellular phone. "Here is the laptop and I threw in a cellular phone. I wanted to make sure you had the right attachments to download the data."

Sloan took it and set it on the bench next to him. "Well, I'm not quite sure what to say. What will you do? Where will you go?"

706-MUCC

"I'll hide out until the information clears me, then who knows what I'll do with the rest of my life. Where will we go? Let's just say that's been prearranged to my liking. Don't be concerned. I'll be safe." Peter turned to the others. "Head to the boat, I'll be there in a moment. Juan, start it up and get ready to cast off."

"Yes sir, captain." Juan saluted him and they all walked down the dock and onto the boat.

"I've got to say," Sloan started, "you beat the odds. You pulled it off. I am very impressed."

"No help from you or the FBI." Peter shrugged. "I gotta go. When we get mid river I'll call you and give you the information so you can download the data." Without shaking his hand or saying goodbye, he turned and walked down the dock. The moment he stepped on board the boat they cast off and very slowly trolled to the center of the river while making their way down stream.

Sloan's cellular phone rang. "Okay Sloan," Peter said, "you'd better have a pen and paper because I'm only going to give this to you once."

"I'm ready," Sloan replied.

After writing down the phone number, user name and password, Sloan hung up. He pushed a button on his cell phone that speed dialed a pre-programmed number. "I got what we need, put an end to it."

Sloan hung up and turned towards the river at the very moment a tremendous flash and blast rocked the water. The cabin cruiser erupted in a ball of flame and exploded into splinters that showered down onto the water.

Sloan stood there, nonplussed at the event that he had just orchestrated. Without any sense of remorse or hesitation he dialed the number on the cell phone Peter had supplied. The connection was made and he was asked for the user name and password, when that was accepted the download started. Ten minutes later the download was finished. Sloan broke the connection and stared at the screen. There was a folder that opened automatically. He read it:

> Sloan, the biggest mistake you made was underestimating me. If you think you've downloaded anything of importance you are mistaken. What you have done is send a code to a server that downloaded the information to a computer that is very safe and is within the hands of the FBI, pre-arranged by my lawyer. You got sloppy, especially at Spencers. I saw you in the van. You will be pleased to know that I did get inside the Cartel and got all the information needed to put each and every one of them, including you, away for a very long time. And yes, the Cartel had a file on you killing Dr. Collas. Have a nice day.

Sloan picked up the laptop and threw it into the lake. "Yeah, well at least I'll be around to be chased. Hope you enjoy being fish food."

706-MUCC

34 | CHAPTER THIRTY-FOUR

Samuel walked slowly down the beach; the fine, powdery, white sand covered his ankles. He marveled at how beautiful Grenada's Grand Anse Beach was. He was very tired. It had been 31 days since Peter's boat exploded. Thirty days since Barbosa was found face down in a tobacco field in South Windsor Connecticut with a bullet in his head, and 27 days since Agent Sloan was apprehended and charged with the murder of Dr. Collas. He was indeed tired. It had been an emotional roller coaster. After he finished his last and most lengthy telephone call, he strolled onto the beach and stopped beside a group of lounge chairs and sat down.

"You need a frosty drink, bro?"

Samuel smiled at Juan. "No, I just had one at the bar while I was on the phone."

"And?"

"Well the Feds were faced with a interesting dilemma. They had two tapes of the Senator's angioplasty. The one the hospital gave them, and one they received in the mail. They checked both of them, and found that neither had been tampered with. They found no overlays, no dubbing. Essentially, they were both clean originals, which didn't make sense. Finally, they talked Mrs. Demind into having her husbands body exhumed and autopsied." Samuel gazed out over the water.

"And what did they find?" a voice to the side asked.

"The pathologist found a very tiny rubber catheter tip occluding a Coronary artery."

"So they know which tape is real, I would guess," the voice said.

Samuel turned his gaze to Peter and smiled. "You are cleared of all charges and free to return any time you like. That is, if you want to leave this paradise."

"Not for a while." Kelsey chimed in. "We need to convalesce on this beach for at least another month."

Dusty and his mother appeared and Dusty sat down, all excited. "Did you hear the news? We can go home anytime we want."

"Yeah, Dust that's great," Juan said to his friend.

Samuel chuckled. "I am still amazed at how you pulled it off. Everyone thought you all were dead."

"Yeah, we're dead and rich," Dusty interrupted.

"Oh, yes, very rich," Samuel agreed.

"I figure," Peter said, "that after what the Cartel put us all through taking 40 million from them and giving it to us was not unreasonable."

"Wiring it through Barbosa's brokerage account was a stroke of genius. How many accounts did you transfer it through after that?" Samuel asked.

"Five. All numbered off shore bank accounts."

"And untraceable," Kelsey said.

"I never really asked you," Samuel said, "how did you know Sloan would blow up your boat?"

"He had to. He had no choice. That was the only time he knew we would all be together. He couldn't chance us splitting up. It was then or never. I had Juan cut a hole out of the side of the boat just above the water line on the opposite the side that faced the dock. It was duct taped back in place. We left the boat there ahead of time, giving Sloan enough time to wire it with explosives. Just to be safe we had already hidden our own explosives on board and if Sloan hadn't blown up the boat we

06-MUCC

would have after we entered the water. We figured he would have thought other members of the Cartel had done it. While I was talking to Sloan on the cell phone everyone, including me, slipped into the water and swam away from the boat."

"So what are you going to do with the money?" Samuel asked.

"We're going to split it four ways. Ten for Juan . . ."

"I'm gonna take it back to the Hollow," Juan said, "and try to turn that place around. There are a lot of smart people there and with this seed money we can do a lot more than sell drugs."

"Ten for Dusty," Peter continued.

"Yeah, Mom and I both are gonna go to school and get education," Dusty said

"And ten for me and Kelsey . . ."

"We're getting married," Kelsey said.

"Yeah, and I'm gonna be their best man." Dusty boasted puffing out his chest.

"That leaves ten million." Samuel said.

"The last ten is for you. You deserve it. Now you can give all the free legal service you want to the people who need it but can't afford it."

"You are one class act Peter Pavano . . . one real class act."

"Got t'at right. T'at's why we are his friends," Dusty added.